AFTER THE DUST SETTLES

by
Cindy Butler

Gotham Books

30 N Gould St.
Ste. 20820, Sheridan, WY 82801
https://gothambooksinc.com/

Phone: 1 (307) 464-7800

© 2024 *Cindy Butler*. All rights reserved.

No part of this book may be reproduced, stored in a retrieval system, or transmitted by any means without the written permission of the author.

Published by Gotham Books (November 22, 2024)

ISBN: 979-8-3306-0344-2 (H)
ISBN: 979-8-3306-0342-8 (P)
ISBN: 979-8-3306-0343-5 (E)

Because of the dynamic nature of the Internet, any web addresses or links contained in this book may have changed since publication and may no longer be valid.

The views expressed in this work are solely those of the author and do not necessarily reflect the views of the publisher, and the publisher hereby disclaims any responsibility for them.

Contents

CHAPTER ONE: The Escape 1

CHAPTER TWO: Taking the job no one wanted 19

CHAPTER THREE: Finding the Forever Home 39

CHAPTER FOUR: Desperation and Jealousy 66

CHAPTER FIVE: Getting to know Beautiful 84

CHAPTER SIX: Cruel Rumors spread through town 104

CHAPTER SEVEN: Pride and Pestilence 118

CHAPTER EIGHT: Innocent Responses 138

CHAPTER NINE: Hiding her Shame 160

CHAPTER TEN: Planning to run Again 183

CHAPTER ELEVEN: Found by Frank and left for Dead ... 205

CHAPTER TWELVE: The Inquest 220

CHAPTER THIRTEEN: Sneaking out of town 243

CHAPTER ONE

THE ESCAPE

Something had gone wrong. Sadie thought she had planned well. Her plan had allowed an extra couple of hours before Frank would know that she was gone. But there was Frank standing in the entrance of Grand Central Station face red with rage. Sadie was temporarily paralyzed with fear, her eyes wide with disbelief but only for a moment. This was Sadie's only hope, and she could not give up this easily. Her maternal instincts told her that she must protect Gus at all costs. The punishment for running from Frank would be the ultimate, and Sadie knew that Gus would not be spared this time. She needed to hide Gus from Frank no matter what.

As Sadie's mind raced for a place to hide Gus or an escape route, her eyes focused on the four-sided brass clock in the middle of the main terminal. The top of the clock was at least twenty feet high, and the base of the clock was surrounded by small wooden doors. The doors were almost hidden by the throngs of people admiring the clock and milling about the terminal. Sadie crouched below the height of the crowd and led Gus to the clock.

"I have to take care of something right now, and I need to know that you will be at the same place when I come back to get you. Crawl behind this wooden door under this pretty clock. Pretend we are playing hide-and-seek. Don't come out until you see me by the clock. That will be our signal that the game is over. Whatever happens, don't come out from behind this door until you see me. You have to promise me!" Sadie whispered to Gus. Sadie tucked Gus safely behind one of the wooden doors under the clock, kissed him one more time, and then walked quickly out one of the porter's exits into the train yard.

    Sadie's lungs stung with the limited air of pure fear. She had glanced behind her as she exited the terminal and caught Frank's eye. He had recognized her. Sade started running as fast as she could away from the main terminal. Away from the lights illuminating the terminals, and away from Gus. Frank was swiftly closing the distance between them. Sadie was running blindly down an unlit alley between two parked trains as fast as her legs would carry her. Her ankles were threatening to turn against her amid the pressure of balancing the tiny heels of her shoes in the loose coal gravel that was so very deep. Sadie wanted to scream, but the sound stuck in her throat and made her choke.

    The noise of the steam engines sputtering to life and the resulting steam rolling across the train yard obscured the terrifying struggle that was playing out between Frank and Sadie. Sadie's petite body couldn't compete against the long muscular legs of her husband, Frank. Frank was running behind Sadie gaining ground with savage speed, pure rage exploding on his face. The night was dark with no stars or moon, unseasonably hot and humid for early April. The bizarre mix of the whistles of the trains, the cars and wagons clicking by on the streets above them, and the cries of the stock market crash beggars screaming about the unfairness of their recent plight heightened Sadie's fear and desperation. She frantically ran and stumbled against obscure silhouettes in the dark, hallway expecting each shadow to rise up and grab her as she fled.

    Frank was much taller, stronger, and faster than Sadie. He quickly caught up with her five-feet-two-inch frame, grabbed her long red hair from behind, and threw her up against the side of the closest railroad car. The back of her head slammed hard against the metal with a dull thud. Sadie slumped into the coal bed beside the railroad tracks and lost consciousness.

Sadie's green eyes opened a few seconds later. She was struggling to breathe. The smog and congestion from the trains was filling her lungs with grit and keeping out the air. Sadie sensed there was something else blocking her airway. Sadie struggled to clear her head, struggled to move. Frank's forearm was pressed against her neck, his other arm restraining her arms against her chest, and his face was so close to Sadie's that the alcohol on his breath burned her eyes.

"I told you if you ever left me, Sadie, I would kill you! You belong to me. No other man will ever touch you. And now, because you have been so stupid, you will never see your son grow up. I will raise him my way, without you. You are such a dumb, stupid wench!"

Frank had Sadie pinned beneath him now, glaring into Sadie's green eyes. Frank leaned the weight of his six-feet-two-inch frame into his muscular right hand that was clasped around Sadie's throat.

Sadie was struggling to breathe, lapsing in and out of consciousness. Sadie was trying to focus all her energy on staying alive and consciously breathing in and out. Sadie's fear was quickly being replaced by painful acceptance. Frank was going to kill her, right here on the train bed. The sharp edges of the rocky coal bed were cutting into her back, shoulders, and head. Her thoughts raced to Gus, who was hiding under the clock in the main terminal. She knew Gus would be peeking through the space above the wooden doors, looking for her and waiting for her signal. The thought of Gus waiting for her and her never returning was excruciating.

 Earlier that evening, Sadie had hastily grabbed the two small satchels of clothing that she had hidden under Gus's bed and the envelope containing the small amount of cash she had taped to the bottom of the bureau in the bedroom. Sadie had been hiding small amounts of cash for over a year. She had chosen the bottom of the bureau as the only safe hiding place in the house. Sadie's husband, Frank, would always move the bureau when he did his weekly dust inspections, but he never turned the bureau over to inspect the bottom. Sadie rolled a bewildered Gus out of his warm bed and dressed him in his Sunday best. They had no time to waste in getting to Grand Central Station, the only surefire escape route that Sadie knew. The train would carry them far, far away from Frank – far enough that even Frank's friends and relatives could not find them and report back to him.

 Sadie and Gus slipped quietly out the back door of the house and walked quietly and silently through the late evening shadows, until they were out of the neighborhood. Once out of the eyesight of any neighbors, Sadie and Gus picked up their pace through the streets of New York City, using the faraway twinkly lights in the west as their road map. The April evening was clear and the air sluggish with humidity as they hurried along. They passed by squatter's shacks, tenements, warehouses, and the stench of slaughterhouses. Sadie held her breath and prayed for safety every time they side-stepped a sleeping figure in the shadows. Sadie and Gus eventually turned onto Park Avenue. She knew she was close, the terminal remaining hidden amongst the enormous skyscrapers. They passed the Biltmore Hotel, the Yale club, the Lincoln Building, and the Chrysler Building. Finally Grand Central Station was in front of them.

Breathlessly, they finally rushed through the front doors into the bustling main terminal of Grand Central station, the end of Sadie's escape plan. The room was massive and overpowering. The walls seemed to rise forever, topped with a blue ceiling covered with twinkling stars. A multi-sided brass clock stood in the middle of the room. Each side of the clock displayed the current time in different time zones. Sadie wasn't sure what to do next, but she knew she had to get as far away from New York City as her small amount of money would take her.

The ticket windows stretched down both sides of the main terminal. Sadie had been to Grand Central Station as a teenager but had not noticed the overwhelming chaos going on in the terminal. At that time, she had been following her parents and did not have any travel decisions. Sadie studied the destination charts, looking for a destination that was a small spot on the map with no recognizable attraction that would draw people to it. Sadie had no idea what final destination she would choose. She wanted a small, sleepy town that simply existed, a town to make a new life for her and Gus where Sadie could forget the past years of abuse and emotional neglect that had molded her into a miserable puppet of humanity. Even though Sadie had lost a lot of herself in order to survive the years with Frank, she still knew enough to know that she would never return to New York City. In her eyes, New York City represented the evil of Frank – loud, drunk and dark.

Sadie's eyes rested on an unfamiliar destination: 'Galesburg, Illinois. One-Way fare - $3.40. Travel time – 30 hours. Boarding – 11:45.'

Sadie had never heard of Galesburg, Illinois. She knew Illinois was in the Midwest and was farther west than Ohio. Sadie had lived in Ohio with her parents before marrying

Frank. She had met Frank when she and her parents had taken a family vacation to New York City. Married in 1921 at the age of sixteen, and kept in virtual isolation ever since, Sadie knew little of the world. It was now late spring in 1930, and Sadie was still wearing the same clothes that she had taken with her when she left her parents' home to live with Frank. She knew that her dress made her look outdated and definitely poor. But they also helped her to fit in with the crowd. The great stock market crash had occurred the previous fall, and now most everyone was poor and struggling. No one had money to buy new clothes since the Depression had started. For once, Sadie fit right in. she selected Galesburg, Illinois, as her destination from the railway map without knowing anything about the place. Galesburg seemed to be unknown, unexpected and far away from New York City. Illinois should be a place where Frank would probably not expect her to be.

Sadie's stomach was full of butterflies as she requested two one-way tickets from the ticket agent.

"Ma-am, you can save fifty cents if you purchase your return ticket now. We have a sale on round -trip tickets." The ticket agent looked up over his horn-rimmed glasses at Sadie, waiting for her response.

"No, sir. I'm visiting family in Galesburg, and don't know when I will be returning. I only need one-way tickets at this time, please." Sadie carefully counted out the money as she began to allow her heart to hope. She and Gus just might make it out of New York City in time.

After paying for her fares, Sadie counted her money that was left. It wasn't a lot, but she would worry about that after they got to Galesburg. Right now, all she was concerned about was getting as far away from Frank as possible before he realized they had gone.

Sadie had one hour before boarding. If the train left on time, she would be well on her way out of the City and toward her new life before Frank even knew she was gone. The local bar was only eight blocks away, and Frank's visits to this bar were frequent and predictable. Every evening after work Frank stopped in for one beer, and a shot of whiskey. Tuesday was his poker night with his buddies at the bar.

Before he left to play poker, Frank had asked Sadie, "You going to be here when I get back?"

Sadie knew that this question was meant to be a seditious reminder that she was bound to Frank forever. But this Tuesday night Sadie had a ray of hope, and this tiny bit of hope brought out a little of the old Sadie that had been buried for years. Sadie had been carefully planning her escape for almost a year. And she had meticulously guarded her words and actions for the entire time. But in an instant, she had almost given her secret away.

Frank always closed the bar down on Tuesday nights. He never staggered in the house before two thirty or three in the morning. Even if Frank was lucid enough to realize they were gone, as soon as he walked in the front door and surmised that they had gone to Grand Central Station, he wouldn't have time to get there before they were long gone from the City. Sadie had cut it close but was confident that time was on her side. They were almost safe.

"Of course, I'll be here. Where else would I be?" Sadie had walked up to Frank with feigned affection, fixed his collar and touched him lightly on the cheek. "I think I will pick up the house and then do some mending. You go have a good time."

Frank did not turn to leave immediately. Instead, he turned to watch Sadie walk away. Sadie felt his eyes on her back and immediately stiffened. She had done something to give her secret away.

"You had better go, Frank. You know the guys are waiting for you to start the poker game." Sadie winced again. She was being too friendly.

"Since when have you been so talkative? Usually, you don't even watch me leave. What's up with you?"

"Nothing is up, Frank." Sadie searched her immediate surroundings, looking for any excuse she could find. "It's just that I wanted to water the flowers on the porch. The watering can is outside the door."

Frank opened the front door and stuck his head out. The watering can was sitting on the flower stand by the windowsill.

"Well, okay then. Maybe you are finally learning how to be a good wife. I was beginning to wonder if you were smart enough to learn anything." Frank hesitated for a few moments and then turned and walked to the bookcase beside the couch. He took Sadie's purse and dumped it out on the dining room table. He took out her coin purse and dumped the coins on the table. Sadie kept her eyes on the floor and did not look up when she heard the coins drop on the table.

"Twenty-seven cents. That is more money than you need to sit around the house." Frank picked up the quarter and put it in his pocket. He threw her empty purse on the couch and closed the distance between them quickly. Once there, Frank grabbed a handful of Sadie's strawberry blonde hair and pulled her face into his.

"Now I'm only going to tell you this once. So you listen and you listen good." Frank tightened and twisted his fist in Sadie's hair until Sadie let out a little whimper in pain.

"I decide when you touch me and how you touch me. You do nothing without getting my permission first. You got that?"

"Yes. Frank. I'm sorry. It won't happen again." Sadie wanted to pull away. She wanted to shove him away. She couldn't bear his breath, his stubbly face, and his bloodshot eyes anymore. It took all her strength to tolerate his rough, hard hands on her. Everything about him repulsed her.

After a long minute, Frank dropped his hand and walked toward the door. Once outside on the porch, Frank grabbed the half-full watering can and threw it inside the door toward Sadie. Water spewed over the floor and Sadie as it tumbled onto the floor.

Sadie picked up the can and went into the kitchen to add more water. She filled the can and went outside on the porch and began watering the geraniums. Without looking straight out at the street, Sadie found Frank's silhouette in the corner of her vision. She moved from flower pot to flower pot, always keeping Frank's body within her sight. Before Sadie was done watering all the flowers, Frank had disappeared around the corner. Sadie smiled to herself in satisfaction as she went back inside the house.

Sadie checked the clock on the kitchen wall again. It was eight thirty. Frank had been gone for thirty minutes. Sadie needed to wait at least another thirty minutes before putting her plan into action. She needed to know that Frank was at the saloon and had a few beers under his belt before she made her move. Once he had a few beers, he would be pretty mellow until he reached the turning point. That usually took five or six beers and more shots of whiskey. Sadie knew that she had about three hours to complete her plan. Once Frank was past the stage of mellow liquor, he would turn into a mean, mean drunk. That was when he usually headed home to Sadie and used her for target practice, especially if he lost money in the poker game. Each beating was more brutal than the last, and she knew her body couldn't take much more and still hide the effects from her son when he woke up on Wednesday mornings. It was getting more and more difficult to crawl out of bed with the accumulation of bruises on her battered body. And Sadie knew, as surely as she knew that she was still alive and breathing, that Frank would move on to Gus when the effects of her beatings were no longer satisfying to him. This knowledge gave her the courage and cunning she needed.

Sadie slowly and meticulously checked each room in the house as she waited for the clock to move. She had to keep busy, or she would lose her resolve. She didn't dare spend more time thinking about her plan. There were too many ways it could go wrong. Sadie needed to just do it before she lost her nerve. She had only one chance. If she failed, the punishment would be ultimate. She busied her mind by making sure every article in every room was spotless and placed in perfect harmony with the surroundings. Sadie thought herself a bit odd for spending all that valuable time perfecting the house that she was about ready to flee from and never return to. But, deep in the back of her mind, Sadie had been taught to be proud of a clean house, and she didn't want Frank's mother thinking ill of her by leaving a messy house.

Sadie had taken a few pennies from the grocery money for almost a year and squirreled it away. She counted her pennies every week, forcing herself not to get too excited or put a lot of detail into an escape plan too early. Frank was very perceptive and knew Sadie better than she knew herself. He watched her so closely and was so completely in her mind that Sadie sometimes answered Frank's questions before he had verbalized the thought. Sadie had been very careful not to betray herself. She didn't plan any further than 'We have to go before tonight. Sadie didn't even decide that today was the day until after Frank had left for work this morning. Only then did she pack the satchels and hide them under Gus's bed. She could not risk spending a lot of time planning or packing until she was ready to bolt.

She couldn't let Frank discover her secret. But somehow Frank knew. He had found her. She had been so close to freedom. And now she was going to die before she could taste it. She had failed. She had failed herself and she had failed Gus.

"You are such a whore, Sadie. You ran from me, but you cannot escape me. You made a vow to spend the rest of your life as my wife, and, by God, that's what you are going to do! You will die as my wife. Right here. Right now! Remember me as you die. I am the only man you will ever know. You will never know another man or feel another man's touch. Not as long as I live and breathe!"

Sadie closed her eyes, bracing for the increase in pressure from Frank's hand that she knew would end her life. She had made a desperate attempt to escape the brutality of her husband and raise her precious child without fear. And she had failed. What would happen to Gus, who would finally find him, who would take care of him, and how would he survive without her? Sadie prayed silently that someone would find Gus before Frank did. All Sadie could hope for was that someone would take him in and raise him as his or her own. A life with a kind stranger would be better than being raised by Frank without Sadie to protect him. Sadie prayed for one more tiny miracle for her son as she waited for the final breath to expire.

Sadie opened her eyes when she felt the weight of Frank's body drop on her like a boulder. Frank had passed out. Frank's battle with extreme physical expenditure of catching Sadie was lost when his inebriated body had sucked up all his remaining oxygen. Sadie's prayers had been answered in an unexpected way. With extreme effort, Sadie rolled Frank's body off of her and stood to her feet. She still had a chance, but she couldn't risk Frank waking up and finding her again before she was on that train. Sadie scanned the dark shadows for something to help, something to keep Frank here until she was safely on that train. Sadie ducked into the shadows close to the empty trains, searching for anything that would keep Frank motionless for at least an hour.

Sadie searched the ground around the closest railroad car and found a heavy chain looped over the coupler at the end of the car. Sadie smiled to herself as she pulled the chain off the back of the railroad car and dragged it across the ground to where Frank lay unconscious. It took Sadie several minutes to wrap the chain around Frank's body and secure the end of the chain to the rail bed. This would serve nicely. Sadie had a brief moment of guilt as she thought about what would happen to Frank if a train came through on the rails before he woke up. Sadie glanced around the scene to ensure no one had seen her tie up Frank. If she could be so lucky as to have a train decapitate Frank, she could rest peacefully on the train, knowing that her search for lasting freedom was really over. Or maybe one of the beggars would take advantage of Frank's helpless state. She wouldn't have to run or hide anymore. Sadie's guilt for thinking such awful thoughts about another human being dissipated as she limped back in the train station toward the clock. Her train was leaving for Galesburg in twenty minutes. She had just enough time to gather Gus and the satchels and find the right train. Those thoughts were all that counted right now.

Sadie had not failed, at least not tonight. She was back into her quest for freedom. Frank's image was still with her, and the thought of him was powerful enough to shake her to her very soul. But she and Gus were on their way out of New York City and thousands of miles from Frank and his evil, brutal ways. Sadie gave Gus a big bear hug as she helped him crawl out from under the clock.

Sadie almost dragged Gus to the departure platform, furtively watching all the figures mingling around the departure platform and searching for anything familiar about them. She cursed the bright light flooding the departure terminal. The two-tiered chandeliers hanging from the ceiling illuminated even the far corners of the terminal room. But she could barely see past her throbbing head and aching body. It took every ounce of her strength to keep moving. Sadie and Gus milled around the terminal room with the crowd of people, trying to stay hidden among the bodies and luggage. Sadie needed to make certain that she saw Frank before he saw them. Sadie's anxiety had traveled through her body into Gus, and he began to whimper and cling to her skirt.

"It's okay now, honey. Mommy is just really tired. And really excited about our trip. It's our first trip together, you know. It will be fun. So many new things to see and do. You'll see." Sadie tried to convince herself while at the same time calming Gus. She had to keep him calm. If he suddenly bolted or refused to move, she didn't think she would have the strength to go after him or to carry him.

"Where are we going, Momma? And how long will we be gone? Will Daddy come too?" The innocence in Gus's eyes tore at her heart. Sadie didn't want to lie to Gus, but she couldn't bear to tell him the truth.

"It's a surprise, Gus. You'll just have to wait and see what happens. But it will be fun. I promise! Our first stop is Galesburg, Illinois. We're going to stop in that town and stay for a while, just to see what it is like." Sadie's words seemed to soothe Gus somewhat, and his whimpering was much quieter. He didn't push for information about his father. And he stood a little farther away from Sadie so he could peek around her skirt and watch the people milling around.

Once they were allowed to board the train, Sadie seated herself and Gus in the middle of the car, their presence obscured by the passengers stowing luggage and picking the prime seats by the windows. The lights were on inside the car, and Sadie wasn't taking any chances that Frank would free himself too soon, and they would be recognized. Once the train began to move, Sadie watched the City lights lumber by until they faded into the distance. As soon as Sadie knew New York City was behind her, she began to relax.

The next morning, Sadie and Gus ate the sandwiches Sadie had brought from home. Later that day, they explored the train. Gus was fascinated with the observation car, so they spent most of the afternoon watching the world roll by. That evening Sadie slept fitfully through the night, the unfamiliar sounds of the train and milling passengers keeping her brain from totally shutting down. She finally allowed herself to drop into a deep sleep as dawn was breaking.

"Momma. Momma. We're here! Wake up. A man just walked by and told everybody that Galesburg, Illinois, was the next stop. We get off here, don't we?" Gus was shaking Sadie's shoulder, concern on his face.

Sadie awoke instantly alert. Sadie blinked her eyes in confusion for a few seconds. The mental images of her narrow escape from Frank had popped immediately into her head, and her brain was having trouble organizing any kind of conclusion. As the fog began to clear in her head and her eyes started to recognize the passenger car, Sadie hastily scanned the unfamiliar surroundings. People were milling around and jostling each other as they gathered their belongings. There was no sign of Frank. The car was swerving sideways as the brakes of the train forced the slowdown on the rails. Steam was rising and surrounding the windows as the train pulled up to the platform in Galesburg, Illinois. Sadie leaned down and reached frantically for the two satchels that contained all she now owned and smiled up at Gus when her fingers recognized the thick paisley upholstery of their bags. She had succeeded.

"Yes, Gus. We are here. This is where we get off to start our new adventure!"

Sadie and Gus stepped off the train and began to weave their way through the crowd of people. They walked past the baggage and freight house toward the main station. The train station complex was built of dark reddish-brown glazed brick with limestone trim. The red Spanish clay tile roof contrasted the blue sky of early morning and seemed to welcome them to their new home.

Sadie and Gus walked across the green lawn to the entrance into the general waiting room. The morning sunlight streaked in through the windows, causing dust particles to dance in the airy spaces between the people. The people inside looked around at the two ruffled strangers as the clicking of Sadie's heels broke the muffling sound of scuffling papers and the sighing of the heavy luggage scraping across the floor. Although the room was crowded with passengers and people coming to meet them, there was familiarity among each other. Galesburg was a bustling, industrious town but also very complete in itself. Faces were known, if not names, and townspeople with business at the train station expected everyday sameness.

Sadie smiled to herself as the realization of her successful escape started to sink in. She had made it to a new life. This was now her home, a small place so very far away from the brutal voice and hands of Frank. As far as Sadie was concerned, this town had to be the freshest, friendliest town she could dream of. Sadie had been living in the bowels of New York City for almost ten years and could only compare Galesburg to her childhood memories of Ohio. This town had to be a good, healthy, bright spot in the world. Sadie felt somewhat refreshed even though she had been wearing the same dirty, sweaty clothes for the last three days. Sadie was now ready for the next step, finding a place to stay.

Across the room, the front door of the terminal opened, and the crisp, pungent early spring air pushed in the smoke and noise from the steam engines. The acrid scent of the steam burned Sadie's eyes and nostrils. As the light breeze pushed the steam away from the open door, Sadie saw the small figure almost hidden behind the stack of newspapers the young man was carrying.

"I'll take one of those papers, please." Sadie was bubbling with enthusiasm and almost skipped across the room to the paperboy who was stacking papers. Female heads turned disapprovingly toward Sadie with her dusty, rumpled clothing and wildly disheveled hair.

Sadie felt the sting of stares, but right now she didn't care what the rest of the world thought. She was free, and her son was free. She had taken the first step toward a new life, and she was not ashamed of what she had done. The next step was finding a temporary place to stay. So much remained unknown, but Sadie was only able to take one small step at a time. Sadie whispered a prayer for help as she flipped through the pages of the paper.

"Gus, here's a room for rent. The paper says it is a well-established rooming house with a kitchen we can use. And it's only eight dollars a month. This sounds like a great place to start. We can stay there for a while until we get to know the town a little better. So, let's go find out where the corner of Maple and East North Street is. On with the adventure!"

Sadie stuffed the paper into her satchel, bought a small Galesburg City map from the ticket agent, and smiled down at Gus as she took his hand and headed for the street. She didn't tell Gus that it was the only room advertised in the paper. All the other rental ads were for tenant housing or apartments that Sadie knew she couldn't afford until she had a job. Once she had secured a job, she could then find a house close to where she would be working. And maybe close to a school for Gus.

The excitement and adrenaline rush of the last few days was beginning to take its toll on Sadie's body. Her body was tired and broken, and she was emotionally drained. She was excited with her victorious freedom, but her body was beginning to feel the toll of all the months of worry and the last three days of her desperate escape. Sadie felt the throbbing of her swollen feet stuffed into shoes that were not meant to be worn for days at a time. Sadie was hot, sweaty, and dirty. Sadie could do nothing else but cling to the hope that the room was still available.

"Come on, Gus. Let's go find our new Home.

CHAPTER TWO

Taking the Job No One Wanted

Gus slipped his hand into Sadie's, looked up at her, and smiled. Sadie felt a sharp pang of guilt as she walked down the sidewalk hand in hand with her son. She had successfully escaped Frank's brutal prison. But in doing so, she had taken Gus away from his father. Frank's relationship with Gus was a cold one, but the only one Gus knew. And for his young years of knowledge, it was a relationship that he would be missing soon. It was just Sadie and Gus now. And she would find a way to fill any void left by a missing father figure. Sadie purchased two ham and cheese sandwiches from the lunch counter in the corner of the terminal room. She handed one to Gus, and they walked and ate as they headed down the bright streets of their new town.

After walking for over an hour in the early April sunshine, Sadie and Gus finally found the street signs for Maple and East North Street. They stopped on the sidewalk and gazed up at the huge Victorian house in front of them.

The cream-colored paint on the three-story house was faded and beginning to peel, but it radiated warmth with the huge wrap-around front porch. Tiny clusters of native roses were beginning to snake up the wood lattice work around the bottom of the porch, and the corner tower rising through the middle of the porch roof reached out to Sadie with strength and safety, engulfing her in its height and watchfulness. The front yard was big and green and reminded her of the front yard she grew up with in Ohio. Sadie was immediately drawn to the house. It would provide safety to her and Gus for as long as they needed it. This home was beckoning her inside, welcoming her home.

Sadie and Gus walked up the sidewalk and opened the gate that blocked their path to the front steps of the house. The white picket fence surrounding the yard seemed to protect the shade being produced by several aged oak and elm trees scattered in the two front corners of the yard. Gus was walking beside Sadie, hand in hand, almost jogging with his short legs to keep up with her.

Sadie and Gus walked up the porch steps, crossed the vast porch floor, and knocked on the large oak door. Endless seconds passed before muffled sounds were heard on the other side of the door.

"May I help you?" The lady had only partially opened the door and was peering out from behind the door as if to guard her from bodily harm.

"We need to rent a room. May we please come in?" Sadie was holding Gus up with her arm. The excitement of the long trip was beginning to take its toll on Gus. Gus started to sit down on the steps, and Sadie bent down to pick him up in her arms. When she looked back at the lady behind the door, she couldn't hide her weariness and worry.

"I don't have any rooms left that are decent for a family. The only sleeping place left is on the main floor with me. You would have to share my kitchen and bathroom. And I don't take kindly to the inconvenience. I'm old and set in my ways. Move on, please." The older lady turned away and started to close the door. Without hesitation, Sadie stuck her foot in the crack of the doorway to keep from being completely shut out.

"Please, Ma'am! Please don't send us away! We've ridden the train all the way from New York City. We are bone tired and so hungry. Please let us stay. At least for a couple of days until we have time to find another place? I can pay in advance. Please! My son needs to rest!" Sadie was not used to begging for a bed, and it rankled her considerably to be in the position of relying on someone else for the care of her children. But she needed a few days to get a job before she could look for a permanent home.

The older lady opened the screen door and came out onto the front porch with Sadie and Gus.

"Please, Ma'am!" Gus's soft voice was garbled as he choked back his fear. Gus couldn't hold back his own tears any longer and began to silently let the tears slide down his cheeks.

The old lady gazed a few moments into Gus' tear-stained face then looked at Sadie, smiled and held out her hand. With her left hand she wiped away Gus' tears.

"My name is Mrs. Blumenthal. You can stay for a few days until you get settled. Your room is down the hall, last door on the left. You can share my bathroom across the hall. You are free to use the kitchen any time. You just need to make sure you clean up when you are done. I'll also fix a space for your things in the refrigerator and in one of the cupboards. Now come on in and get settled. "

Sadie sighed with relief. As she shook Mrs. Blumenthal's hand, the relief she felt almost overwhelmed her into years.

"Thank you. Thank you so much! We'll be no bother. I promise! It will just take me a few days to find a job and a permanent home. Then we will be out of your hair."

"Let's just take this a week at a time. See how we get along." Mrs. Blumenthal smiled at Gus and tousled his hair. "Been a long time since I've been around any children and young folks. Might be a nice change for a while. Come on in. I'll show you to your room. And I'll even make some sandwiches while you two freshen up."

Sadie and Gus inhaled their sandwiches, thanked Mrs. Blumenthal profusely, and then crashed on the bed, still in the rumpled clothes they had worn on the train. It was early afternoon, and the rest was to be a little nap, enough sleep to give Sadie the strength to check out the job ads in the paper safely tucked in her satchel. Sadie knew the rooming house was a temporary place to stay, but she was already getting attached to the warmth and cheerfulness that exuded from the house. She was sure it had beckoned her as they walked up the steps. The rooming house was full, and she would just have to find another place that was just as warm and inviting. At least she and Gus had a wonderful place to rest first.

The sun was slipping under the horizon when Sadie woke up. She looked over at Gus, and he was fast asleep on the other pillow, curled up in a tiny ball. Sadie decided the job could wait until morning. She tucked a blanket around Gus's body up to his chin, and unrolled his little body into a more comfortable position. Sadie felt safe for the first time she could remember. And her child was safe. Sadie could sleep peacefully and not worry about Frank finding Gus in bed with her.

It had only happened once. Gus was four years old at the time and Frank had decided to make a man out of him.

"No son of mine is going to cry at the drop of a hat. When I raise my voice to you, boy, don't cry and run to your mother. Look me in the eye and say, 'Yes, sir". It was Saturday morning, and Frank had decided it was time for Gus to grow up. This was the third Saturday in a row that Frank had monitored and corrected every minute of Gus's day.

"I'm sorry, Daddy. I'm trying to be good." Tears were streaming down Gus's face, and his little body was shaking so hard he could barely stand.

"I don't want you to be good. I want you to be tough!" Frank had shoved a chair behind Gus with his foot.

"Now sit down and eat your breakfast. Eat all of it. You and me are going to clean up the garage, so you need to keep your strength up."

Sadie had watched in pain as Gus had gulped his food down. She knew he wasn't hungry, and she knew he was terribly frightened. But she didn't know how to help him.

Sadie had spent the day in the kitchen so she could be as close to Gus as she could without interfering. She had cried more than Gus did that day and hugged him close for hours that evening after Frank left for the bar.

Sadie had taken Gus to her bed early that evening as he couldn't stop crying. Sadie fell asleep soon after Gus did and did not wake up in time to move Gus to his own room. When Frank flipped on the light in their bedroom, he exploded in rage.

"Get that child out of my bed! What on earth are you thinking? He will never be able to stand on his own feet as long as his mother keeps coddling him!" Frank took the two steps to the bed swiftly.

"I'm sorry Frank. We were just so tired that I didn't think it would hurt anything." Sadie had jumped out of bed and started to reach for Gus. But Frank moved faster.

"That's right, Sadie, you didn't think. You never do. You aren't capable of a single organized thought." Frank reached down and grabbed Gus by the arm. Gus was screaming in fear as Frank lifted him out of the bed by one arm, took a step into the hallway, and threw Gus into his room. Gus had landed with a thud on the edge of his bed.

Sadie had worried about Gus all night, but Frank had her body pinned down. He had one leg thrown across her stomach and one arm across her chest. His face was two inches from her ear, and she couldn't move without waking Frank.

Sadie could let that fear go now. Sadie kissed Gus lightly on the cheek, crawled under the other side of the blanket, and closed her eyes. Sadie sighed and drifted off to sleep. Her body was completely relaxed, and no dreams awakened her.

Sadie awoke to the sound of crackling bacon frying and the wonderful mix of smells of bacon, eggs and fresh bread in the oven. The desire to run into the kitchen and sample was almost overpowering. Two days of nothing but cold sandwiches and water, coupled with the stress and activities of actually completing her escape, made for a very empty stomach,

"Oh, Momma, do you think Mrs. Blumenthal is cooking that breakfast for us? It smells so good!" Gus was sitting up on the bed, trying to smooth the wrinkles out of his shirt and combing his hair with his hands.

"No, Gus. We can't take advantage of Mrs. Blumenthal. She was nice enough to let us stay here. We must be very polite and not intrude on her. We were invited to share the kitchen. We mustn't expect Mrs. Blumenthal to cook for us too." Sadie found her comb in the bag and winced as she started working out the tangles in her red hair. She needed a bath, a long, hot soaking bath to wash off the dirt of New York and begin her personal cleansing of removing Frank from her head, her heart and her life.

"Well now, you two. I'd love to invite you both to have breakfast with me, but I don't even know your names." "Mrs. Blumenthal was smiling in the open doorway, spatula in one hand, and a glass of milk in the other.

"My name is Gus, and this is Sadie, my momma. We came all the way out here from New York City on the train. It took us two days!" Gus smiled his appreciation as he took the milk that Mrs. Blumenthal offered him. He drank half the glass in almost one gulp and then handed the rest to Sadie.

"My husband died recently, and Gus and I felt we needed to find a new home. There wasn't much left for us in New York." Sadie watched Mrs. Blumenthal's face intently to see if the lie was believable. Mrs. Blumenthal looked into Sadie's eyes intently, smiled faintly, and turned toward the kitchen.

"No need to explain. I make it a point not to get too familiar with my houseguests. I run a rooming house here, and no one stays around long, but I wanted to get your first day in Galesburg off to a good start. Don't expect this every day! Breakfast will be ready in five minutes." Mrs.

Blumenthal smiled at Sadie and Gus, and then turned toward the kitchen.

Sadie hurried Gus through breakfast and kept the adult conversation focused on very harmless topics.

As soon as Gus had swallowed his last drink of milk and the dishes were washed and replaced in the cupboards, Sadie thanked Mrs. Blumenthal profusely and shuffled Gus back to their room.

Sadie pulled the crumpled Galesburg newspaper out of her satchel and quickly found the job ads. Disappointment grew as she checked off job after job that she had no qualifications for. Close to the bottom of the column was an ad that peaked Sadie's interest: 'Wanted. Live-in housekeeper. Widow with no children. Apply at Charles Boarding House for Boys.'

Sadie considered her options. She was not a widow, but they would never know that. She had already lied about her marital status, and she could probably do it again. Sadie did have a child, but she didn't have to accept the live-in arrangements, and they would never know otherwise. Sadie knew she could do this job if just given the chance. Housekeeping was the one thing she knew she was very good at. And no boss could be more of a perfectionist than Frank. And she could make arrangements for Gus, so that her employer would never know he existed. Sadie decided to take a chance and see if she could get an interview. If she got the job, she would figure out what to do next. She wasn't sure what she would do, but she didn't travel halfway across the country to give up now. Sadie hoped that each small victory would open that next door of opportunity. It had to work. She had no other way to go and knew no other paths to take. And she wasn't going to turn back now just because she didn't know what to do next.

Sadie dug into her satchel looking for the proper outfit to wear. She had never been to a job interview, so she wasn't sure what was appropriate. Sadie pulled out her best outfit of the three that she had brought with her. The drab, brown dress was originally made to hide any possible curves a woman might have. The dress had a wide, scalloped-edged collar that buttoned all the way to the chin. Boxy, squared shoulders and a hemline that dropped to her ankles completely hid any hint of a body shape. Frank had brought the dress home to her after she had given birth to Gus. The preparation for motherhood had brought a new maturity to Sadie's body. Her curves had enhanced themselves and rounded out over the additional flesh worn by a grown woman. Frank had been insistent that she cover any glimpse of beauty and grace.

The dress was quite worn, and the faded brown of the color added to the drabness. Sadie giggled to herself as she slipped it over her shoulders. 'Well, at least this dress will make a statement that I do need the job!' Sadie slipped into her thick brown heels with the scuffed rounded toes. Sadie's hair was a bright strawberry red, naturally curly and glowing in loose curls halfway down her back. Attempting to make herself look older, Sadie pulled her hair into a bun. She fussed with her hairpins, trying to poke the unruly wisps of ringlets into the thick bun. She finally gave up when she ran out of hairpins.

Sadie's mind was racing as she tried to find a way to let Gus know that she was gong to have to leave him alone for a while and gently ease his fears, especially now on their first full day in their new town. Gus had been through so much in the past few days. She wasn't sure how much more Gus could handle. She wasn't sure how much more she could handle, and she was supposed to be the grownup.

"Gus, I need to go out for a few hours to see if I can get a job. I need you to stay here in the bedroom until I get back. You can keep busy here with your sketch pads. See, I brought your sketch pads and your charcoal." Gus spent a lot of time by himself with his drawings. It seemed to be his way of staying out of Frank's way and being able to ignore the noise of the beatings when Frank would come home drunk. On many occasions Sadie would find Gus sitting on the floor of his bedroom drawing by the light from the streetlights that shined in his windows. There were never words spoken between them on those nights. Gus never looked up from his sketch pad, but he would smile, and Sadie would know he was okay.

"Please, Momma, let me go with you. I'll be good, and I'll be quiet. Please let me go with you!" Gus was clinging to his mother's waist as tears started to form in his eyes.

"No, Gus. You need to stay here. I won't be gone more than a couple of hours. And when I get back, we can walk around Galesburg for a while and see what is here. I promise. I'll be back soon! Draw me a picture of what you think our house will look like. Okay?" Sadie couldn't tell Gus that she needed to appear childless to get the job. She would not crush his little heart by letting him learn of her pending betrayal.

"Momma, I want to go with you. I can help you!" Gus looked so desperate and forlorn that Sadie picked him up and squeezed him as hard as she dared. She felt Gus's little body tremors and knew he was so very afraid. All this was new and foreign to Gus. She wished she could explain it all to him so he could see the future and be less afraid. But she had to be able to explain it to herself first. And Sadie's plan did not extend beyond getting the job at the boarding house. If she got the job, she and Gus could plan. If she didn't get the job, she just didn't know.

"Gus, listen to me. It's going to be just you and me for a while now. Your father isn't going to join us for a long time. So we need to build us a new life here in Galesburg, just you and me. And since we don't have your father here to bring in money to buy food and pay for clothes and such, Momma is going to have to go to work for other people. They will pay me for my work, and then we can buy food, clothes and a place to live. It will be fun, and adventurous. Just you and me! But first I must go see about finding some of that work. And I can't take you because you are too little. So, you have to stay here and wait for me. I will be back in a couple of hours. I promise! Do you understand, baby?"

The 'Yes Momma' that came out of Gus's mouth completely belied the look on his face. Sadie's heart went out to him as she watched him try to understand. She knew this might be too much for him. But nonetheless, she would work on Gus's understanding later. Right now, she had to get that job. It was the only one she had any hope of getting.

The walk to Charles Boarding House for Boys seemed much farther than it looked on the map. Sadie had walked for almost an hour before she saw the sign in the yard. Walking up the sidewalk, Sadie hurriedly straightened her skirt and ran her fingers through her hair. She had rolled her hair into a bun in an attempt to look older, but her red stubborn strands kept sneaking out onto her neck and face. The combination of the early spring moisture in the air and the natural curl in Sadie's hair resulted in bouncy little ringlets around her ears and the back of the neck. Instead of looking older, the effect made Sadie look very young, naïve, and fragile. Sadie timidly knocked on the heavy wooden front door.

After several minutes, the door cracked open, and a middle-aged, bespectacled woman stuck her head through the crack.

"Whatever you are selling, young lady, I am not interested. I only purchase from my regular salespeople." With that said, the door started to close.

"I'm not here to sell anything. I'm here for the housekeeping job. Please tell the mistress of the house that Sadie Adams would like to speak to her about the position."

The woman opened the door and glared at Sadie over her glasses.

"The ad called for an older widow. You do not qualify."

"I am a widow, and older than I look. I will repeat my request. Would you please let the mistress of the house know that I am here for the job?" Sadie was losing her patience with this woman. She was anxious to get this job and get on with building a new life for herself and Gus.

"I am the mistress of the house, missy! And I don't tolerate such insolence!"

"My sincere apologies, ma'am! I didn't realize. Please forgive me for my hasty judgment. My name is Sadie Adams. I am here to apply for the housekeeping job." Sadie winced inwardly. She was definitely starting off on the wrong foot. Things were not looking good.

"Oh, all right. Take a seat here in the hallway. I'll get to you in a few minutes. I'm Doris Steinway. I do the hiring, and I do the firing. I decide who lives here, works here, and who doesn't. Is that clear?"

"Yes, ma'am." Sadie instinctively dropped her eyes to the floor. The tone in Doris Steinway's voice struck a chord in Sadie deep within her soul. Frank's training had been quite effective. But Sadie just had to get this job. Housekeeping was the only thing she knew how to do. She didn't have enough cash to get by on for very long. She needed to start working right away. But right now, things were not looking good. She was not making a good impression, and she knew it.

Sadie sat in the hot, stuffy hallway for what seemed like hours. The hard, walnut straight-backed chair was very uncomfortable, and sweat beads were seeping down between her shoulder blades, down along her spine, and settling into the elastic waistband of her panties. Sadie wanted to find a mirror. She knew her face and hair must look as bad as her lower back felt.

Doris finally dropped a piece of paper and a pen in Sadie's lap as she walked by with a prospective college student.

"Here's an application. Fill it out. We'll talk when I get back." The ice was dripping from Doris' voice. Sadie shivered in the aftermath.

Sadie filled in as many of the blanks she could, leaving previous information blank. Sadie wanted nothing in writing that somehow might betray her whereabouts to Frank, nor did she want anyone in this new place to know about her past. Sadie hesitated only for an instant before writing 'widow' after the question on marital status.

"Come with me." Doris whisked quickly by Sadie's chair. Sadie jumped to her feet and rushed forward to stay in step behind her. Doris was almost six feet tall and towered over Sadie. Her appearance was starkly different than Sadie's. Doris was easily in her mid-forties, had a ruddy, blotchy complexion, and piercing green eyes. Her nose was the most prominent feature on her face. Doris was not overweight in any sense of the term. But the shape of her body was not pleasant to look at. Her wide shoulders were bent inward and slumped downward toward her chest. And her breasts were way too large and way too loose for the tight-fitting thin silk blouse. Her body continued to display unnatural bumps and corners. Her waist was tightly belted, giving it an unnatural sunken look. Her lower belly had developed a middle-aged protrusion that poked through her tight plaid skirt. Doris was not exactly an ugly woman but definitely not a comely woman. She had already blossomed, and the flower was wilting on the vine.

Doris motioned Sadie to a straight-backed chair in front of a huge oak desk in a small office. The one window in the room was open, but the blinds had been pulled down over the opening, stopping any fresh air from entering. Two bookcases graced one wall, with their books stacked neatly, proportioned by the height and the size of the books. Tall, fat books were on the left, and the small, skinny books were all on the right. A small fan sat on top of the file cabinet, and a tiny ceramic music box was the only personal adornment on the desk. On the opposite end of the room was a small living space in front of the fireplace. It had a small loveseat and two Victorian straight-backed chairs with a dark, oak-stained coffee table between them. A large black and white commercial clock ticked loudly on the wall.

Doris walked around to the other side of the desk and sat down carefully in another straight-backed chair just like the one Sadie was sitting in, only bigger. Sadie waited motionlessly as Doris carefully straightened her skirt and her hair and began to study Sadie's application.

The minutes ticked by. Doris used her finger to guide her eyes as she read each line of the application. Doris would use the same finger to push her reading glasses back up her nose each time they slid down with the sweat on her face. Between every few lines, Doris would pause her reading, study Sadie's face over her glasses, and frown. Sadie shrunk into her chair in reaction to the frown, making her look and feel tinier and more frightened than ever. It took all of the resolve Sadie could muster to keep from bolting out the door.

"You didn't include your previous address. I know you aren't from Galesburg because I know everyone in this town. Where did you come from? Who did you work for there? Did you bring references with you?" Doris frowned at Sadie over her reading glasses.

"I asked you for your references. You haven't provided them. Obviously, you have none. Does this mean you had no experience, or you were such a poor housekeeper that no one would give you a reference? Which is it? Speak up! I don't have all day to waste on your silly little notions of working for me!"

Sadie recoiled from the venom that spewed out of this woman's mouth. Even if she got the job, she didn't think she could measure up to this woman's expectations. Life would be miserable, as this woman expected no less than perfection. Sadie wasn't sure she wanted to do that again. And she knew the first time she messed up this woman would delight in firing her.

But she had to get the job. It was the only one in town at the moment. The only decent job, anyway. Sadie was determined to be a good mother to Gus and provide a home and an income that he didn't have to be ashamed of. Sadie wanted Gus to live in a modest, quiet, calm and loving home from now on. She knew that she had to provide Gus that stability if he was ever going to get past the years with his abusive father. Sadie knew that truth with all her heart.

Displaying all the courage and confidence Sadie could muster, she leaned over Doris's desk and faced the bitter woman, looking steadily into Doris's green piercing eyes.

"I came here from New York City, and I am a widow. My husband recently passed away and left me little. I came out here to heal and start my life over. I have no formal housekeeping experience in that I have never been paid for it. However, I have spent every day of my married life keeping a perfect house, keeping a house the way, my husband demanded it be kept. I can take orders very well and can work long hours."

Doris scrutinized Sadie's face and body language.

"Look, I pay ten dollars a week for my housekeeper. That's top dollar. Better than you can get anywhere else in town. And I don't pay top dollar for mediocre help. I pay for the best, and I expect the best." With that said, Doris watched Sadie's face for any flicker or recognition of other places in town.

"Ms. Steinway, I don't know what it will take to make you understand that I am perfectly capable of doing this job and doing it well. I know I seem young to you, but I am experienced beyond my years! Tell you what. You pay ten dollars a week? I will work for you for seven dollars a week. You pay me seven dollars a week for three months on a trial basis. If you determine at any time that I am not doing my job, you may fire me. If, however, you determine at the end of the three months that I am qualified, then you raise my pay to ten dollars a week." Sadie met Doris's gaze with her own steady green eyes and didn't blink until Doris turned away.

"Seven dollars a week, huh? For three months?"

"The ad also stated no children. You are too young not to have children lurking around some corner, I don't have the patience or the room for children in the boarding house. The housekeeper's quarters consist of a very small bedroom and a bath at the end of the hall. And since we board college boys here, it would not be appropriate to have young children under foot. So, where are your children?"

Sadie sat up straight in her chair, folded her arms on the front of Doris' desk, and leaned in close, so close that Doris flinched and backed away a bit. Sadie would have really enjoyed that fleeting feeling of power had she not been so afraid of losing her attention and the momentum of the moment.

"I don't have any children. My husband had been ill for a long time, and God chose not to bless us with children. Also, I don't need the housekeeper's quarters. I have found quarters of my own and would prefer to stay where I am." Sadie was still meeting Doris's gaze, but her eyes were beginning to tear. She felt like she had just betrayed Gus in the worst way. Sadie needed to protect and love Gus, and here she was denying his very existence. The tears were going to spill over onto her cheeks really soon if Sadie didn't do something quick. Deftly Sadie bowed her head and turned her chair sideways, with her face away from Doris as she began to dig in her purse. Sadie then feigned a sneeze with a muffled, 'Excuse me', as she swiftly blew her nose and quickly wiped the tears into her handkerchief.

Doris pretended to reread Sadie's application very slowly, page by page.

"All right, we'll give it a try. Today is Thursday. You start on Monday. Report to my office Monday morning at six thirty. Your hours are six thirty to five, Monday through Friday, or until you work is finished. You will have thirty minutes for lunch. Your lunch hour will vary according to your duty schedule for the day, and you will not leave the premises. You can eat in the kitchen. Please dress appropriately, and conduct yourself in a lady-like manner at all times. We have young boys in this house who are paying to stay here to be near the college. No fraternization! Remember, you are the hired help. If at any time I deem your actions, appearance, or conversation in appropriate, I will fire you without hesitation. Do I make myself clear?"

Sadie breathed a sign of relief. She had the job!

"Yes, ma'am. You have made yourself perfectly clear. I will be here at six thirty sharp Monday morning!" Sadie held out her hand to Doris as she stood up to leave. Doris simply glared at Sadie over the rim of her reading glasses.

Sadie felt the burden of the world lift from her shoulders. She had her first real job, and she had gotten the job with no help from anyone. She had convinced a hardened spinster that she was capable and worthy of the position. She knew offering to work for a lower salary had definitely swayed Ms. Steinway. And Sadie also had no doubt that this job would be very hard work, with very long hours. And perfection would be demanded. But Sadie knew she was up for the task. She had no other options.

As Sadie almost skipped down the sidewalk toward her temporary home and Gus, she giggled out loud. The very thought of Sadie fraternizing with the college boys! If Ms. Steinway had any inkling of what Sadie had been through the last few years, she would have never entertained the thought, let alone the verbal warning. All Sadie wanted was honest work and a chance to make a home for Gus. Life for Sadie included only Gus now. Sadie had had a man of her own for many years. Frank was exciting and irresistible at first, a man who had put her on a pedestal and showered her with attention. A man of every woman's dreams. Until Sadie succumbed and married him. Then he turned on her.

The happy moments in Sadie's marriage were so far removed from Sadie's memory that she couldn't remember what she had ever seen in Frank. And she had tried so hard to remember. The last few months of Sadie's life in New York City, as she planned her secret escape, had been filled with frustration and doubt as Sadie tried to recall why she had ever fallen for Frank. Some minute part of Sadie's heart had wanted, and still wanted, to love and believe in Frank. She couldn't have been so very wrong in choosing a man absolutely devoid of any goodness, love or compassion. There had to be something inside Frank that Sadie had seen to attract her to him. Some shred of goodness somewhere in Frank. Something that would give Sadie a reason to stay and hope. Breaking marriage vows did not come easily, and Sadie had searched her soul for answers. But search as she did, Sadie found no answers. All Sadie could find were trace memories. Memories so weak that she couldn't bring the pictures into focus.

The vivid pictures in Sadie's memory were those of meanness and hatred. Frank was mean, evil and avenging. There was no good anywhere that Sadie could see. Any glimmer of hope that Sadie had for Frank had been all but snuffed out by repeated physical beatings and constant emotional abuse.

But Sadie was done with that. She had rescued Gus and herself from a life destined for early death. She was making a loving home for Gus, and he would grow up to be a fine young man. Her quest for freedom from the shackles of abuse and humiliation, and to live her life as a respected and contributing member of society, had been won. Sadie could now relax and enjoy her life to the fullest.

Sade picked up her pace as she turned onto the street of Mrs. Blumenthal's boarding house. She forgot about the scratching of her wool skirt on her legs and the humiliation of the interview. Sadie had a job. A well-paying job. She couldn't wait to tell Gus. She couldn't wait to see him. Life was good. No, life was wonderful!

CHAPTER THREE

Finding the Forever Home

Sadie was up at dawn the next morning, combing through her rumpled newspaper under the dim glow of the bedside lamp. Gus was sleeping contentedly beside her in the bed. She wanted to begin her search for a permanent residence and a place for Gus. Surely this town was big enough to have a settlement house with day nursery. A few days ago, Sadie would have scoffed at living in a settlement house, let alone considering a day nursery for Gus. Sadie now justified her thinking. Galesburg was not nearly as dirty as New York City, so any settlement housing here had to be much more respectable. And if she had to, Sadie would leave Gus home alone. She shivered at the thought. Then she put her options to the back of her mind. She had found work easy enough. The rest would work itself out also.

But her new, unfamiliar situation nagged at her. Husbands were expected to take care of their families. And a woman's place was definitely in the home. Women who were married and had children only did volunteer work outside the home. And the children were usually cared for by other female family members while the mothers were out of the home.

With the fallout from the stock market crash, many women were seeking work to help put food on the table. And devastating stock market losses for some families meant that their status went from affluent to penniless overnight. Other women were forced into the working world as a result of the alarming number of men who chose suicide over admitting failure and defeat. Sadie may have been a prisoner in her own home, but she had been able to keep abreast of current events by devouring the daily New York Times that was delivered to Frank. Frank had modest investments in the stock market that had lost almost all of their value after the crash. Frank read the stock market reports religiously before going to work each day. Sadie then read the paper cover to cover as her only connection with the outside world.

Settlement houses with day nurseries were dotted throughout communities and were easily obtained in New York City, but judging by the local newspaper, it could be difficult to find in the small town of Galesburg. If settlement houses weren't called that here in Galesburg, then Sadie would look for an apartment community. Sadie refused to be daunted. She had been successful in escaping Frank and finding a job, and she would be successful in finding a home and a place for Gus while she worked. He would be in school soon, so she would only need to find a mother in the neighborhood who would be willing to help out a few hours a day.

Sadie dressed, combed her curly hair, and again carefully rolled it into a bun. She had learned quickly from her experience with Doris Steinway that the appearance of maturity had a better chance of getting her respect. The newspaper ads for housing had been circled, and Sadie carefully folded the housing section of the newspaper and placed it in her purse. This newspaper was Sadie's only link to her new world, and it had become her security blanket.

Gus was still sleeping as Sadie paced back and forth across the tiny floor of the bedroom they shared. She didn't want to waste any daylight, and she needed to get busy. She only had a few days before she had to go to work, and today was a Friday. She was pretty sure that she wouldn't be able to find what she wanted on a weekend. Sadie was completely unfamiliar with her choices here in Galesburg and wanted to check out as many as possible quickly. She knew she could stay at the rooming house for a week, so she wanted to be ready to make her choice by next weekend.

The house was still quiet as Sadie padded barefoot into the kitchen. Mrs. Blumenthal had been so generous and gracious to Sadie and Gus. Sadie felt indebted to her for allowing her and Gus to stay there and for watching over Gus yesterday while she went for her job interview. Sadie had not asked Mrs. Blumenthal to take care of Gus, but she knew Mrs. Blumenthal had stayed home and peeked in at him several times to make sure he was okay. Sadie was extremely grateful to this stranger who had so graciously accepted the silent responsibility for her son. She would have left Gus alone even if Mrs. Blumenthal hadn't been there, but knowing she was there made it so much easier on her conscience.

Sadie had decided to surprise her and cook breakfast as a gesture of repaying the kindness Mrs. Blumenthal had showed Sadie. And Sadie didn't want to be more of a burden than she had already been. Sadie had the table set, the bacon cooking, and was just popping the bread into the toaster when Mrs. Blumenthal appeared in the doorway.

"Well, this is a surprise!" Mrs. Blumenthal smiled approvingly at Sadie as she wrapped her housecoat around her waist and cinched it tight. Mrs. Blumenthal was a small, fragile woman in appearance. Her oval-shaped, thin face still had the hint of modest beauty even though thinning strands of gray and white curls now surrounded it. The white was beginning to outnumber the gray hair and created a sparkling accent to the gray-blue of Mrs. Blumenthal's eyes. Eyes that still sparkled of the dreams of youth that could only be tempered and softened by the wisdom of many years of patient experience.

"It has been a very long time since someone has cooked for me. Not since my husband was alive. This is nice. Thank you!"

"Your husband cooked for you?" Sadie's incredulous look of surprise made Mrs. Blumenthal laugh out loud.

"Yes, my dear child. My late husband used to cook breakfast for me every Sunday. He would demand that I stay in bed while he destroyed the kitchen cooking a huge breakfast for me. And then he would deliver my meal to me in the bedroom and help me eat it. We would sit on the bed and eat our breakfast while discussing how we would spend the day. We always spent Sundays together, usually taking long walks, spending afternoons in the library reading, always so very relaxed and enjoyable. Sometimes he would jump back in bed with me after breakfast, and we would just cuddle and talk for hours. He used to say that Sundays were a day to recharge our batteries. I miss him so." Mrs. Blumenthal wiped a tear from her face as she smiled back at Sadie.

"I tried to keep the tradition alive after my husband died. I would make a huge breakfast for myself and then jump back into bed to eat it. I thought that this tradition would bring him close to me, but it just made my missing him worse. You just can't bring them back. Anyway, thank you again for breakfast. This is really a nice surprise!" Mrs. Blumenthal popped a piece of bacon in her mouth as she poured milk into the three glasses at the table.

"We are so very grateful to you for giving us a place to stay. Cooking breakfast is only a token, but I don't have any other means of repaying your kindness right now." Sadie's face flushed with humiliation. She was beginning to realize that she had no one but Gus. She needed a friend. No, she wanted a friend more than she needed one. Someone she could share this awful burden with. Someone who could maybe give her some guidance and relief from the weight of it all. Sadie was really lost. She didn't know what to do next, how to do it, or what to expect. She had spent the last nine years doing exactly as Frank had demanded, which left no time or energy to pursue any interests or education. And whenever she showed any initiative or expressed her own ideas and creativity, Frank would beat it out of her.

"Don't dwell on my kindness. Goodness knows we all need a helping hand once in a while. There had been many times in my own life that I don't think I would have survived to tell the tale if it hadn't been for someone reaching out to me. But enough of that. Tell me a little about you. How did you end up in Galesburg of all places?" Mrs. Blumenthal stirred the sugar into her coffee and looked expectantly at Sadie.

"There is no really big story here." Sadie turned her back to Mrs. Blumenthal and proceeded to remove the bacon strips from the cast iron skillet. She removed them individually, blotting each one on a kitchen cloth slowly. She continued to speak to Mrs. Blumenthal with her face hidden. Sadie was new to this business of lying and wasn't sure her facial expressions would match what was coming out of her mouth.

"My husband died unexpectedly, leaving Gus and me with no visible means of support. Neither of us had much of a family left to count on, so I took a chance and hopped the train. Besides, I really didn't want to raise Gus alone in the City. It's not safe, you know." What she didn't tell Mrs. Blumenthal was that she had no other place to go. Sadie had met Frank on an excursion to New York City with her parents. She had just turned sixteen, and the attentions of the older, dark stranger had flattered Sadie beyond even her own vivid imagination.

Frank had won her parents approval with the loving attention he had bestowed on the entire family during their visit. Frank was a passenger train porter and had ample opportunities to drop by their home once they were back in Ohio. He kept in touch and quickly won Sadie's heart. In one day, Frank proposed to her, married her, and whisked her off to New York City. Her parents had been upset that Sadie wasn't being married in the Catholic Church, as was the family tradition. But Frank convinced them that the quick marriage was a necessity and that he would bring Sadie back in a few months to be remarried in the traditional church ceremony. Nine years had come and gone since then. Sadie had never been allowed to visit her family and had never returned to Ohio.

Sadie's parents had never approved of her courthouse marriage, and Frank had never approved of her parents. Frank had pushed Sadie's family out of her life a long time ago. Sadie had made the decision to marry Frank and move away from everything that she had known. And Sadie had made the decision to stay with Frank. She carried the regrets and the weight of responsibility of that decision every day of her life.

"Have you lived in Galesburg a long time?" Sadie was anxious to get the conversation onto something, and someone, else.

"Most of my life. I was a teenager when I met Saul, my late husband. We were married here in Galesburg and bought this house soon after. So I've pretty much spent my life here in this very house. After my husband died, I made the house into a rooming house, partly for the income and partly for the company."

"What's on the agenda for today? You are up and around awfully early and seem to be in a hurry."

"Gus and I are going to look for a more permanent place to live. We very much appreciate you taking us in and letting us stay. But I have a job now. I can take care of Gus and me. I don't want to take advantage of your kindness. And I really need a place of my own." Sadie also needed the privacy that came with her own place. She needed to be able to reach out to Gus and talk him through the traumatic experience of leaving his father behind. And she needed Gus to be able to be himself and let things out and question and heal with no fear. That was one of her goals when she left Frank, a home where there were no secrets and everything was discussed and decisions made as a loving family. At least there would be no secrets inside their home. Outside their home was another story. Sadie had already started building her external shell to protect her secret world. But she would sort that world out later. Not now. Sadie could only handle planning one day at a time right now. Every time Sadie tried to think ahead more than a day or two at a time, she felt like her brain would simply explode, so she refused to go there.

"Well, don't let your pride get in the way. There really is no hurry. And that woman you are going to work for is a hard woman. She is notorious in town for destroying housekeepers in an amazingly short amount of time. She won't go easy on you. And the women of this town have already judged you. You are too young, too pretty, and too alone. You'll make them uncomfortable and cause them to lash out at you. I know. I've watched them destroy more than one young woman in your shoes. I can help you if you let me.

You need to slow down a little and take this one step at a time. Trust me, I know these things." Mrs. Blumenthal reached over to pat Sadie's hand, but Sadie pulled it away. Tears were threatening to brim over and down Sadie's cheeks, but she wouldn't let them.

"I'm a grown woman. I know what I am doing, and I will take care of my son! I know you mean well, and I appreciate your concern. I have nothing to be ashamed of, and the ladies of the town will soon see that. You'll see. We'll be fine!" Sadie was thankful that Gus had just walked back into the kitchen. Sadie hid her face in Gus's neck as she hugged him, and Mrs. Blumenthal respectfully turned away.

Sadie's face was flushed. The previous conversation with Mrs. Blumenthal had caused her fear and agitation to rise so close to the surface. Sadie was concentrating completely on holding back her feelings. She must not lose control now when she had no safe place to allow herself to be vulnerable. Once she had a home of her own, it might be easier to convince herself that the new life that she had dreamed about for so long was really hers. Sadie had no experience as to what her life should really be like, only dreams. Sadie's plans and dreams were so very incomplete, as she didn't have enough knowledge to make her sketchy dreams a reality. Only a sketch could she envision now. And all that the sketch contained was her and Gus alone in a house of some kind with clean clothes to wear and food on the table. A home where there would be no need to hide her face inside for days until the bright colors of the bruises healed. Sadie's hands moved lightly over her bodice, smoothing out the material over and down her breasts. Sadie's very light touch caused the muffled pain of the most recent bruises on her chest and ribs to rise to the surface. The emotional stress of her flight from Frank and the physical toll it had taken on her body had made her rib cage absolutely rigid. The light touch caused her delicate flesh to wake up and remember.

Sadie longed for a day without pain, a day where she could roll out of bed in the morning and go about her normal chores without wincing. Sadie looked forward to the evenings when she could go to bed at night looking forward to peaceful sleep with no worries about Frank violently waking her up. She wanted no more days where the only incentive for getting up was to protect Gus. A good day, up until now, was to end the day still being able to walk upright and keep Frank away from Gus. And an even better day was one of Frank's poker nights. They always gave Sadie and Gus time alone without fear. And Frank was usually drunk enough when he came home that his violent outbursts would be shortened, and he would pass out quickly.

Sadie shook the memories out of her head. Enough of dwelling on the old memories. She must be persistent and strong. Sadie had been very successful in the last few days, but she still had a long way to go before she could completely relax.

"Okay, Gus. Let's get moving. Let's check out our new town and see if we can find a home for us. We're going on an adventure today! It'll be such fun. Come along, you must wash up and comb your hair before we leave. We mustn't give the wrong impression to our new neighborhood. They need to see what a wonderful family we are right from the beginning!" Sadie spoke to Gus as if in direct defiance of Mrs. Blumenthal's previous warnings. In spite of Mrs. Blumenthal's dire painting of the local societies, Sadie found herself getting excited about her outing. This was a new life. A place where she could be a respected citizen of the community. A new start and a new life. Sadie glided down the hall, holding hands with Gus and swinging their arms together.

"Sadie, please. You don't need to find another place to stay. You are more than welcome to stay with me as long as you need to. I know I made it very clear when you arrived that my house was full and I didn't want to take on any more boarders. But I'd really like the chance to help out a little. Please spend the day here. We'll go for a picnic, and I'll show you and Gus the town, and you can take plenty of time to find your new home. What do you say?" Mrs. Blumenthal smiled ever so engagingly at Sadie. Yes, Sadie would eventually have to face the bitter truth of being different. But she didn't need any more disappointments this soon. She was still too new at this and did not realize what her limits were.

"Mrs. Blumenthal, we'll be fine. We know what we are doing. After all, we came from New York City. I really think we can manage Galesburg!" Sadie tossed her head back, red curls bounding across her neck and down her back. Galesburg was a very small town. She and Gus would be fine.

"I have my map that I bought at the train station and the ad for the tenant houses. We'll find one with a big green yard and lots of trees!"

Mrs. Blumenthal stood in the doorway and waved to Sadie and Gus as they bounced down the sidewalk.

Sadie and Gus walked the ten blocks to West Berrien Street using the map to guide them to the first tenant house. The tenant housing block was only ten blocks from Sadie's place of employment, a short distance to walk to work every day but still far enough away to live in privacy.

There were five tenant houses that comprised that side of the City block. There were all of the same architecture, color, and landscaping. What little faded, white paint that was left on the outside of the houses was cracked and peeling from many years in the blistering sun. The houses were one story, narrow, and had few windows. Two rotting wooden steps led up to the front doors. The front yards were small with tiny patches of yellowed, thin grass splotched off and on against the bare soil. A small group of grubby children were playing kickball in the street and stopped to watch Sadie and Gus approach. They parted slightly to let Gus and Sadie pass and then banded together behind them as if to forbid the newcomers from encroaching on their territory.

"Are you sure this is the right street, Momma? I don't see any big green yards. All I see is dirt and dirty, yellow houses." Gus looked up at Sadie, squinting his eyes against the sun. "You said we would be living in a pretty place. This isn't pretty."

"Well, Gus. Maybe I spoke too soon. This is the right address according to the newspaper. And that third house has a for rent sign. That must be the place. I know it doesn't look that great outside, but maybe the inside is better. And we can make curtains and paint and plant flowers. We can have the prettiest house on the block!" Sadie's spirits rose as she knocked on the door of the house with the management sign tacked beside the door.

No one answered. Sadie grew anxious. The sign on the door said 'Housing Manager'. Someone just had to be home. Sadie needed to move forward before she lost her nerve. She was afraid that if she hesitated or something went wrong this soon, her delicate lifeline would break. Sadie knocked again, this time much harder. Sadie winced and shook the pain out of her finger from the splinter that jumped from the dried cracked wood on the door into her hand.

The door opened, and a portly middle-aged woman with wispy graying hair filled the doorway. She wiped her hands on a soiled towel as she looked Sadie up and down.

"Whatever you are selling, I don't want any. Just move on down the road." The lady pushed a wisp of gray hair back over her forehead and wiped the sweat from the side of her face with the back of her hand. She frowned at Sadie over her droopy eyelids as she began backing into the house. Sadie held out her hand and smiled.

"Wait! What I am looking for is a house to rent. You see, my son and I just arrived in town, and we need a place to live. I can pay an advance."

"Well, now we do have a couple of places, but they are a bit small. Not sure they would be good for the boy. Is your husband working? That why he isn't here?"

"Ma'am, my husband died recently and didn't leave us with much. I have a job now, but need to find a place to stay. We won't be any trouble. And I can pay."

"Ma'am? You want to live here? Where is your family? Why are you not living with your kin?"

"I don't have any family here. And Gus and I like Galesburg, and we would really like to stay here."

"Well, where is your family? Any decent woman would go back to her family or her husband's family until she could get another man to take care of her. You sure you had a husband, or are you just a tramp that got caught and ended up in the family way? And now you are trying to pass yourself off as a decent woman? I got enough of the likes of you already living here."

"Ma'am, I'm not even sure I want to live here! If I decide that I want to live here, I can pay my rent in advance. Just show me what is available." Sadie was getting disgusted with this woman and having a hard time keeping her composure. She was not used to begging for a place to stay, especially from some old hag who was passing judgement without knowing the facts. How dare this woman decide what kind of woman Sadie was when she hadn't even spent fifteen minutes with her!

"What kind of job you got? You going to take your son to work with you? He doesn't look old enough to stay home by himself. What you going to do with him? We got a few women here with children, but they don't have no permanent child care. They just take turns with each other's kids. And they ain't too swift about paying the rent on time. I don't need another washed up floozy here adding to the mess." The woman was still standing in the doorway, sweat trickling down through the wrinkles on her neck and following the cracks in her skin down into her bosom. Sadie was watching the sweat travel down its path while trying to compose herself and not burst into tears.

"You know what, I've changed my mind. I really don't want to live here. I'm better than this! Your place is rundown, there is no grass in the yard, and I'm sure some of those dirty little children there belong to you. We'll keep looking. You just lost a tenant. Come one, Gus. Let's check out some other places." Sadie grabbed Gus by the hand and flounced down the steps towards the street. There was one other place in the paper to check out. Sadie was hoping with all her heart that the housing manager was a little more open minded. And hopefully a little more kind.

Sadie knew that tenant housing was not the best place to put herself and Gus. But they needed a temporary home. They couldn't stay with Mrs. Blumenthal very long. She had taken them in out of pity. And Sadie greatly appreciated the help. But Sadie could take care of her own son now. She didn't need any help. The day she left Frank, she knew that Gus was her responsibility, and she was up to it. It might be a little ugly until she saved up enough money to get the perfect house, but she would make it up to Gus by loving him and keeping him safe. Besides, she had a job. All she needed now was a nice, comfortable home to rent until she could buy her own.

Sadie and Gus walked the tree-lined streets of Galesburg for another hour and then stopped in a little park to rest. The breeze was light and fragrant with the spring flowers, and the grass was spongy soft and green under their feet. Sadie and Gus took off their shoes and walked barefoot in the sun, enjoying the clean air and quiet of the late Friday morning. Soon Sadie and Gus were lying on their backs on the green grass, checking out the clouds for familiar animal shapes.

"Momma, why can't we just stay with Mrs. Blumenthal? She has a really nice place, and she seems friendly. I like it there. I don't want to live in one of those places that we just went to. It was ugly and dirty. And I don't think that lady liked you. I think Mrs. Blumenthal likes you. Why can't we stay there?"

"Honey, I really wish we could stay. But Mrs. Blumenthal's home is not our home. It's her home, and she was really nice to help us out. But, you know, the first place we live might not be exactly what we want, but it's a place to start. And soon we will have a place of our own, and we can do whatever we want!" Sadie hugged Gus tightly and tried not to worry. They would make it. They would take it a day at a time, and someday they would look back on this day and smile.

Sadie's mood was lifted when she and Gus finally turned the last corner and gazed on the for-rent sign in the lush, green yard. The neighborhood here was clean, there was a park across the street, and the small children playing outside were clean and sunny with cherub faces dancing in the afternoon sunlight. Sadie Squeezed Gus's hand in anticipation.

"This looks like our kind of home. There's lots of green grass, and there are lots of other children to play with. It looks like what I remember from my childhood. Let's go check it out." Sadie's childhood memories were bittersweet on this bright sunny day in the Midwest. Sadie had nothing but happy memories of her childhood growing up in the countryside of Ohio, with a doting grandmother and lots of cousins to scrap happily with on the long summer days. But the good memories ended the day Sadie left with Frank.

Frank had been the porter on her train car on the trip out to New York City with her parents. He had told her of stories of his big Italian family, the glitz of New York, and had showered her with attention and gifts. Once in New York City, Frank had volunteered to be their tour guide and was nothing but absolutely charming to Sadie and her family. In a grand, impressive gesture meant to sweep Sadie off her feet, Frank had even changed his work schedule so he could be the porter on her train back home to Ohio. With this he pretty much cemented the relationship and Sadie's adoration for this handsome dashing older man was blooming. The day

Frank had shown up with flowers and a marriage proposal was the end of her idyllic childhood.

Someday maybe Sadie would go home, after she had made a successful life for herself and Gus and after she no longer had to worry about Frank finding her. If she went home now, she also felt she would be putting her entire extended family in danger as her former home in Ohio would be the first place Frank would look for her. It was better this way. Safer for everyone. Someday she would go home.

A pleasant young woman with a flushed face and a baby on her hip answered Sadie's knock, instantly smiled, and held out her one free hand in greeting.

"Hello. What can I do for you today?" The young woman blushed slightly as she shifted her baby a few inches up on her hip and smoothed out her apron as if to be more presentable.

Sadie smiled back appreciatively and took the young woman's hand graciously.

"My name is Sadie Adams, and this is my son, Gus. We are new in town and looking for housing. Your place here is very appealing. May I inquire as to the cost and conditions of renting?" Sadie was encouraged by the friendliness and cheeriness of this manager woman. This place was just what she was looking for.

"Will your husband be stopping by later? Where will he be working here in Galesburg? We only rent to families; you know. We don't want any of the other class of people spoiling our neighborhood."

Sadie was stunned. All she wanted was a place to live. She was a decent person, and she didn't need a husband to make her respectable. Sadie knew a house in such a nice neighborhood would be rented quickly. She also knew that most tenant housing places would be more like the first place she had visited. This was the kind of place she wanted to live in.

"Gus, why don't you go check out the grass and those big oak trees while I talk to this lady? We need to talk grownup talk, and you should be enjoying the nice spring day." Sadie shooed Gus down the front steps as she hastily appraised the situation and made up her next lie.

"Ma'am, my husband is finishing up business in our old town and will be arriving in Galesburg in a couple of months. He sent us on ahead so he could sell our home and tie up loose ends." Sadie told her lie while she stared at the flowered curtains in the window beside the doorway. Sadie found it impossible to look this woman in the eye and lie outright. She needed a lot more practice before she could do that on a regular basis. Sadie's stomach churned with guilt and anticipation as she waited for the reaction.

"You sure you have a husband? Where is your wedding ring?"

Sadie instinctively pulled her hand behind her back in shame. Damn Frank. Damn him. She had escaped his brutality only to be continually punished by his apathy. Frank had promised that they would pick out matching bands once they were back in New York after their wedding. But that never happened. Frank never had the time to spend with Sadie, and less time at home after Gus was born. And he would never spend that much money on things for Sadie. Any extra money was spent at the taverns and the pool halls with his cronies.

"We had a whirlwind romance and marriage ma'am. And then after Gus came along, it just didn't seem that important anymore." The words were almost spat out of Sadie's mouth. She had to snicker to herself under her breath. Even she wouldn't have been able to swallow that one. She really needed more practice.

"I bet you did! And you sure you are really married? It is extremely unusual for the wife and children to come into town before their men. Usually the men come in first, find work, and get settled before bringing their families. Where is your husband going to work when he gets here?"

Sadie couldn't answer the question. She didn't even know what the local industries were. All she had thought of since arriving in town was her own job and her own living space. She searched her new memories quickly for something familiar to key off of. Nothing came to mind.

"Ma'am, I'm sure he told me where he would be working. But I just don't seem to recall the name of the place at the moment. I just arrived in town after a two-day train ride and am a bit exhausted. I'm sure it will come to me when I have had some rest." Sadie looked pensively at this young woman, searching her face for any kind of reflection.

The reflection that came back to her was not what Sadie expected or wanted.

"Of course it will come to you, dear. But whether it does or not, I don't have any openings right now. Thank you for stopping by. Have a nice day now." With that, the woman turned, took a final full-length glance at Sadie over her shoulder, smiled slightly at Sadie, and firmly shut the door. Sadie was still standing on the top porch, frozen with surprise, when she heard the bolt lock slide into place on the other side.

Sadie nearly stumbled down the stairs as she tried to hold back the tears. She scooped Gus up in her arms and held him tightly to her breast as she worked at regaining her composure. She couldn't let him see her disappointment. After all, he was just a boy, and this was not his worry. It was hers. She would find something else. But at the moment, she knew of no place else to turn.

Suddenly she was weary, so very weary of the road dust and the unfair treatment she had received for so many years. It had taken a good long time to convince herself that she was a good person and did not deserve to be beaten repeatedly by her own husband. She just knew deep inside that the problems were not hers but his. She wasn't a bad person. She was a good person who just wanted a chance to raise her son in peace and solitude. Right now, her resolve was a little shaky. Maybe there was something in her that she couldn't see in the mirror's reflections. She was mentally fatigued and emotionally drained.

"Are we going to be living here, Momma? Which house is going to be ours?" Gus grinned up at Sadie from her arms. He was so very trusting in her.

"No, Gus. We aren't going to be living here right now. Things didn't quite work out. Let's go back to Mrs. Blumenthal's, and we'll work something out later in the week. It's about suppertime, and I'm getting hungry. How about you?" Sadie did not tell Gus that there were no other places to rent. He didn't need to worry about that. It was her job, and she would take care of it. Somehow.

An hour and a half later, Sadie and Gus walked up to the front steps of Mrs. Blumenthal's boarding house and were greeted with the smell of fresh, warm cookies. Mrs. Blumenthal was stacking the cookies on a dinner plate and setting out glasses and napkins around the table when Gus burst through the doorway, his eyes searching for the cookies that his nose had already located.

"Hey, slow down, young man. There are plenty of cookies for you!" Mrs. Blumenthal laughed as she poured a glass of milk and set it down in front of Gus.

"You must have had a busy day. You're a hungry guy!"

"Yup! Momma and I checked out some places to live, but they weren't nice. One place was pretty, but Momma said it just didn't work out. But that's okay. I like your house. I want to stay here!"

Sadie tousled Gus's hair as she reached for her own glass of milk and dipped her cookie. She hadn't been able to dip cookies since she left home almost ten years ago. Frank didn't approve and said it was disgustingly childish. Sadie felt a kinship with Mrs. Blumenthal, but she didn't know why. She felt a warmth in this house that made her want to kick off her shoes and sit on the front porch for hours, watching the world go by.

"So, Sadie, how did it go? Did you find a permanent place to stay? There really aren't many places around here, you know. And a lot of the tenant complexes are quite nasty. This is the Midwest, and they seem to have a problem accepting people who were not born here or that don't arrive with a full pedigree. The only way to get accepted around here is to visibly have lots of money or live here for seventy or eighty years!" Mrs. Blumenthal chuckled to herself.

"I really don't want to talk about it right now, Mrs. Blumenthal. It was a long day. I'm tired and my feet hurt. I need to get Gus fed and off to bed soon. And I need to get a good night's rest. I start to work very early Monday morning." Sadie was exhausted.

"Hey, it's okay. There's no hurry to find another place, I'm rather enjoying having children in the house. More so than I had imagined. Let's put a light supper on the table, get this little guy off to bed, and then we can talk." Sadie didn't understand why this older woman was showing so much kindness to two straggly strangers, but she was grateful. She didn't think she could handle another disappointment today.

Sadie and Gus enjoyed a meal of warmed-over ham slices and fresh peas from Mrs. Blumenthal's Garden. Sadie had relaxed on the porch earlier and watched as Mrs. Blumenthal showed Gus how to find the ripe peas and radishes and remove them from their vines without disturbing the rest of the plant. Sadie yearned for her own yard and garden for Gus. A place where she could teach Gus these important life lessons, and not watch a stranger do it because she couldn't.

Sadie washed the dishes and laughed with Mrs. Blumenthal as Gus insisted on standing on a chair and putting the dried dishes in the cupboard. Gus was lively and happy and comfortable as he made animal noises for Mrs. Blumenthal's entertainment. He counted the plates and arranged the glasses in straight lines as he put them in the cupboard. Sadie tucked Gus into bed and kissed him good night. He sighed and was fast asleep before she had removed her shoes and turned off the light. Sadie sat on the bed for a while and watched Gus sleeping peacefully. He was safe here and happy here. Sadie knew she had made the right choice in leaving Frank. She just didn't know what her next step would be.

Sadie padded through the house in her bare feet and found Mrs. Blumenthal on the front porch with a cup of hot tea and a crocheted lap robe waiting in the extra wicker rocking chair.

"Sit down, child. You need to relax. I'm sure you must be exhausted by now." Mrs. Blumenthal patted the rocking chair next to her and motioned for Sadie to take a seat. Sadie appreciated the gesture and kindness and wrapped herself up in the lap robe as she cupped the warm cup of tea with both hands. She stared into the tea as if searching for an answer in the tea leaves.

"Thank you again, Mrs. Blumenthal, for your kindness. Please do not think that I am not tremendously grateful. But I need a home for Gus. I want him settled and in a routine as soon as possible."

"Sadie, you have a home for now. That's enough for today. It will all work itself out soon." Mrs. Blumenthal smiled at Sadie from the chair next to her.

"I don't know what to do next. I guess I didn't think this through very well when I left New York City. I have a job, but I lied to Mrs. Steinway and told her I didn't have any children. It was the only way I could get the job. I know I shouldn't have lied about it, but I am desperate. I need that job. I guess I just thought I would be able to find a tenant house and someone to look after Gus by Monday. I don't know what I was thinking. I wasn't planning very far ahead, I guess."

"What is so hard, Sadie? I think the worst is behind you now. It's going to be better every day now." Mrs. Blumenthal gently pulled one of Sadie' arms down from her face enough to see her tear-stained eyes. She leaned in close and smiled. But Sadie pulled way, very agitated.

"I guess Galesburg hasn't much caught up with the times. Everywhere I went today, I was turned away and scorned. All because my big, strong protector of a husband wasn't doing the talking for me. If it wasn't for my husband, I wouldn't be in this mess in the first place. And these women walk around like they own the world. Hah! They are no better than I am. They are worse! They hide behind their husbands and pretend that just because they have a ring on their finger, they have been elevated to a particular judgeship status and can look down on the rest of us! I am not a threat to them. All I want is a home, a job, and a quiet life with my son. I don't want their lives, their homes, or their husbands!" The tears finally escaped and began pouring down Sadie's face. She was too tired to care who saw her pain anymore. She had reached the end of the line.

"Honey, I don't know why you left New York. But it sounds like you may be running from something. Probably a man. Perhaps this man could be Gus's father? I'm not asking you to tell me your secrets, but I am asking you to let me help you." Mrs. Blumenthal reached across and laid her gnarled hand on top of Sadie's young, supple fingers. This display of caring only made Sadie feel sadder and lonelier.

"Why would you care? No one else in this town seems to worry about anything other than where my husband is or isn't. I can't believe this is happening! I have a job. I can pay my rent. I bathe regularly. My son is clean and well-mannered. Do I look like a tramp to you?" By now Sadie was pacing back and forth across the porch as she talked to Mrs.

Blumenthal. The more she searched her mind for answers and tried to formulate a plan, the more frustrated she became. Sadie had no experience with this kind of complete rejection. Rejection that was based on nothing that she knew she had done wrong. If she could only figure out what everyone saw that was so wrong with her, she could fix it. But she couldn't see anything but a mother trying to protect herself and her child.

"Sadie, leaving New York is not your problem. Your problem is that you blew into this neurotic little town and immediately threatened the matriarchal regime. You are young, you are pretty, and you are alone. All of these things threatens the little women out here who like to think that they rule their world. If they let you in, then they would have competition. They cannot allow that. Besides, you don't have a past or a history here. They can't find a familiar little box to put you in. Just because you are young and pretty and trying to make it on your own, you threaten their very existence. By accepting you as an equal, they would be forcing themselves to rely on their own sense of well-being and confidence in who they are. And they've never learned that they needed that. Or should even want it. They've always hidden behind the societal rules. These rules afford them no accountability and no responsibility. That is a very comfortable and safe place for a lot of people to live. You are unknowingly attacking their traditions just by walking down the street."

"But all I am trying to do is take care of my son and protect him! I'm not hurting them! I just want a chance to be free!" The fear in Sadie's heart rose to the surface uncontrollably. Sadie stopped pacing and looked directly at Mrs. Blumenthal. The trapped, wild animal in her was finally cornered.

"What are you trying to protect him from?" Mrs. Blumenthal gently asked.

"I ran away, Mrs. Blumenthal. I took my son and ran away from my husband! If he finds me, he will kill me! I have been planning and scheming for months on how to escape. Maybe I subconsciously thought I would never get this far. I don't know. I don't know what I thought. I don't know anything. Frank was right. I can't do anything right. And I can't do anything on my own." Sadie sat down and pushed her head back in the chair and looked out over the evening shadows. She was now just done. She had no more thought. She had no more plans.

"I don't know what to do. It's hopeless. I have no home and no one to watch Gus while I work. I can't take him with me. Miss Steinway would fire me on the spot for lying to her. And since this is such a small town, I know I would never be able to get another job once the gossip got around. And I don't have enough money to go to another town and start over. I'm at a dead end." Sadie sank to her knees at Mrs. Blumenthal's feet and cried. Her cries came from deep within a part of her soul that she hadn't dared open up since the first beating she had received from Frank shortly after their marriage.

"Sadie, you don't need to find another home right away. You can stay here as long as you need to." Mrs. Blumenthal stroked Sadie's hair and patted her shoulders. "Sadie, I understand where you are. I ran away once myself. I'll tell you about it someday. Someday when things are better and you are not so tired. I really do know how you feel. And I also really know that when you hit that wall, all you have to do is look up, and the wall will come down." Mrs. Blumenthal laughed out loud when she saw the surprised look on Sadie's face.

"Sadie, you have stepped out and taken a major step forward. Don't look back, and don't try to see too far ahead. Keep moving forward. All you have to do is just move. The exact 'where' in forward will come to you when it's time. And don't worry about Gus. He can stay with me while you work. I really enjoy having Gus around. I'm even starting to look forward to getting up in the mornings again. I never realized how much I missed having someone to take care of since Saul passed on." Mrs. Blumenthal smiled at Sadie when she raised her head from her lap and looked at her through tear-stained eyes.

"You would do that for me? Why?" Sadie was incredulous. She couldn't believe her own ears.

"Yes, I would do that for you. Goodness knows we all need a friend to lean on once in a while. I've needed a friend a few times in my own lifetime. Guess you could say I'm returning a favor. And, please call me Laura."

"Thank you, Mrs. Blumenthal. Or Laura, rather. You are a godsend! I don't know about the next life, but you are definitely an angel of mercy in my lifetime." Sadie was so appreciative of Laura and her offer. She didn't understand why a perfect stranger would reach out to her like this lady just did. But whatever the reason, Sadie was going to accept the help. Laura was the only thing that stood between her and the street corner. Or going back to Frank. Which was a much worse fate than the street corner. Sadie would accept Laura's offer for an open door until she could repay the kindness.

Sadie looked up at Laura, who was quietly rocking in her chair and staring off into the street. Tears of gratitude began to fall.

"I don't know how I will ever be able to repay you." Sadie was so relieved that her immediate problems were temporarily solved. She was suddenly very, very tired. So tired that she could no longer hold back her exhaustion. The stress of the past few days began pouring out of her body through her sobs. Sadie cried exhaustion and relief into the crocheted lap robe on Laura's lap. Laura stroked her hair and clucked softly into the night, contentment filling her heart.

"Just let it out, Sadie. Just leave it be here so you can move on."

CHAPTER FOUR

DESPERATION AND JEALOUSY

The early morning air was crisp, the coffee rich and hot, and Gus was safely tucked away in their bedroom. Sadie thought about her own mother as she prepared for work on Monday morning.

Sadie thought about her mother and the front porch she played on as a child, much like the front port she was becoming so familiar with here in Galesburg. She did miss her mother terribly and wondered if her mother would have been proud of her for having the nerve to finally strike out on her own. Traveling far in a few days with a young child and no means of support. Or would her mother have been fearful for her? Sadie held on to the thought that if her mother knew the full truth about Frank, she would have her blessing now.

Someday she would go home again. Someday when she was established in her own right and Frank was a distant memory. Someday she would like to really get to know her mother as a person. She had spent a lot of her childhood with her grandmother and sometimes even pictured her grandmother in her mind when she thought of her mother. Sadie was old enough now to know that her mother had a life and relationships beyond her children. And Sadie really wanted to know more about her. Especially now. Sadie wanted to know if her mother had ever lied or had any deep, dark secrets that she kept even from her own children.

Sadie waited for the sun to peek over the horizon. She paced back and forth across the kitchen floor as she drank her morning coffee and waited for her toast. She had bathed, fashioned her hair back in a bun the best she could, and had only to slip on her dress over her undergarments after eating. Sadie had decided against any makeup other than a little rouge on her cheeks. She was going to be cleaning up after college boys. Makeup would be inappropriate. And Doris Steinway had already made it clear that she would fire her in a heartbeat if given the chance. So Sadie had decided to mousy down as much as possible for the first day. She knew how to mousy down. Frank had made that rule his first priority as soon as the teachings had begun. She had already messed up on the first impression with her new boss, and she was going to do everything in her power to make the first day of her new working life perfect.

Sadie was lost in her thoughts and did not hear Mrs. Blumenthal walk quietly into the kitchen. She jumped slightly at the sound of Laura's voice.

"Good morning, Sadie. Are you ready for your first day with the Galesburg witch?" Laura asked.

"Come on, Laura, you are not helping me, here! I am having enough trouble as it is. This is a first for me, and I have no idea what to expect. Is Ms. Steinway really that bad? Have you ever worked as a housekeeper before? Is it hard?" Sadie took a sip of her coffee to have something solid to rest her lips against. It gave her an instant pacifier and kept her lip tremors from vibrating all over her face.

"Oh, Sadie. I never had the privilege of working as a housekeeper. My first job was working in the back room of a laundry. I think housekeeping has to be much better than that! I guess it all depends on how you look at it. She will expect you to work very hard, she will expect absolute perfection in your work, and you will put in more than a full day. But she will pay you a fair wage, so to speak, and this job will allow you to begin your new independent life and make a home for Gus. So It's not all bad."

"What's the so-to-speak part? Sounds like there is an underlying threat here."

"Well, you'll work a lot harder for her than you would as a housekeeper for any other boarding house in this town. You will not be allowed to stop and chat with any of the other staff or salesmen. But remember that it is a real job, and it pays money." Laura rested her hand on Sadie's arm as they sat at the kitchen table and talked in the early morning predawn.

"I remember my first day on the job like it was yesterday. I remember every minute. I was fourteen years old." Laura smiled at Sadie as she picked up her coffee cup.

"You were fourteen? Why on earth ware you working at the age of fourteen? Tell me about it!" Sadie pulled up a chair and sat across the table from Laura. She put her elbows on the table and her head in her hands, ready to take in every word.

"Well, I would have to give you a little background first so you would understand the circumstances." Laura shifted uncomfortable in her chair. "I've never told anyone this story. But I want to tell you now. You see, my childhood was not all that great. My uncle started sexually abusing me when I was seven. And he wasn't just sexually abusing me. He used me for a punching bag regularly. He teased and tortured me by burning cigarettes on my back and pouring hot water on my chest. He was my father's brother and lived in our house. My parents knew about the abuse, even watched it happen. But did nothing. My mother was too afraid of my father and my uncle. And my father would never cross his older brother. I was the expendable one." Laura rubbed her hand across her chest while talking.

"Do you still have the scars, Laura?" Sadie had tears in her eyes. She wanted to hug Laura, but she also wanted to hear more of the story.

"Oh, yes. Some of the scars are still on my body. And a lot of the emotional scars have never quite healed. I just push them back down when they start to push their way up. Time does make a lot of things tolerable, Sadie." Laura looked at the surprise on Sadie's face and laughed out loud.

"But on with the story. At the ripe old age of fourteen, I had convinced myself that I had to get away from my family or die trying. Death was more welcome than spending another day with my uncle and parents. So, after one particularly malicious assault, I just left. I just started walking. I slept in a cornfield the first night and then walked until I came to Galesburg."

"So, your family didn't live very far from here. Why didn't you go somewhere else?"

"Because I didn't know where I was going. I was just going."

"So, what did you do when you got to town? How long did it take to get your job?"

"Oh, the job just happened. It was dark when I got to town, and I was cold. I wound up behind a steam laundry because the steam coming out of the vents into the alley was warm. And there was a big, shaggy, friendly dog sleeping on a mat by the back door."

"You slept with the dog to keep warm? Oh, Laura!" Sadie's tears were now running down her face."

"Oh, don't feel sorry for me. The dog was very nice and friendly. He became my best friend! The next morning when the owners of the laundry came to work, they found me and their dog on the back step. They never asked why or asked me to leave. They took me in, fed me, and put me to work. I even had my own room in the back of the laundry. It was a great job!"

"Did your family ever come looking for you?"

"I don't know. I never saw them again. I guess I never missed them much either."

"Well, if you can weather that and come out on the other side, I can do this." Sadie was smiling now. She really liked Laura and felt like they were quickly becoming very close friends.

"I didn't just weather it, honey. I thrived. I met my Saul there." Sadie had to smile. The older woman was glowing like a young teenager after her first kiss.

"So, what did Saul think of your childhood and your life before him? Surely it would have made him very angry."

"He never asked, and I never told. He asked me to marry him on my sixteenth birthday, and I said yes. The next day we were married in a private ceremony, picked up my things at the laundry, and I moved into this house and never looked back." Laura got up from her chair and took her cup to the sink. When Laura turned to face Sadie, Sadie thought she had a look on her face that signaled the story was over. But Sadie had one more question.

"Didn't it bother you that he never asked? That he never wanted to know that part about you?"

"I don't know that he didn't want to know."

"All I know is that he never asked. And I was so appreciative that he loved me for who I was. I never wanted to disturb that. I never wanted to risk losing him or damaging what we had. So that was that."

"Laura, you are one fantastic lady. I so admire your strength." Sadie felt truly blessed to have found such an inspiring person and to be able to call her a friend.

"Well, if you want to make a good impression on the first day, don't be late. You have a long walk ahead of you. It's already five thirty, so you had belter wash down those butterflies with the rest of that coffee and finish getting ready. Don't worry. You will do fine." Laura squeezed Sadie's arm as she walked past the table and smiled reassuringly.

"You are a lot more confident than I am. I certainly hope you're right." Sadie took a deep breath, quickly washed out her coffee cup and headed down the hall toward her bedroom.

"I just hope that I don't get fired the first day. That Steinway lady didn't hire me because she was convinced I could do the job. She hired me because I agreed to work cheap. What a great way to make a good first impression." Sadie threw the words over her shoulder toward Laura.

"Well, then look at it this way; if she hired you because you work cheap, she will keep you around long enough to get her money's worth. By then you will have proven to her that you are worth your salary. So stop worrying about getting fired and get going!"

Sadie quickly pulled on her best house dress. It was at least four years old and definitely outdated. It was fairly comfortable and matched her low-heeled brown pumps. Frank had always matched Sadie's outfits with her shoes when he shopped for her. Or maybe the color of brown was just easy to accidentally match. Every piece of clothing Sadie had was some shade of brown. The bright side was that Frank no longer controlled what she wore. Someday soon she would be able to buy her own clothes and dump these reminders of Frank. She would buy bright dresses and hats with pink feathers. Someday she would celebrate her freedom every day.

"Morning, sweetie. Did you sleep well? I'm leaving now for my first day of work. You just roll over and go back to sleep. Laura is here and will take care of you while I am gone. I just want a good morning kiss from my sweet little man." Gus kept his eyes closed as he squished up his face and smiled. He reached up and squeezed his arms around her neck.

"Love you, Momma. Bye-bye." Gus was still smiling through his closed eyes when he released his hug and rolled away from Sadie. His little body curled around itself in contented sleepiness, and Sadie kissed the back of his head as she tucked the covers around him.

This would be the first day that Sadie and Gus had ever been apart for more than a couple of hours. Sadie was a bit disappointed that the pending separation seemed so easy for Gus. But the last few days, Gus and Laura had begun to form a strong bond. Gus really needed a grandmother, and Laura was proving to fill that need very successfully. Sadie wasn't sure who needed whom the most. Sadie squelched the twinges of jealousy as she gently shut the door behind her.

Right now it didn't matter. Gus was safe and happy. That was all that mattered.

Sadie slipped out the front door into the early morning mist and started her brisk walk to work. She looked up at the fading moon and allowed herself to listen to the morning waking up. She took in deep breaths of the April air. She relished the force of the brisk air chilling her nostrils as she appreciated the clean smell of spring, the clean smell of freedom at last. Her life was finally beginning.

Sadie knocked on the front door of the boarding house at ten minutes before six thirty. This was good. At least she was early and would begin the day on the right note.

It seemed like an eternity before Doris answered the door. Sadie struggled to hide her amusement as she took in the sight before her. Doris stood in the doorway in her faded flannel nightgown and housecoat, curlers hanging loosely in her fizzled graying hair, a deep frown accentuating the dark hair creeping across her upper lip as she opened her mouth to speak.

"What on earth are you doing here?" Doris's voice was more shrill and harsh than Sadie remembered.

"I'm here to report to work. It's Monday, and you told me to be here at six thirty. I'm here."

"You stupid little tramp! You obviously don't know your place. The hired help does not use the front door. Ever! Go around to the back. Mrs. Goshen, the cook, will let you in and get you started. Your first chore is to help with the breakfast chores." With that said, Doris unceremoniously turned and slammed the door in Sadie's face.

Sadie was still stinging over Doris's rebuff when Mrs. Goshen unlocked the back door. Smells of fresh rolls, frying bacon, and hot coffee greeted Sadie as she walked into the warm, cluttered kitchen.

"You must be Mrs. Goshen, the cook?" Sadie questioned as she tried to regain some of her composure and hope for at least one friendly face.

"Yes, I am. You must be the new housekeeper. Come on in, hang up your coat over there on the coat hook, and roll up your sleeves. The boys will begin to wander downstairs in about thirty minutes, and we have a lot of work to do." Sadie removed her coat, arranged it on the coat hook, and turned to the disapproving face of Mrs. Goshen as she walked back toward the stove.

"Where's your uniform, girl? That dress will never do! Mrs. Steinway is very strict that the hired help look like the hired help. Why didn't you wear your uniform? And where is your apron?" Mrs. Goshen was a rather large, plump woman and looked quite foreboding with her hands on her hips and the sweat on her face trickling down from her forehead between the frowning eyebrows

Sadie instinctively looked down at the floor and quickly assumed the slumped shoulder position, crossing her arms in front of her body to shield the blows. She was not going to make it on her own. Maybe Frank was right after all. Maybe she just wasn't smart enough to be out on her own. When she spoke, her voice was barely audible.

"I'm sorry. I didn't know. This is my first housekeeping job. I don't have a uniform."

Mrs. Goshen let out a deep welcoming belly laugh. The very loud noise of the laugh made Sadie instinctively jump backward. Recognizing the warmth in the laugh, Sadie looked up at Mrs. Goshen and smiled.

"Now I get it. I wondered how Ms. Steinway found a replacement so quickly. You must be new to Galesburg also. Nothing like fresh meat to make Ms. Steinway sit up and take notice. Don't worry, little girl. The last housekeeper left a couple of her uniforms here. You'll find them hanging in the pantry down the hall. Go slip one on, and I'll cover for you. Hurry now. Breakfast is to be ready promptly at seven."

Sadie smiled her thankfulness as she scurried down the dark hallway. She wanted to ask why the other housekeeper left but decided not to push her luck. She decided that she didn't want to know. She had a lot to learn in a very short time and didn't dare allow any more doubts and fears to cloud her mind. Sadie was already teetering on the edge. She had all she could handle on her thin shoulders. One more worry or one more fear might very well crush her soul.

Sadie grimaced as she found the uniforms, and held one up to her body. Besides the fact that the uniform was a least three sizes too big, the uniform was made out of a heavy, beige sackcloth with horizontal sea green stripes that did not meet at the seams. There were several grease stains down the front of the dress and leftover body oil on the collar and the sleeve cuffs. Sadie slipped it on over her slip, added a long, faded brown apron over the top, and wrapped the apron ties around her waist twice in an effort to make the outfit feel more fitted and allow her to move with less constriction. She then carefully hung her own dress on the hook behind the door, took a deep sigh, and headed back to the kitchen to begin her day.

The morning flew by as Sadie and Mrs. Goshen served breakfast, cleaned up, and begin early preparations for dinner. Two meals a day went with the monthly boarding house fee, which left Sadie free to pursue her own duties most of the day.

Doris was quite distant with Sadie on her first day, which Sadie was very thankful for. Immediately after breakfast had been served for the boys, Mrs. Goshen whispered instructions for Sadie's next task. Sadie's first task that she was completely responsible for every day was to serve Doris her breakfast. Doris sauntered into the dining hall as soon as the group breakfast activities were completed and the dining room cleaned. Doris expected to be served privately with Sadie's full attention to her needs.

Sadie soon realized that this first task on the list could become the most distasteful task of the day. Sadie became Doris's personal waitress for the entire breakfast ordeal. She was required to wait just outside the dining hall, ready to respond as soon as Doris rang the small brass bell that Doris had set at her plate. Doris did not speak to Sadie during breakfast and provided instruction to Sadie with hand gestures, heaving great sighs when Sadie did not respond quickly enough and gave hard, disapproving glances toward empty plates and loose crumbs on the table. Once Doris was finished, she stood up, gathered her paperwork in her arms and dropped Sadie's daily task list on the table. The task list could not be started until the dining hall was cleaned again.

The task list was daunting. There were three pages to the list and Sadie's nervousness heightened. She knew she had to do this and do it well. When Sadie looked up from skimming the pages, Doris had left the dining hall, making it clear to Sadie that she was expected to already know what needed to be done.

The day flew by as Sadie concentrated on her tasks at hand. She completed each task as quickly as possible, and as thoroughly as possible. Doris checked Sadie's list several times during the day with an occasional direction or correction to Sadie's tasks. These directions came out of Doris's mouth in a very monotone, authoritative voice and usually were hurled in Sadie's direction as Doris flew by on her hurried way to somewhere.

By Wednesday afternoon, Sadie was becoming comfortable in her routine. She had received three of the five daily list of her chores and had not been informed of any serious wrongdoing by Doris. Doris would always check Sadie's work three times a day, and each day Sadie had managed to have her work completed on time and also pass the inspections.

Sadie had taken the extra uniforms home and with Laura's help altered the uniforms to fit her thin, wisp-like body. Laura surprised Sadie by working her magic on the stains and discoloration to make the required uniforms look very nice and definitely passable. Sadie knew what it was like to be poor, but she didn't have to be dirty.

Sadie looked forward to the first few minutes of work each morning when she got to help the cook finish the final preparations for breakfast. The kitchen was so warm and cozy, and the smells were always a welcoming reminder that Sadie had a job and was making it.

This Thursday morning, Sadie was clearing the dishes from Doris's breakfast. She had received her task list for the day, and it was longer than the previous days. There was an extra chore of waxing the dining hall floors. Sadie knew this task would take another couple of hours, and she knew she would have to move quicker today if she was going to be finished on time. Her final task every day was to help Mrs. Goshen put the evening meal on the table, and the floor had to be waxed, dried, and polished before dinner was started.

Sadie was balancing all the final dishes in her arms to save a couple of trips back to the kitchen and hurried through the narrow hallway toward the kitchen. As she reached the swinging doors into the kitchen, she turned around and started backing through the door, using her backside to push the doors open.

The doors didn't budge as Sadie attempted to back through the doorway. Slightly irritated, Sadie stepped forward a half step and pushed the doors hard this time. The doors still didn't budge. Sadie then turned sideways and positioned her hip to bang the doors open if necessary. Just as Sadie took one last quick look over her shoulder to make sure she was positioned to make the last attempt count, the doors swung open on their own.

Mildly surprised, Sadie walked through the doorway expecting to see Mrs. Goshen holding the doors with a grin on her face. She liked to play pranks every now and then, and Sadie could usually expect to be on the receiving end of her jokes at least twice during the day. Standing just inside the doorway, with his hand holding the door open and an impish grin on his face, was one of the most handsome men that Sadie had ever laid eyes on.

This man was not a big, burly masculine man like Frank was. This man was only a few inches taller than Sadie with a slight build. He had black wavy hair that touched the tops of his ears, just long enough to flirt with social rules of the day. His thick, black mustache did little to hide his beautiful smile, and the bright green piercing eyes overshadowed his large Jewish nose and seemed to blaze right through to her soul.

Sadie was able to break his gaze and, after some very long seconds, dropped her eyes and walked into the kitchen.

"I'm sorry, I didn't know anyone else was here. I apologize for my rudeness." Sadie spoke with her back to the young man as she stacked the dishes in the sink, feeling safer standing next to Mrs. Goshen.

"Apology accepted. So you are the new girl Doris hired? Turn around and let me take a look at you!" The young man had merriment in his voice, with a slight hint of invitation.

Sadie accepted the challenge and turned to face the young man.

"Yes, I'm the new girl. My name is Sadie. And who might you be?" Sadie attempted to add some strength to her voice by dropping it half an octave and stood to her full height to face him. As Sadie met his eyes again, she instinctively felt the need to protect herself and folded her arms together in front of her. Sadie was responding to a silent power struggle that made her feel awkward.

"Honey, I'm the best memory you will ever meet. Guaranteed. My name is Howard, and you are one of the lucky ones." Howard quickly crossed the kitchen floor, smiled even broader at Sadie and held out his hand.

Sadie instinctively took a step backward before taking Howard's hand. He was standing much too close and smelled much too good. The edge of the kitchen sink was digging deep into the small of Sadie's back, and she was cornered. She heard Mrs. Goshen giggle as she stepped sideways away from the sink, took Howard's hand, and met his gaze.

Howard laid his other hand over Sadie's and stepped toward Sadie, closing the safety gap that Sadie had just created for herself. His hands were warm and soft, not at all like Frank's cold, hard callused hands that Sadie was used to.

Since Sadie had married Frank, she had had very little contact with other men. Frank had kept her sequestered and had only allowed limited interaction with the few male friends that Frank had occasionally brought home to dinner. And most of them were old, crinkled, and smelly. And there was absolutely no physical contact between them and Sadie. Frank would not have tolerated that. He considered Sadie his property. Any man caught even looking at Sadie, let alone touching her, would have been severely beaten by Frank. And probably killed. Sadie had no doubt that Frank was capable of killing without conscience.

Sadie was completely unprepared for Howard's touch. She had no experience with men and had no idea what to do with the warm tingles and the rushing heartbeat. Sadie dropped her gaze to the floor and blushed profusely as she pulled her hand out of Howard's grasp. Sadie was totally startled with she heard Doris's voice coming from the kitchen doorway.

"Well, Howard, what a pleasant surprise! You're early today. Well, I see you've met the new housekeeper, so we can dispense with the formalities. Mrs. Goshen, please bring our coffee to the sitting room. Sadie, you need to get started waxing the dining hall floor. Now!"

Sadie stood still for a few seconds and looked deep into Doris's eyes. Doris was jealous! Sadie almost laughed out loud.

Howard's charm had not been lost on Sadie. Sadie enjoyed the looks and the sparks from Howard. But she also knew he was a salesman. Charming people was part of his job. Even thought it was directed straight at Sadie, Sadie knew that it wasn't real. But it was enjoyable nonetheless. Sadie could easily understand how Doris could be jealous about sharing the attention.

"But, Ms. Steinway, the dining hall floor is last on the list. You have strict orders to complete my chores in the order they are on the list." Sadie was confused. She wanted Howard out of the kitchen and out of her sight. He made her very uneasy, and she did not know what she was supposed to do next. Sadie was so new at being on her own that she had no idea how to deal with any man. And she certainly did not understand how Howard's arrival at the boarding house had affected the order of her daily routine.

"Young lady, you were hired to be the housekeeper, not question my authority. And if you really must know, I want the dining hall done first to guarantee its completion on time. You haven't been doing very well, and this is one chore that must be perfect and must be done on time. The dining hall is where all our guests are entertained and is a direct reflection on this house. So, if you must know, you need to do it first so you will have time to do it again if it isn't right. Now get to it!"

"Yes, ma'am. I understand." Sadie ducked quietly out of the kitchen and headed toward the pantry to gather her cleaning supplies.

Sadie was working on scrubbing the hardwood floor and had started her cleaning at the public entrance into the dining hall. Sadie was on her knees, balancing her body with her left hand on the floor, as she scrubbed the floor with a huge sponge in her right hand.

Sadie could see Doris and Howard across the hallway. She giggled to herself as she watched Doris take her cup of tea from Howard and then slide her body closer to him on the couch. Howard looked uncomfortable, but he didn't move. Sadie wondered if Doris was engaging in the public display for Sadie's benefit. Sadie had only known Doris for a short time. But in the time Sadie had seen nothing but cold, hard interactions between Doris and everyone in the house.

Doris was smiling a lot as Howard reached across her lap and picked up the book on the coffee table. Sadie watched Doris lean in when Howard reached across her lap. Howard did not move away from Doris, but he looked like he had accidently put himself in a position that he didn't know how to get out of. For a few seconds, neither Howard nor Doris moved. Sadie watched Howard place his arm on Doris's shoulder momentarily as he regained his balance when he picked up the book. His hand was dangling only a few inches from Doris' large breasts. As Howard looked up, he caught Sadie's gaze from across the hall and smiled ruefully at her. Sadie ducked her head and went back to work.

Sadie shifted positions so she could reach around the corner of the doorway with her sponge. This position put her on her knees directly across from Howard. As Sadie worked she felt Howard staring. She tried to subtly look busy and not be noticed. But it didn't work. Her eyes caught Howard staring at her. But he wasn't looking at her face. Sadie mentally followed his gaze. As soon as she realized what he was looking at, she turned her body away quickly. Her oversized dress was hanging down off her shoulders and exposed way too much of her chest. No one but a husband should be able to see what Howard was looking at.

Sadie decided she would rather listen to the conversation then see the interaction between Howard and Doris. So she ducked back inside the dining hall, adjusted her dress, and went back to work.

The conversation carried on with dull business transactions until Howard was ready to leave. Sadie heard him stand up and then heard a teacup crash to the floor. Sadie giggled as she heard Howard gently tell Doris he had had enough of her attentions. Doris was definitely a desperate and deprived woman.

CHAPTER FIVE

GETTING TO KNOW BEAUTIFUL

As the late spring moved into early summer, Sadie and Gus began to relax and enjoy their new world. Gus and Laura were getting along famously and were becoming inseparable. Sadie was comfortable in her routine at work and had mastered her chore list to perfection. She was smiling and laughing more than she had in years. She was even beginning to enjoy Howard's flirting and found herself looking forward to his weekly visits to the boarding house.

Sadie's new life was very satisfying for her, and she found her work at the boarding house very gratifying; except for the day when the Galesburg Ladies' Aid Society held their monthly meetings at the boarding house. Sadie felt like she was on display when the women were there. The sideways glances from the women and lowering of voices when Sadie walked into the room told her that she was frequently the topic of conversation.

Sadie never had to check the calendar to know when Doris was hosting the society. For several days prior to the meeting, Doris would pencil in more chores on Sadie's daily list. The morning of the meeting Doris would follow Sadie around wearing one white glove to check for even a hint of dust or a little extra wax buildup. Sadie and Mrs. Goshen would joke about the arduous afternoon they knew they were going to have.

Howard also always seemed to know when the ladies were coming. The week of the meeting, Howard would spend more time in the kitchen with Sadie and Mrs. Goshen than he did with Doris. And he always seemed to be withdrawn. He would dispense with his normal jokes and flirting and stick strictly to business. Mrs. Goshen would joke that even Howard was afraid of Doris when she was preparing to face the prying judgement of the Society.

This particular Thursday in early June, Doris was even more meticulous. Sadie's dining room wax job had not passed inspection. Sadie was still working on the second pass of waxing the dessert bureau as Mrs. Goshen was well into preparing dinner for the college boys. Sadie was beginning to fret that she would not be able to complete her chores on time and was deep in concentration. Sadie was peering intently into the sun's reflections on the bureau, checking for sun streaks from the window. She felt a warm hand on her shoulder and reacted instantly. Sadie let out a barely audible gasp as she jumped and turned to face the intruder. As Sadie turned to face the person, she instinctively threw her arms up defensively in front of her face.

"Hey, it's just me. I'm sorry, I didn't mean to startle you. I thought you saw me come in."

"Oh, Howard. I'm sorry, it's just that you startled me. What can I do for you?" Sadie was still shaken enough from the episode that she couldn't bring herself to look up at Howard. She continued to stare at the freshly waxed cracks in the floorboard.

"Well, I've been thinking. You have been working so hard today getting ready for the ladies. And tomorrow is going to be an especially long day for you. You must be exhausted. How about I take you to dinner after you are finished here? That way you won't have to worry about cooking for yourself, and I won't have to worry about you not taking care of yourself. I have nothing to do this evening. And Mrs. Goshen and I always go out to dinner the evening before these events. So it would be the three of us if you could come."

"You two will have to go to dinner by yourselves. I have special plans with my husband tonight. Don't worry, Sadie. Howard and I do this all the time. He is an absolute gentleman, and he always pays for the meal. He knows lots of out-of-the-way places that are quiet and serve great food." Mrs. Goshen did not look up from the stove as she threw her words down the hall towards Sadie.

Sadie was secretly pleased that Howard would even consider inviting her. It sounded innocent enough on the surface, what with dinner being a regular event with Howard and Mrs. Goshen. But Howard didn't look at Mrs. Goshen the way he looked at Sadie. And Sadie found herself excited just to be talking to Howard.

But she knew it would never work. After all, she was still married to Frank. And Howard didn't know about Gus. Sadie couldn't risk that secret getting out. If the truth were known, she could lose her job. And she could not allow that to happen just because of a little vanity. Besides, she knew Howard wasn't serious. He was just talking like he always did, saying things to her to make her feel good but not really meaning any of it. Sadie picked up her cleaning supplies and headed back down the hallway to the kitchen. She still needed to help Mrs. Goshen get dinner ready, and she was running behind.

"Thanks for the thought anyway, Howard. See you next week." Sadie threw the words over her shoulder and didn't look back.

"Wait a minute, Sadie. I was serious!" Howard headed down the hall after Sadie.

"What's the harm in dinner? You've been working hard ever since you landed in Galesburg. I bet you don't even know where any of the restaurants are in town!"

"Okay, so I don't know where all the eating establishments are in this town. Big deal. Eating establishments are not real high on my priority list right now. And having dinner with you isn't even on my list. I really like things the way they are."

"So what is on your priority list? Working your fingers to the bone? Dying at an early age because you didn't take care of yourself? Having dinner with me isn't going to change things. I'm not asking you to jump in bed with me or anything. I'm just suggesting two tired adults take a break from the daily grind and relax for a few minutes. I think we deserve that. And furthermore, I will not take no for an answer. If I need to, I will follow you home and park myself on your front step until you agree to dinner. That could make for a long night for both of us!" Howard folded his arms across his chest and planted his body squarely in front of Sadie, blocking all her exits.

"Oh, Howard, please don't do this." Sadie couldn't begin to explain to Howard why she couldn't go to dinner with him. The temptation was definitely there. But the need to protect Gus and her secret was greater.

"I can't Howard. Maybe some other time." Sadie's hope was that she could put him off this time and indefinitely postpone any future requests.

"Why can't you? Do you have big plans? A date perhaps? Or do you really dislike me that much? I am just looking forward to getting to know someone new in town. And I know this great place behind the college campus that no one that is anybody goes to. So you don't have to worry about being seen with me if that is what is worrying you."

Sadie was visibly distraught. She was not used to this attention. She had spent many years completely isolated by Frank and had not known what it was like to have the attention of male friends. So she hadn't missed those relationships. But now that she had started to develop new relationships, she was curious as to how it would feel to spend time with a man who wanted to spend time with her. A man who was nice and normal. Sadie really did enjoy Howard's company and attention. And she would have to continue to deal with him as long as she worked at the boarding house. Judging by the way Doris's face lit up whenever Howard made a sales call and the way she always dressed a little more meticulously on the days Howard was due, Sadie was pretty sure that Howard probably had the power to get her fired if he wanted to.

"Okay. So I don't have big plans. I just don't want to get involved with anyone right now. Okay?"

"I'm not asking you to get involved with me. I'm asking you to have dinner with a friend." Howard's pleading eyes and pouty smile finally got the best of Sadie. And she laughed out loud at the pathetic, begging picture before her.

"Okay! I'll go to dinner with you. But I will meet you at the restaurant. I have to run a couple of errands first. Okay?" Sadie could only hope that Howard would accept her conditions. This was the only way that she could possibly have dinner with him. She could not risk him finding out about Gus, and she also could not risk his following her home in the evenings. Hopefully having dinner with him would satisfy his curiosity enough to keep him from pursuing her. Sadie needed to keep her two worlds separate for now. Someday soon she would be established enough to be able to find a better job or maybe even run a boarding house of her own. And by then, the town of Galesburg would have accepted her and her son, and she would be able to hold her head up in the town with respect. The people of this town would soon stop worrying about where she came from and start accepting her for what she was. Then maybe she would be able to live completely out in the open, and her secrets of the past would be forgotten. Forgotten by the townspeople and most importantly forgotten by her. But until then she would just have to work a little harder to keep her two worlds separate and secret.

"Well, if you are ashamed to have me pick you up at your house, then I guess I'll just have to settle for your terms. There is a little restaurant a few blocks from here called Guido's. It's on the corner of West Simmons and East Main Street. It's a little Italian restaurant that serves great pasta. I'll meet you there about eight. Is that acceptable?"

"I can find it, Howard. I'll see you then. I really have to get back to work now." Sadie smiled a farewell to Howard and disappeared through the swinging kitchen doors. The remainder of Sadie's afternoon went quickly as she worked tirelessly to help Mrs. Goshen make sure that dinner was on the table in time.

Sadie pondered her predicament on her way home. She wasn't sure how to ask Laura if she would sit with Gus and wasn't sure if she should. Sadie felt like she was maybe taking advantage of her landlord, and she and Laura were becoming good friends. But she was pretty sure Laura wouldn't mind at all.

"Hi, Momma! Grandma Laura and I had such fun today. We worked in the garden, went shopping for groceries, and even picked you some fresh flowers for the dinner table. See? Aren't they pretty?" Gus was waiting on the porch for Sadie and bounded down the sidewalk as soon as she turned the corner onto their block. Sadie had instant pangs of guilt as she took the bouquet of fresh daisies and carnations from Gus's grubby little hand.

"These are really, really pretty, Gus! Thank you! I'm so glad you had such fun today. But I need to talk to Laura for a second. Where is she?"

"She's in the kitchen starting dinner. We bought chicken today at the market, so she's making fried chicken, mashed potatoes, and gravy that she says will be better than anything I have ever tasted." Gus was beaming from ear to ear. His little round face was browning from the early summer sun, and his clothes were getting tighter and shorter. This midwestern small-town life was certainly agreeing with him. Amid the pangs of guilt for her dinner plans, she also took great comfort that Gus was blossoming in his new life. This was proof to Sadie that she had made the right decision in leaving Frank.

Gus took Sadie's hand as they walked up the steps together and into Laura's kitchen. The smells of frying chicken filled the kitchen with wonderful scents and caused Sadie's empty stomach to roll and toss under her dress. At this moment, dinner with Laura and Gus was much more appealing than dinner with Howard. Mainly because she wouldn't have to wait so long to satisfy her hunger.

"My Laura, dinner smells absolutely superb! I am so hungry! But I received an invitation to dinner tonight and was hoping you would not be offended if I had dinner later with my friend?" Sadie posed the question and braced herself.

"Oh, this is news. Dinner with a friend? So is this a male or female friend? I know it's not your boss, Ms. Steinway. She only has dinner with the society when they invite her. Other than that, she hides in her little boarding house, pretending to be important. Out with it. Tell me the gossip!"

"It's not a big deal. Just someone I met at the boarding house. Just dinner with a friend." Sadie tried not to be too evasive as she knew that would only produce more questions. And she didn't want too many prying questions. She didn't want to lie to Laura, but she also didn't want Laura to think she was dating someone. And she was still married to Frank. Having dinner with Howard was simply a delay tactic to keep him from snooping into her private life. Dinner with Howard was a necessary survival tactic right now. And Sadie was almost convinced that Howard really didn't want anything more than to get to know her.

"Well, since you seem to be reluctant to give me a name, that means you are having dinner with a man. Is this somebody special? Anybody I know?" Laura continued to tease Sadie as she watched her squirm under the questioning.

"It's just a guy I met at the boarding house. We're just friends. Do you mind if I skip dinner tonight with you and Gus? And would it be too much to ask if you could watch Gus for me while I'm out? I won't be gone long. Dinner is at eight, and I plan on being home by eleven at the latest. Tomorrow is the ladies Society meeting at the boarding house, so I have to be in tiptop shape to be able to deal with my day tomorrow. Every time the ladies meet at the house,

Doris is an absolute madwoman. And Mrs. Goshen and I work our tails off nonstop. So, I cannot start work tired." Sadie watched Laura's face to see if there was any concern about watching Gus. Sadie didn't want to take advantage of her and was prepared to call off dinner if Laura had any hesitations about watching Gus.

"Sadie, I'm just teasing you. You most definitely deserve a night out. You have done nothing but work since you got to Galesburg. It's time a young thing like you got to relax a little. If you keep working all the time you'll get old long before your time. Gus and I will be fine. We'll have a good time tonight. After all, grandmas like to spend time with their grandchildren!"

"Oh, thank you so much! I do so appreciate everything you have done, and are doing, for me and Gus. And I won't be late getting back. I promise." Sadie gave Laura a quick hug as she started back to her bedroom to decide what to wear.

Sadie decided quickly on her brown dress and low heels. Since it was a warm evening, and she didn't have to pretend to be anybody, Sadie decided to leave her hair down and not wear a hat. She knew this was not exactly an accepted fashion trend, but she was tired of wearing her hair up all the time. And she was feeling a little freer and more independent than she had felt in a long time. There would be no one at the restaurant who knew her except Howard, so there were no appearances that she must keep up. And, after looking in the mirror, Sadie added a bit of blush to her cheeks and lips and cinched the belt on her dress a bit tighter to accentuate her tiny waist.

Sadie had never felt beautiful, except for the brief courtship she had with Frank before they married. He had swept her off her feet but never complimented her on her physical beauty. Frank had made her feel wanted and needed and special at first because he was focused on her. Once they had married, Frank told her how to dress, how to eat, how to keep house. And if she didn't follow Franks instructions to the letter, there was always a gutful consequence. At first it was just verbal abuse. Frank was adept at putdowns, lectures on proper respect for her husband, and constant reminders that Sadie owed Frank for taking care of her. And Frank reminded Sadie at least once a day that she had no place else to go and that no other man would want to take on used goods. After childbirth the beatings started. Sadie had wanted to put the child first in her life, and be the perfect mother. But Frank wouldn't tolerate Sadie giving her attention to anyone but him first and foremost.

Sadie kissed Gus good-bye and bounded out the door in the warm summer evening. Laura had loaned her a shawl, and her shiny, curly red hair bounced across the stitched yarn as she walked down the sidewalk. The sun was just beginning to set, and the scent of the prolific little wild roses created a natural perfume that settled lightly in her hair. Sadie was lost in her own peaceful thoughts and smiling to herself when she arrived at the front door of Guido's.

Sadie had never been to a restaurant by herself and was not sure if she should go in or wait for Howard outside.

"Hey there."

"Oh!" Sadie jumped as she turned around to see Howard standing just a few inches from her.

"You startled me. I wasn't sure if I should go in and meet you, or wait outside. I guess I don't need to worry about that anymore." Sadie smiled up at Howard.

Sadie took the arm that Howard offered, and they strolled into the dimly lit restaurant. She didn't notice that the din of the conversation suddenly became much smaller when she walked in. Heads turned to look at the glowing young woman whom they had never seen before.

Sadie and Howard were led to a small table near the corner of the room, conspicuously farther away from the other tables and outside the reach of the dining room's chandeliers. A small candle was burning on the table, illuminating a small vase of fresh yellow roses and an accompanying plate of rich, unwrapped chocolates. Sadie noticed that their table was the only table with a candle, candy and roses. Sadie looked at Howard's face. He was watching her intently with a slight smile on his face. Sadie was immediately flattered and somewhat grateful for the special attention. No one had ever gone to this much trouble for her. She knew that starting a relationship with Howard would be extremely dangerous and could expose her dark secrets to the entire town. Besides, married women did not consort with other men, even if the husband was no longer in the picture. But, then again, Frank was many miles away. And no one knew she was married. Sadie decided she was really going to enjoy the evening. Just this once. She would be very careful not to expose her situation to Howard and would enjoy the special attention just this once. One time certainly couldn't hurt.

"How about a glass of wine while we check out the menu?" Howard helped Sadie into her chair. Sadie felt his slight touch and tingled with instant delight. This evening could provide enough dream stuff for at least six months. This would be much better than the nightmares she had regularly about Frank finding her and Gus.

"That would be wonderful. You choose for us." Sadie watched Howard signal the waiter and stayed amused as Howard and the waiter discussed the wine menu. Shortly, Howard made his choice, the waiter nodded in agreement, and Howard turned again to Sadie. Sadie was hoping that Howard did not ask her opinion of his choice. She had no experience with wine tasting. With Frank everything was hard, cheap liquor or beer. And Frank had never invited Sadie to drink with him, nor would she have wanted to. But tonight, Sadie wanted Howard to assume that she was a lady with worldly knowledge. She was hoping he would be less bold if he thought she had experience and understood everything that was going on. Howard proposed a toast with the wine glasses as soon as the waiter left the table.

"How about a toast to new friendships? There is always a reason for meeting new people in the strangest places. And I never expected to find someone like you at Doris's boarding house. So let us give a toast to fate." Howard and Sadie's glasses tinkled when they connected, and Sadie sipped her first taste of the chardonnay and let it slowly slide down her throat, concentrating on the warm tingling that was spreading down her throat and chest. She knew she had better savor this. Her body's reaction to the first sip warned her to be very, very careful.

"I hope you don't mind, Sadie. I took the liberty of ordering for both of us. They have great spaghetti and meatballs here. Everything is made from scratch, including the spaghetti. And besides, you were so adamant that we not go out on a date. Ordering spaghetti should prove that we are not on a date. First rule of etiquette for men as taught to me by my father: Never have spaghetti on a first date. It can be very messy and embarrassing for the couple to try to manage a forkful of spaghetti and remain graceful. And spaghetti sauce stains are very hard to get out of clothing. So, we are having spaghetti, which means we are just friends out together for the evening."

"I didn't hear you give our order. You set this up before I got here, didn't you? When did you have time to plan this? You were still at the boarding house when I left!" Sadie was amazed and a little concerned. Either Howard had done this many times before and the people at the restaurant knew his routine, or Howard had planned this before today and just assumed that she would accept his invitation. Either way, Sadie was a little irritated, and her light mood sank a bit. She had really believed that Howard's dinner invitation was really a spur-of-the-moment suggestion between two friends.

"Okay, yes. I planned this. But you are misinterpreting this! I planned for a nice evening with a friend. I thought you deserved a little attention and something special for yourself! And I didn't know until this afternoon that Mrs. Goshen wasn't coming along. Just trying to do something nice for someone I care about. Like a good friend." Howard tilted his head and stuck out his bottom lip in a mock pout. Sadie had to laugh.

"Okay, then. Thank you for thinking of me. This is really nice." Sadie's heart melted in spite of her good sense sending up a red flag in her belly. This was nice. It was really nice to have someone think of her. And do something to make her feel good. She really, really liked that thought.

"But I do have just one more question. What would you have done if I had told you no? What would you have done with all this planning and stuff?" Sadie was intending to back Howard into a corner, but instead he smiled slyly.

"Well, I would have had to just go out on the street at the last minute and find someone else who might be interested in flowers, wine, and wonderful conversation with a friend. So, tell me about yourself. How did you get to Galesburg, Illinois, from the Big Apple? It seems a bit unusual at best. And most likely juicy gossip!" Sadie didn't look up from her salad as she carefully responded.

"Well, It's not that difficult. My husband died suddenly, and I needed to make a fresh start. Neither one of us had much family left, and I didn't want to be a burden for those who are left of my family. I'm young and very able to work. Why would I want to lounge around in someone else's house and expect them to take care of me? That just didn't seem to be the right thing to do." Sadie knew the proper path for young widows was to stay with family until they remarried. Or died. But she could think of no other way to explain her unusual circumstances. And since Howard knew she was from New York City, Sadie knew Doris was talking about her. She had to keep her stories straight.

Even if it were true that Frank was really dead, Sadie was pretty sure she wouldn't allow herself to be taken in by her in-laws. They were old, bitter, spiteful people. Franks' father treated his wife in much the same way Frank treated Sadie. Sadie knew he beat her because she, like Sadie, always wore long sleeves and walked with her head down. If Sadie had been lucky enough to outlive Frank, she certainly wouldn't voluntarily walk back into the same hateful environment.

"Was your husband's family not able to take you in? And if so, why didn't you go back home to your parents for a while? Where did you grow up?" Howard's line of questioning mirrored Sadie's thoughts and was expected. Howard was simply carrying on the conversation as society would expect him to, using standard acceptable questions.

"You are certainly a nosy friend. Do I have to pass an accountability test here? Not that It's any of your business, but my husband's family and my own family were not options for me. I can take care of myself, and I needed a change in my life. So, I jumped on the train in New York City and off the train here. Galesburg just looked like a good place to start a new life." Sadie wasn't exactly lying outright to Howard. She was simply omitting the reasons behind the truth. And she needed to move this conversation to another subject soon.

"Enough about me. Have you lived in Galesburg long?" Sadie was honestly curious about Howard. She had never had a male friend and needed to know why Howard would want to be friends with her. And how dangerous it might be for her to have him as a friend.

"Galesburg is the only place I know. My grandparents immigrated to the United States from Russia, and Galesburg is where they finally settled. My father is a banker here in town, and my mother died shortly after my brother was born. I was raised by nannies and cleaning ladies, and that's probably why I sell and deliver groceries and kitchen supplies now instead of working at the bank with my father."

"Do you live at home with your father, or do you have your own place?" Sadie felt compassion toward this man who had lost his mother so young. Sadie felt her own mother had been dead to her since she married Frank, and that loss was painful.

"Oh, I don't live at home anymore. Haven't for years! God Forbid! There is no room in my father's house for those who don't follow the rules to the letter and show absolute respect. I've had my own place for years."

"So you have your own place, huh? I bet there are women in and out all the time. You probably have a revolving front door!" Sadie was intrigued when she noticed him shifting in his chair. And his eyes were down on the table when he responded.

"Well, so to speak."

"I rather like living alone. No one to answer to but me. And if I want to take a pretty lady to dinner on the spur of the moment, I can." Howard winked at Sadie and gestured a mock toast to Sadie as he took a sip of his wine.

"Spur of the moment? Right." Sadie smiled across the table at Howard and returned his toast.

"I'll follow your lead. Let's just not worry about each other's dark past and just relax and have some great food and great company. What do you say? Agreed?" Again, Howard was raising the mock toast as he was speaking.

Sadie tried to swallow, but the wine lodged in her throat. She put her glass down on the table so hard and so fast that the bottom of the goblet clinked loudly against her table knife. A chip of the glass flew across the table and landed in the middle of Howard's plate of spaghetti. Sadie's face was flushed and her eyes wide with fear.

"What do you mean dark past?" Sadie sputtered as soon as she was able to speak. She was absolutely shocked that her secret may be out already. She had never told anyone! How could Howard know already?

"Sadie, calm down. I didn't mean anything by it. It was just a figure of speech. I was just making conversation!"

"Oh, okay. Apology accepted! I just simply chocked on my drink and lost my head for a minute. Oh, I am so sorry! I didn't mean to throw glass chips at you!" Sadie flashed a feeble smile as she delicately dabbed her mouth with her napkin. She was still not used to hiding her secret and had no confidence that she could pull this off. Years of mental conditioning by Frank had convinced her that she was stupid and inept. Trained subservience always rose to the surface when she was in the presence of men. She was going to have to work on that if she was ever going to be able to hold her head up and be accepted on her own.

"So anyway, Howard, what are the summers like here in rural Illinois? Are they as wonderful as I remember from my childhood in Ohio?"

"Depends on what you remember. If you remember heat, humidity, and bugs, then I'm sure you won't be disappointed." Howard graciously signaled the waiter for another plate of spaghetti and a fresh wine glass for Sadie. Once the evidence of Sadie's nervousness was removed from the table, the tone of the conversation lightened considerably

"That is not what I meant. I know that comes with the territory. What I meant was the good things. I've spent so many years in New York City that I have come to despise summers. The houses are built so close together that you can't get any breeze through the house on a hot summer day and can't sleep at night because of the stale City smells that just seem to hang on forever. And what little grass there is turns brown by the middle of June. Most of the City is just dirty, littered cement. I'm really looking forward to the summer breezes, green grass, and lots of wonderful inviting shade from the big oak trees." Sadie was enjoying her reflections of past summers in Ohio and looking forward to her first summer outside the City. Her face reflected her contentment.

"Well, if that is what you are looking forward to this summer, I doubt that you will be disappointed. Summers are pretty predictable around here. Sun comes up, it gets hot, sun goes down, and it's not quite so hot. And yes, we do have those gentle breezes that keep the heat from being unbearable and do help keep the bugs from sticking to your skin, along with the violent summer thunderstorms and a tornado every once in a while."

"Oh, Howard, you are such a poop. Don't you enjoy the summer breezes and the smell of nature? And being able to walk through the meadows and the hills and hear nothing but the wind and your own footsteps?" Sadie was beaming at the thought of taking walks with Gus in the early evenings and being able to bask in her freedom and good fortune. She was beginning to forget about Frank and his threats and relax in the thought that that part of her life might truly be over. She held on to the belief that her fears would soon fade completely away. Her secret and her past would fade with them. Someday soon she would even be able to stop looking over her shoulder.

"Well, I think I would thoroughly enjoy walking through the meadows with you." Howard reached across the table and let his fingers rest on the back of Sadie's hand. Sadie blushed as she pulled her hand back into her lap.

"You are making me a little uncomfortable, Howard."

"Well, underneath this nasty exterior, I am a gentleman. Your wish is my command. So that's the end of that. Would you like me to pour you a little more wine, madam?"

For the remainder of the evening, Howard concentrated on keeping the conversation light and casual. Sadie would only drink two glasses of wine, so Howard knew that she was not going to waver.

Howard helped Sadie with her shawl as they walked out of the restaurant into the cool night air.

"Would you like me to drive you home, Sadie? My car is just around the corner."

"Howard, no. But thank you. I had a lovely evening tonight. It was just what I needed. Thank you for a lovely dinner. I will be fine walking home. I really don't mind at all. In fact, I look forward to the lovely stroll." There was no way Sadie was going to allow Howard to see where she lived. Even though Gus would be fast asleep by now, and there was no chance of Howard spotting him. Sadie didn't want to risk the chance of Howard dropping by unexpectedly at some other time. She did not want to have to explain Gus to Howard and didn't want to have to explain Howard to Gus. It was a lovely evening, and Sadie wanted to leave it at that.

"Well, maybe I mind. I'm not used to being denied the gentleman's need to see his date safely home."

"I'm not your date, remember? I distinctly remember you saying that you don't take dates out for spaghetti. And besides, this is Galesburg. After nine years in New York City, I think I can make it home in Galesburg. Thank you again for a lovely evening, Howard. Good night." Sade touched Howard's sleeve with her hand and started to turn away.

"Howard reacted with instinct and took hold of Sadie's arm with his left hand. Sadie turned back to him with a puzzled look on her face. Howard reached out and gently touched the side of her cheek with the back of his hand. He then pulled her forward and placed a kiss on her forehead.

"Thank you, Sadie, for a wonderful evening. And good night to you." Howard's voice was lower than normal, with a slight guttural sound. Howard smiled his farewell, bowed slightly to the lady, and walked down the street and disappeared around the corner.

Sadie smiled in the middle of the sidewalk, unable to move as Howard sauntered away. She was absolutely stunned at her body's reaction to Howard's touch. The wild tingling sensation and the difficulty breathing were feelings Sadie had buried years ago, feelings that Sadie thought she would be incapable of ever feeling again. After Howard was out of sight, Sadie closed her eyes, took several deep breaths, and forced the feelings back down deep. Way down deep for safety.

The wonderful evening of attention and the awakening of those wonderful delicious feelings left their mark on Sadie, if only for a moment. She smiled to herself as she walked home through the quiet residential streets. Her step was light, and her heart was alive. She knew there was no future with Howard, but it was a really good feeling to know that her company was enjoyed by a man other than Frank. A really nice man who totally enjoyed her company.

Tomorrow would be another hard tedious day at the boarding house. But Sadie knew it was worth it. She was convinced the worst was over and that she was well on her way to a good life. A life she was building for herself and Gus. And she now had a pleasant memory of her own to hang on to. She could use this memory to produce pleasant summer dreams for many nights to come.

CHAPTER SIX

Cruel Rumors spread through town

Friday morning dawned bright and crisp. Sadie was up early after having slept soundly the night before. Dinner with Howard created an aura of contentment and confidence in Sadie's independent heart. It seemed to be the seal of approval that Sadie needed to begin to trust her decision and accept success in her new life. Sadie bounced through the kitchen as she readied herself for work. Smiling broadly, Sadie patted Laura's shoulder each time she passed by.

"Well, I see dinner out last night agreed with you. I've not seen you this bright since I met you. So, Sadie, spill your guts and give me the dirt. Tell me what happened last night. Where did you go, what did you have to eat, and what did you talk about? Come on, girl, talk to Grandma Laura."

"Laura, it wasn't that big a deal. We just had dinner and visited for a while. It was a really nice break from everything. And it wasn't a date! We had spaghetti, if that helps. You don't order spaghetti on a date. So there. It was just a really nice break." Sadie smiled at Laura triumphantly and turned to head back to the bedroom to finish dressing for work.

"Well, I guess you don't usually order spaghetti dinners on a date. Or on a dinner outing that you don't want to look like a date. Wonder which it was." Laura threw out the challenge to Sadie's back, but the only response she got out of Sadie was a shrug as she disappeared into her bedroom.

Sadie arrived at the rooming house almost thirty minutes early that morning. Mrs. Goshen welcomed the extra help, and breakfast was served and the dining hall cleaned in record time. When Doris arrived in the dining room at the appointed time to be served her breakfast, she was mildly surprised to find the tables all cleaned, shined and dried. Normally Sadie was still finishing the cleaning of the tables when Doris sat down to be served. This had always given Doris an opportunity to be extra critical if her food was not exactly the right temperature or when Sadie's wait service was a little slow. But today she didn't have the opportunity to nag on Sadie, which Doris found a bit of peace in. She had other things to think about today. The Society would be arriving this afternoon for their monthly meeting, and Doris had to make sure that everything was exactly right. She didn't have time to dawdle over breakfast.

Doris hovered over Sadie as she finished her morning chores. Sadie soon learned that the short click-click of Doris's tongue meant the white glove inspection had failed. But by the time Sadie's chores were finally finished, she was cringing with every inspection. It took Sadie three attempts to get the furniture just right in the sitting room. Doris ordered Sadie to re-dust the floors and wood furniture as she left to check her hair and makeup. It was almost time to assume her position as head mistress.

The door chimes began to sound at fifteen minutes before two o'clock. Sadie rushed down the hall to perform her new duties. She was not at all comfortable meeting the women of the town this way. Her house dress was clean and it fit, but it would not have been what Sadie would have chosen to wear to entertain in her own home. Sadie felt like these new duties were a signal to the Galesburg female Society that she definitely worked for Doris and was not quite good enough to be included in the inner circle. Sadie had learned very quickly that she was to be seen and not heard. And she was to be especially prompt. Sadie was glad that all she had to do was just escort the ladies in. Mrs. Goshen would serve the ladies, and Sadie would reappear after they left to clean up after them. Staying out of sight in the kitchen was just perfect for Sadie.

"Good afternoon. Please follow me to the sitting room. Ms. Steinway is waiting for you there." Sadie felt silly being so formal. It wasn't like these women didn't know exactly where to go in the boarding house. Sadie resisted the urge to giggle and curtsy in a flirtatious manner. Sadie was still in a good mood from her wonderful dinner the evening before. Once she delivered everyone to Doris, her publicity work was done. She couldn't wait to be through with these ladies.

"Why thank you. You're the new girl, aren't you? What name do you go by?" Sadie had already started walking toward the sitting room when the crumply little woman behind her spoke very softly to her back. Sadie turned and looked at the woman. She was shorter than Sadie and easily someone's grandmother. She was wearing much too much makeup for her age and much too much for the early summer weather. Her hair was colored with a very dark pigment that made the wrinkles on her face very prominent. The short bob of her hair curled just across her cheeks from the corners of her mouth and made it look like someone had painted a fake smile all the way across her face.

"Yes, I am the new housekeeper. My name is Sadie. And what is your name?" Sadie attempted to help the lady off with her coat, but she pulled her fox fur around her body and signaled that she wanted to keep it on.

"No, what is your professional name? We don't call the hired help by their first name in this town. It signals that we are friends, which we will never be. Obviously, you haven't had any professional training, have you?" The lady looked Sadie up and down and frowned at her disapprovingly.

"And furthermore, you don't ask me for my name. If you ever need to know my name, Ms. Steinway will deliver any necessary messages. And by the way, there are never messages from the likes of you that are necessary. I'm not here to socialize with the help. Now, please, take me to Ms. Steinway."

"Yes, ma'am." Sadie rolled her eyes as soon as she had turned away from the lady. This was not going to be a fun time. But at least it would be short. There were usually only about ten or fifteen women who came to these meetings, so this duty should end shortly. And Sadie knew none of them were ever late. So she would be finished and back to the kitchen within the next few minutes.

Sadie was kept busy escorting women as they arrived and successfully got everyone into the sitting room. Most of the guests arrived in groups of twos and threes, so Sadie found it was easy to avoid repeating the unpleasant incident of the first guest. Soon they were all seated comfortably in the sitting room, surrounding Doris in her chair that was slightly larger and taller and definitely the most elegant chair in the room. With the escort of the last woman into the room, Sadie excused herself and fled back to the kitchen, thinking the rest of her afternoon would be pretty much predictable. She did not expect to be summoned again until everyone had left and it was time to clean up.

The business meeting was finally concluded when Mrs. Lear ran out of women to assign tasks to. Doris signaled for Sadie with the small silver breakfast bell as soon as the business meeting was officially concluded.

"Inform Mrs. Goshen that we are ready for the tea and dessert to be served in the dining hall." Her orders were brisk and succinct as usual. Sadie nodded her acceptance and backed out of the room. Mrs. Goshen laughed as Sadie mimicked Doris's orders when she was safely out of earshot in the kitchen.

"My lord, girl. You really need to work on your patience. Stay here much longer and you'll get good at letting it go in one ear and out the other. Stop taking her personally. All you need to worry about is doing your job and doing it well. Ms. Steinway will never treat you any better than she treats you now. It's just not in her nature. I don't think she could be genuinely nice if her life depended on it." Mrs. Goshen added the finishing touches to the tea tray and then brushed the flour out of her hair and off her apron before picking up the tray.

"Come to think of it, she is never going to fire you either. As long as you do your job and do it well you have a job here forever. Besides, you can't hire anyone to work for her unless they are new to town. Word has spread!! So in some sense of the term, you are pretty much protected."

"Well, at least I'm almost done for the day. I've had about all I can handle for one day. All I have left to do is help you clean up after they leave. Have fun, Mrs. Goshen. Better you than me. Those women give me the creeps. "Sadie popped a piece of broken raspberry scone in her mouth as she watched Mrs. Goshen back through the swinging doors into the hallway.

"You aren't done yet, girl. I believe there are a least six more chores on your sheet for the day. And one of those chores is helping get dinner started. So just don't be getting too cocky over there in the corner!" Mrs. Goshen winked at

Sadie, letting her know that she considered her a partner in enduring the endless days at the boarding house.

"I know I'm not done with my chores yet. But I am done with the ladies. I can enjoy the rest of the day in peace!" Catching Mrs. Goshen's disgusted look, Sadie laughed outright.

"Okay! Enjoy is maybe the wrong words to use here. Let me rephrase. At least the rest of my day will be quiet as I finish my chores. Every time I walk into that room with those women, I feel like everyone is staring at me, and none of them approved of me. I think Ms. Steinway had me doing the pick-up and delivery today so she could show off her new slave and make a statement to me that she is definitely higher on the food chain. How do you stand it, Mrs. Goshen?"

Mrs. Goshen shrugged her shoulders. "Hold that thought. I need to get the tea out there so they can get started while I get the scones ready. Be right back." Mrs. Goshen disappeared down the hallway. A few minutes later she was back with an empty tray.

"Okay girl. I've been working for her almost ten years. In that time I've seen many a good, and bad, housekeeper come and go. The secret to keeping this job is to not worry about fitting in with Ms. Steinway or those women she runs with. Just keep your place. It's not a bad thing, Sadie. We're getting paid to do a job. That's it. We aren't getting paid to make friends or fit in. And we don't have to take any of those people home with us. All we have to do is a good job. And take personal pride in that we do a good job. That's all. We do this for the paycheck, not for the payback. I just smile on my way to the bank every week." Mrs. Goshen wasn't even looking at Sadie as she filled the tray with raspberry scones and deep, rich chocolate brownies. It was as if she was repeating her daily mantra. The mantra that had kept her going every day for the last ten years.

"Wow, you've really got this down to a science. I really admire your stamina. I don't think I'll ever get that comfortable here."

"Yes, you will. In time. You just got to learn to accept the cards that life has dealt you and just live with it." Mrs. Goshen finished arranging the tray of desserts and held the tray out to Sadie.

"And speaking of those nasty cards, Ms. Steinway says you are to serve the desserts instead of me."

Sadie looked across at Mrs. Goshen with surprise.

"Me? That's your job! You're the kitchen help, not me. Why does she want me to do this?" Sadie crossed her arms in front of her and refused to accept the tray.

"Don't be so stubborn, girl! It's not up to the hired help to ask questions, Sadie. You are supposed to duck your head, say 'Yes ma'am', and do what you're told. So now, Sadie, take the tray and do what you're told. I won't tell Ms. Steinway that you didn't show proper respect and duck your head!" Mrs. Goshen and Sadie both giggled as Sadie took the tray, bowed to Mrs. Goshen, and started down the hallway toward the dining hall. Sadie was still giggling to herself when she entered the dining hall.

The room was quiet as Sadie delivered each dessert exactly as Mrs. Goshen had instructed her. She remained behind the women with her tray and carefully placed each dessert plate to the left of each woman, being careful to make sure her fingers did not touch the food. Sadie had just finished setting the last plate down and turned to go back into the kitchen for the next set of plates. Her face burned red with the embarrassment of all the silent attention. But the difficult part was done. She had managed to serve Doris and most of the table without incident and had noticed no disapproving glances from Doris.

Sadie consciously raised her head in personal defiance as she started to exit behind the head table with the almost empty tray. All that remained on the tray were some empty tea glasses and used silverware that she had picked up from the tables on her rounds. Sadie was concentrating so fully on maintaining her exit composure that she did not see the foot move from under a table and placed directly in her path.

Sadie was walking quickly when her left ankle hit the foot with a solid blow. Her balance immediately dislodged, and Sadie threw the wooden tray to her right as she grabbed for the floor a few seconds later. Sadie hit the floor with a thud a few seconds after the tray crashed to the floor. As her head and chest hit the floor first, Sadie's dress flew up over her rear, exposing Sadie's lean legs contrasted against a pair of old and tattered panties. As Sadie continued her downward spiral to the floor, she rolled slightly to her right side to gain the ability to rest on her backside. Sadie pulled her dress down over her hips a few seconds after she stopped rolling, and felt the draft on exposure.

Sadie came to rest flat on her back on the floor, banging the back of her head hard against the polished wood floors as her body came to rest. Sadie was grateful that her back was to the women in the room as she heard the cruel snickers echo in the distance against the thunder pounding in her head.

Sadie lay on the floor for a few seconds trying to collect her thoughts. The blow to her head had caused her to be slightly disoriented, and she had to concentrate on blinking her eyes and forcing the foggy haze from her head. Sadie moaned quietly and was greeted by a pair of warm, helping hands as she attempted to collect her thoughts.

Sadie had recognized the foot that had tripped her. It belonged to the same woman with the fox fur who had refused to give Sadie her name earlier in the day. Sadie remembered the highly polished shoes as she looked at the floor during the lecture on remembering her place. This woman was sitting right next to Doris.

"Sadie. Sadie. Are you okay? I'm so sorry. Please let me help you up." Sadie turned her head to be greeted by a woman's concerned face. The woman had rushed to Sadie's side when she saw her fall, and was now kneeling on the floor beside Sadie. Although she was a petite woman, she had strength in her arms as she forced Sadie to remain flat on the floor and began checking for broken bones.

"I'm okay. Nothing broken but my pride." Sadie was blinking back tears and trying not to imagine what an entertaining image she must have provided to the Ladies Aid Society. She was sprawled on the floor like a big-footed hound dog pup with absolutely no grace. The remnants of the broken tea glasses from her tray were splattered over Sadie and the floor. Sadie took the kind woman's hand and allowed her to pull Sadie to a sitting position.

"You didn't embarrass yourself. You just had a cruel trick played on you. You were purposefully tripped. Such a childish prank to be played by these women who pretend to be the cream of the crop. I apologize for them and must admit that right now I'm the embarrassed one. I'm embarrassed to admit that I am part of this group. Here, let me help you up." The woman stood up and leaned down to offer Sadie her hand. Sadie, completely humiliated, accepted her offer but could not lift her head to meet the woman's concerned gaze. On her way to her feet, Sadie was working to regain her composure and prepare for the verbal onslaught that she knew would be coming from Doris any second.

"Thank you. I really appreciate your concern and kindness. I'm fine, really. Just let me clean up this mess quickly and bring out the rest of the desserts. My clumsiness shouldn't ruin your lunch." Sadie straightened her dress, quickly located the wooden dessert tray that she had thrown out of her way, and turned her back to the snickering, whispering women as she began to gather up the broken glass. Sadie jumped when she felt Doris touch the back of her arm. She turned to Doris with her eyes to the floor, fully expecting an immediate tirade of chastising. Instead, Doris seemed actually concerned about Sadie's welfare.

"Sadie, I certainly hope you are okay. I heard Grace tell you that you had been tripped on purpose. And I too must apologize. I'm really sorry that some of us could be so childish."

"Thank you, Ms. Steinway. But it wasn't your fault. Or anyone else's. I just stumbled. I broke your dishes, and I'm so sorry." Sadie was surprised that Doris was not berating her for being so clumsy, and she actually still had her hand on Sadie's arm, helping to steady her as she bent over to pick up the broken glass.

"Don't worry about the broken glass, Sadie. You can clean this up after they all leave. You've suffered enough humiliation for one day. Go back to the kitchen and tell Mrs. Goshen to bring out the rest of the desserts and finish serving. You don't need to see these ladies again today. Now go.

Scoot!" Doris pushed Sadie gently toward the door and turned back to her table.

Sadie ran down the hall to the kitchen and burst through the swinging doors into the kitchen, tears streaming down her face. She was so upset that she could barely talk.

"Mrs. Goshen, you need to finish serving the ladies. I, uh, I had a small accident. I'll stay here in the kitchen and then clean-up for you when they leave." Sadie was grateful Mrs. Goshen didn't ask any questions. Sadie was still feeling the humiliation and knew that if she tried to talk about it she would burst into tears.

Sadie stayed busy finishing her chores as she fought to put the humiliation behind her.

The remainder of the day was uneventful and very quiet. Sadie was silent as she helped clean up and finish her chores. She was absolutely seething inside from the embarrassment. The humiliation she had endured earlier in the day hung over and around her like an invisible, impenetrable wall. She knew that she had been purposefully tripped. Sadie felt smaller than she had felt in a long time. This day needed to end as soon as possible.

When Sadie walked in the door at home, she went straight for Gus without saying hello to Laura. She hugged him tightly and buried her face in his neck as if looking for sanctuary.

"Sadie, what's wrong? This is not the happy Sadie from this morning. What happened today?" Laura put her hand on Sadie's shoulder.

"Give me a second, Laura, and I'll tell you about my day. But first I need to hug and kiss my little boy. It helps remind me of why I'm doing this. And gives me a reason to go back to that hellhole tomorrow." Sadie smiled sheepishly at Laura over Gus's head and hugged him a little tighter for a few seconds more.

During dinner Sadie told Laura and Gus every detail of the day. She was eating wonderful food and sitting at a table where she felt welcome. The events of the day didn't seem to be quite so awful any more, and the sting of the humiliation was beginning to subside. Tomorrow would be a better day. As long as she could come home to Gus and Laura every night, she would make it. And building a life for Gus and herself would be worth everything that those ladies could throw her way.

"Well, Sadie, those women will never accept you no matter what you do or how long you live in this town. And from what I can see, they are not worth your time. They are mean, cruel and full of themselves. You don't need them. Look at me!! I've lived in this town for over thirty years, and they have never accepted me. And I've done just fine without them."

"You know these ladies? Were they as mean to you as they are to me?"

"Oh, yes. My husband, Saul, was a history professor at Knox college. Even though I preferred to stay home, I always felt obligated to attend events with Saul at first. I was a lot younger than Saul, so it always raised eyebrow when I walked in on Saul's arm."

"I bet part of the reason the eyebrows raised was because you were so beautiful! You are still so gorgeous. Did they ask lots of questions and try to humiliate you?" Sadie was still stinging a little over the events of her day. The thought of having to deal with these women on a regular basis made her sick to her stomach.

"Saul was pretty good at keeping me out of harm's way. He knew who had the sharpest claws and always kept me away from them. But he couldn't keep all the barbs away from me. It didn't matter how early we left the event; I always came home feeling sad and worthless. We never talked about it, but Saul knew. He would go out of his way for the next few days to make me laugh and feel better."

"How often did you have to go? Did you start dreading going as soon as you got the invitations?"

"For a while. After a year or so, Saul helped me to learn to be choosy about where I went with him. When we would get an invitation he would say to me, 'Laura, I believe your attendance at this event is optional'. So then I knew I didn't have to go. If he didn't say anything, then I knew he wanted me to go with him. I stopped going to all the events the Ladies Aid Society sponsored, and after a while they forgot about me and quit sending invitations. I am sure they found someone else to focus on, which sounds kind of selfish. But it was fine with me."

"Yeah, well, you were lucky enough to have a wonderful husband to be with. That will never be possible for me." Sadie sometimes longed for the kind of man and marriage that Laura must have had. Even though Saul was gone, Sadie could see and feel his love for Laura all over the house.

"Never say never, Sadie. You keep up your dinner dates, and you just might be surprised. You are so very lucky and blessed now, Sadie. You have a wonderful son. You are truly blessed." Laura tousled Gus's hair and kissed the top of his head as she walked by.

"You are so right, Laura. We are blessed, aren't we Gus? Blessed by this wonderful woman who so graciously took us in off the streets." Sadie was not about to miss a chance to thank Laura for her kindness and friendship.

"Okay, enough slobbering. I think we've beat that subject to death. Let's get dinner put away so Gus can have a nice, long bath before bedtime. If he doesn't get washed up, garden weeds might just start growing out of the top of his head!" Laura, Sadie, and Gus joked and laughed as they cleaned up the kitchen. Later that evening, after Gus was sound asleep, Sadie and Laura sat in comfortable silence on the front porch in the cool evening air.

The friendship between them had evolved into a comfortable routine. They laughed and talked together and shared a love for Gus. They had reached a point in this evolution where they could talk about the hurts and disappointments in their daily lives. The trust and sharing was deeper than the surface, but still not strong enough for the real pain of both women to surface. Sadie knew there was more to Laura and could feel the walls coming down between them. They respected each other's privacy and accepted the foreboding shadows as one of the conditions of friendship.

CHAPTER SEVEN

Pride and Pestilence

The weekend had been very relaxing and enjoyable for Sadie. She had begun to look forward to the normalcy that weekends had become with Laura. Weekends were family time, and Laura made sure that Sadie and Gus got to spend a lot of time together. Sadie had made arrangements to do extra housework to help out with their board and keep, but Laura always managed to have the majority of her housework done during the week. She liked to tell Gus that by helping her with the housework during the week, he was helping his mother. Sadie felt like she should be doing more for Laura, but Gus was so proud of his work. Sadie had to accept the arrangement.

Sadie tackled her work at the boarding house on Monday with precise silence. Sadie was still very careful around Doris. She needed her job and was careful to do it well. She gave Doris the respect that was required but was careful to keep any conversations with Doris strictly business.

Thursday was always the bright spot in Sadie's week. Howard usually showed up right after lunch. Sadie would arrange her cleaning schedule so that she was working in the kitchen and bath areas. That gave them a few minutes of conversation without the watchful eye of Doris.

Howard was especially jovial on this Thursday afternoon. He spent more time than usual in the kitchen with Sadie and Mrs. Goshen. Howard paced back and forth between the kitchen cupboards waiting for Sadie to move out of ear shot of Mrs. Goshen. This took some time, and Howard was starting the kitchen inventory for the second time before he got his chance.

"So, Sadie girl, are we on for this evening? You look like you could use a nice evening out. Would you have dinner with me tonight?"

Sadie was quick to accept. She didn't tell him, but she looked forward to the weekly dinners with Howard and was expecting, and hoping, that he would ask.

"Great! I'll meet you at our restaurant at eight. Will that work for you?"

"Yes, Howard. I'll be there at eight. Are we having spaghetti again? You know this is not a date." Sadie was really beginning to enjoy flirting with Howard. She had convinced herself that as long as nothing was official it was simply two people having dinner. That was socially acceptable and would never go any farther. But it created a little excitement in Sadie's life and made her feel good. She was entitled.

Doris was coming down the hall, so Howard had to end the conversation quickly.

"See you tonight then, Sadie. I have a surprise for you. But you'll have to wait until tonight. Got to get to work. See you soon!" Howard smiled slyly at Sadie and winked as he turned away to give his attention to Doris.

Sadie's interest was definitely piqued. She couldn't wait to tell Laura about the suggestion of a surprise.

"Well, Sadie. What do you think it is? Do you suppose he bought you a present?"

"A present for me? Surely not. It's probably something new on the menu that he wants me to try. Or maybe some new wine that he found that he wants to share." Sadie hadn't even considered that the surprise would be something exclusively for her. No one bought Sadie gifts. Even when Frank was courting her, most of the gifts were something useful and practical. Even the flowers that Frank gave her were potted plants. Frank expected to see the plants permanently in the ground and thriving the next time he visited. Any frivolous gifts such as jewelry never materialized. They were always future promises in return for some obedience from Sadie. The gifts were always a carrot dangling for the good girls who deserved it. And Sadie was never quite good enough.

"Well, Sadie, you could be surprised. If he made a point of telling you about a surprise, my guess would be that it is something special, just for you. I'm going to be on pins and needles until you get home tonight!" Laura laughed as Sadie wrinkled up her face at her in response.

"Don't lose any sleep over your curiosity. I'm sure that whatever the surprise might be, the news can wait until morning." Just having the conversation with Laura caused Sadie's heart to skip a beat. The surprise was probably nothing special for her. But it sure would be nice if it was.

Sadie was right on time for dinner. Howard met her at the corner and took the liberty of draping his arm around her shoulder as they walked into the restaurant together. The public display of affection made Sadie feel self-conscious. But she liked the dangerous way it made her feel. She said nothing to Howard.

As soon as the wine was poured and the meal was ordered, Howard pulled a small velvet box out of his shirt pocket and held it out to Sadie.

"For you. To match your beautiful red hair."

Sadie blushed as she took the box from Howard. Inside was a small pair of ruby earrings. The tiny rubies danced at the end of tiny gold chains, with another ruby holding the chains together at the top.

"Oh, Howard. These are absolutely beautiful! But I can't take them. These are way too expensive. And I have nothing to wear them with. Howard, I really can't!" Sadie had never owned a pair of earrings. Frank would have never allowed her to spend the money on such frivolous things. And Frank had never allowed Sadie to draw attention to herself in that way.

"Sadie, these are a gift to you because I like you and enjoy your company. You cannot refuse a gift. That would just be so rude. And you do have something to wear them with. They match your beautiful red hair perfectly. So you can wear them every day." Howard took the box from Sadie's trembling hands and gently removed the earrings. He then quietly walked behind Sadie's chair and pinched the clasps shut on Sadie's earlobes. Sadie visibly trembled as Howard's hands brushed her neck as he moved her hair away from her ears. Howard then briefly caressed Sadie's hair as he arranged it to show off the rubies.

Howard sat back down in his chair, picked up Sadie's hand, and gently kissed the back of it.

"There. Beautiful earrings for a beautiful lady." Howard's eyes were dancing with the closeness of the last few minutes.

Sadie's eyes were glistening when she finally looked up at Howard.

"I don't know what to say, Howard. Except thank you. Thank you from the bottom of my heart."

"Seeing the happiness that I have just brought you, Sadie, is all the thanks I need. You are very welcome, pretty lady."

Sadie lost track of time this evening. She was enjoying the warm and tingling sensations of Howard's company so much that it was after ten before she suggested it was time to leave.

Howard walked Sadie to the corner before saying goodbye. She had let his arm drape over her shoulders again without pulling away. On impulse Howard pulled her body to him with his arms and kissed her quickly on the mouth. Sadie hesitated for just a split second. The warm wonderful feelings of the evening were strong and good. Sadie was not ready to let them go and gave into the temptation. Howard took Sadie's cue and allowed the quick kiss to turn into slow passion.

Sadie looked up into Howard's eyes and smiled slightly. She put her mouth on his and instinct took over. Responding to the warm electricity flowing through her, Sadie moved her body into Howard's, barely touching his. Howard reached around Sadie's waist and pulled her roughly to him. The force of his pull broke the spell, and Sadie quickly pushed herself out of his arms and held her head down in shame.

"Howard, I am so sorry. I should not have done that. Please forgive me." Sadie knew that Howard's response to her was all her fault. She had been conditioned for years to believe that the woman was responsible for everything that happened between a woman and a man. And good women did not lead a man on. They accepted small tokens of affection before marriage, but never let their passion show. And most definitely never took the lead in being as forward as Sadie had been. Sadie was absolutely ashamed of herself and her behavior.

"Sadie, please don't apologize. It was wonderful. You are wonderful." Howard reached out to push Sadie's beautiful red hair behind her right ear. Sadie quickly pulled back.

"Howard, please. No, I can't do this." Sade cast a worried look in Howard's direction, smiled faintly as the tears welled up in her eyes, and swiftly turned away. Howard's face was full of disappointment as he watched her quickly walk out of sight.

By morning, Sadie's guilt had subsided somewhat. She still felt she had really led Howard on last night, and that was bad. But she also didn't think she should not enjoy her gift from Howard. Sadie had not owned a pair of earrings for such a long time. Even with her unruly red hair captured in a bun, Sadie liked the sparkle from her ears as she took that final look in the mirror.

The new earrings were not lost to Laura's watchful eye. Laura turned Sadie's face to the side for a better look as Sadie walked into the kitchen.

"Wow! That must have been some dinner last night. Those earrings are absolutely exquisite!" Laura was happy for Sadie. She really wanted Sadie to be happy. Laura wished happiness for Sadie as much as she wished happiness for herself.

"Why, thank you, Laura. Howard gave them to me. A token of friendship." Sadie blushed slightly as she looked up at Laura.

"Sadie, you don't have to be ashamed of having dinner with a male friend. Or of the gifts he gives you. It's perfectly legal, you know. Who knows, keep this up and maybe you and Howard will get married and give me more grandchildren. I'd like that." Sadie's face paled with a stricken, frightened look, and she rushed out the door to work before Laura could question her any more.

Sadie was halfway through her morning chores when the doorbell rang at the front door of the boarding house. It was unusual for anyone to ring the front door unless an afternoon gathering had been planned. During the day most visitors were service people who came to the back door. And the college boys never rang the doorbell. Frowning slightly to herself, Sadie put her dust cloth in her apron pocket, felt her hair for strays, and went to answer the doorbell.

The woman who tripped Sadie the other day, who Sadie learned was named Mrs. Lear, was standing impatiently on the front porch and frowned at Sadie when she looked up at her.

"Well, are you going to let me in or not? I'm here to see Ms. Steinway."

"Oh, yes. Please come into the sitting room. I'll get Ms. Steinway. Is she expecting you?" Sadie started to walk in front of Mrs. Lear to lead the way to the sitting room.

"Does it matter if she was expecting me or not? I'm here, aren't I? Get out of my way. I know how to get to the sitting room. Just go get Ms. Steinway." Mrs. Lear walked quickly around Sadie and into the sitting room.

Sadie dutifully left the front entryway and went to find Doris. She found her in the office, staring out the window. Sadie knocked lightly on the door jamb to get her attention.

"Ms. Steinway."

"What?" Doris's tone was sharp and loud.

"There is someone here to see you. She wouldn't give me her name. She just pushed past me. She said she would be in the sitting room."

"Oh, all right. I'll take care of it. Bring tea and scones to the sitting room immediately."

"Yes, ma'am." Sadie lifted her eyes from the floor and rushed to the kitchen to do as she was told. Sadie quickly put the tray together and was coming down the hallway as Doris rushed by.

Doris was visibly frustrated with this unexpected visit as she rushed into the sitting rom, straightening her blouse and her skirt as she gave her greeting.

"Welcome, Mrs. Lear. This is certainly a pleasant surprise. Is there something I can do for you today?" Doris waved Sadie to the coffee table as she set down the tea and cookies. As soon as the women were served, Doris again waved Sadie out of earshot so the women could continue their conversation in private.

Sadie stepped out of the sitting room, put her tray down on the lamp stand in the hallway, and turned to shut the French doors that opened into the sitting room. As the doors were closing, Sadie heard the woman called Mrs. Lear begin to speak. So, she let the doors glide to within a few inches of closing and stood at the side to listen.

"Spare the pleasantries, Doris. I'm here to find out what you know about Sadie. You have had plenty of time to snoop, so tell me. Who is she, and what is she doing in our town?"

"Well, I haven't found out much more than we already know. I've been trying to be friendly, but Sadie hasn't said one word to me in conversation since the last Society meeting. She has been completely all business. She's very guarded and very silent with me. I know she talked to Mrs. Goshen, but Mrs. Goshen wouldn't repeat a grocery list, let alone tell tales out of school."

Sadie was incensed. How dare they pry into her business! As long as she was doing a good job, that is all they should care about. Sadie was breathing heavily, and her heart was pounding fast. She had a lot to lose if they ever figured out who she was and why she was in Galesburg. Her safety and the safety of her son were at stake.

Sadie leaned against the wall and silently slid closer to the partially open doors of the sitting room. She had to hear the rest of the conversation.

"Is she really a widow? I can't believe that a woman as pretty as Sadie would stay single very long even if she was once widowed. We have to know. This woman has a secret, and I have got to know what it is."

Just then, Sadie heard footsteps coming toward the hallway. She hastily picked up her empty tray and composed herself when Mrs. Goshen appeared at the end of the hall.

"Sadie, girl. Can you come help me? I am fixing lasagna for dinner tonight, and I need help assembling the pans. Your help would make these preparations go so much quicker."

"Okay, Mrs. Goshen. I'd be glad to help you." Sadie patted Mrs. Goshen's shoulder as she passed her and went into the kitchen. She put her tray down and joined Mrs. Goshen at the kitchen counter.

"Can I ask you something, Mrs. Goshen?" Sadie wasn't sure if Mrs. Goshen would tell her anything about Doris. But she was going to ask anyway.

"You can ask me anything, Sadie. But that doesn't mean I will answer it. But go ahead and try. What's your question?"

"So, tell me about Ms. Steinway. She seems so lonely and bitter. Has she always been this way?"

"So, you have noticed, have you? It's not like she tried to hide it. Doris petty much wears her heart on her sleeve. What's left of it, anyway."

"What do you mean, what's left of it? What happened to her?" Sadie was now very, very interested.

"Doris was in love once. She almost married. She was already being called a spinster by the time she found her man. But she did find a good man and she was happy. Smiling all the time, believe it or not." Mrs. Goshen chuckled. Sadie had to join in as she tried to imagine Doris just smiling because she wanted to.

"So, what happened? Did he die?"

"Oh, no. Nothing so noble. They were engaged to be married, and the wedding was only a few months away. Doris's beloved was a young farmer who was very young and very naïve. He lived a way's out in the country, so when he would come to town to visit Doris, he always stayed a few days. He loved the glitz and glamour of the theater and parties and was more attracted than most to the seedy bars on the edge of town."

"Oh, let me guess. He quickly became an alcoholic and he cheated on Doris. So Doris broke off the engagement?"

"Well, not quite. It all happened in one weekend. A group of young socialites came into town one weekend on a country tour. One of the girls was a beautiful, vivacious redhead. She flirted with Doris's man all weekend. Right in front of Doris! Doris got her feelings hurt and went home, but her man stayed at the bar. I suppose she thought her man would get it out of his system and then come groveling back to her door."

"Did he?"

"No, he did not. He disappeared. No one ever saw him again after that weekend. Everyone just assumed that he went back to Chicago with the redhead. And Doris grew into who she is now. As far as I know, Doris never dated again."

"How sad for Doris. I feel sorry for her." Sadie really did feel sympathy for Doris She could identify with the humiliation and loneliness. She decided to make an effort to be a little more kind to Doris.

Sadie's relationship with Howard was growing significantly. Even though Sadie had convinced herself that they were just friends and nothing more, other people were beginning to notice. Mrs. Goshen seemed particularly annoyed and concerned that Howard's name came up so often in the conversation.

"Sadie girl, I don't know what is going on between you and Howard, but you are playing with fire. You are only the housekeeper here. You need to learn to keep your place. If Doris heard you talking about Howard this way, or knew you and Howard were spending time together outside this building, she would fire you immediately. You know how she is with him when he is here. She would consider you a threat to her territory. She's the only one allowed to lay claim to anybody around here."

"Oh, pshaw, Mrs. Goshen. Howard and I are just friends. Nothing more." Sadie grinned over her shoulder as she pulled plates out of the cupboard for the evening meal.

"Just what is it between you two? I see his little green eyes light up like Christmas trees as soon as you walk in the room."

"Nothing. We're just friends. Really!"

"Does Howard know you are just friends? If you ask me, you are awfully close friends for only seeing each other a couple hours a week in a business setting. I've been seeing Howard once a week for years now. But his eyes don't light up like that when he sees me."

"Mrs. Goshen, just what are you accusing me of?" Sadie was really getting irritated. She and Howard were just friends, and she was surprised that Mrs. Goshen could be so accusatory. And Sadie was also surprised about Mrs. Goshen's comment that people were beginning to talk. Sadie thought her life was secret, and she couldn't, or wouldn't, take the chance of getting fired. She needed this job.

"Sadie, girl. I'm not accusing you of anything. I'm just trying to point out to you what the others in this town may be thinking. And how they may interpret your familiarity with Howard. I'm just trying to help. There is more to Howard than you know, and you could be setting yourself up for heartache." Mrs. Goshen patted Sadie on the arm as she passed through the kitchen, signaling the end of the conversation.

During dinner that evening, Sadie was recounting the events of the day to Laura and Gus. Sadie mentioned the conversation she had had with Mrs. Goshen and asked Laura if she agreed that it was improper to go to dinner with Howard.

"I don't know, Sadie. You are free to choose who you want to spend your time with. And I don't believe I know anyone by the name of Howard. So I can't offer any advice in that arena."

"I believe his last name is Hager. I think I heard Mrs. Goshen call him by his last name once. Howard gave me these beautiful earrings last week." Sadie reached up to touch the earrings as she smiled to herself, distracted by her memories.

"Oh my, Sadie. Howard Hager? I do know a Howard Hager. I've known him for years. Oh my. Oh my. Are you really dating Howard Hager?"

"I'm not dating Howard. We are just friends. we go out to dinner once a week. There is nothing wrong with two unattached people sharing dinner and conversation." Sadie wasn't sure where the conversation was headed, but she knew she didn't like the tone in Laura's voice.

"Did Howard tell you he was unattached?"

"Well, not in those specific words. But he told me he lives alone. He never mentions a wife or children. The only family he talks about is his father. And he doesn't wear a wedding ring. And Doris Steinway slobbers all over him like he's a trophy for sale. But why are you asking? He is single, right?" Sadie already knew the answer. But she needed confirmation from Laura. She held her breath hoping against hope that Laura had good news to tell.

"Sadie, the Howard Hager that I know is very married. He lives with his wife and his mother-in-law. His father is the president of the bank downtown. Sadie, you've been lied to. As far as I know, he is the only Howard Hager in this small town. I believe he is taking advantage of the fact that you are new in town and don't know anybody yet."

"Oh, Laura, please tell me that isn't true!" Sadie's heart felt like it would pound through her chest. She could feel an anger rising up that she hadn't felt for a long time.

"It's all a lie! He has lied to me from the beginning! He was using me and pretending to be someone he isn't. How dare he treat me like that! I feel like a piece of dirt that Howard has been crunching under his feet. And everyone in town probably knows it." Sadie's hands were clenched into fists, her face was flushed deep red, and she was hissing spit between her teeth. She felt like she was going to explode.

"Sadie, you need to calm down. I'm very sorry for you. And very angry at Howard. But you need to calm down and think this through." Laura was holding both of Sadie's shoulders, and her worried face was very close to Sadie's.

Sadie looked in Laura's eyes and suddenly lost all composure. She leaned into Laura and let her arms comfort her. She laid her head on Laura's shoulder and sobbed. She cried for all the lies she had believed. Not just the lies from Howard, but lies from Frank and probably Doris too. The lies from anyone who Sadie felt had deliberately hurt her.

Sadie soon cried out all the hurt and moved away from Laura. She sat down at the table and stared at her dinner plate. She should have known. Who was she to think that she could have a normal life and enjoy the companionship of a man other than Frank? She was getting exactly what she deserved. When you live a lie, you attract others who are also living lies.

"Well, so that's that. It was fun for a while. I guess I just expected way too much from my new life here. I should just be content to be safe and have a good job."

"What do you mean by the word 'safe', Sadie? You know you and Gus are safe here with me."

"Oh, Laura. I meant nothing by it. It was just a figure of speech." Sadie hoped Laura would believe her and drop the subject. She was in no mood to defend the rest of her own life after hearing about Howard.

"So, what are you going to do about Howard?"

"Stop going to dinner with him, for starters."

"So, you will be home with Gus and me this Thursday? I can fix a special meal. And then the three of us can make homemade ice cream. Gus would like that too, I am sure."

"Yes, Laura! That would be great! I've never made homemade ice cream before. Is it hard?"

Sadie wasn't sure exactly how she was going to stop seeing Howard. She really wanted to be angry with him, but she had also lied. She had pretended to be a widow, and Howard did not know that Sadie had a husband back in New York City. A very violent, vengeful husband. Sadie didn't want to tell Howard at the boarding house that she didn't want to see him anymore. She wanted a little privacy so she could let herself off the hook easily. And she wasn't sure how she would react the next time she saw her married friend called Howard.

"Well, Laura and Gus, can we wait until Friday evening for the homemade ice cream? I think I really want to break it off with Howard at dinner on Thursday. The boarding house is just not a good place to be telling secrets. God forbid if Doris or Mrs. Goshen should overhear us!" Sade shuddered at the thought.

"Well, Okay. We can wait one more day. Can't we, Gus? Then we can teach your momma how to make homemade ice cream herself. How does that sound?"

The days passed slowly as Sadie agonized over what to say to Howard. She knew she couldn't see him anymore. Now that she knew he was married. She was absolutely convinced that things had already gotten out of hand. She thought of the very personal present Howard had given her. And that very, very personal kiss that they had shared. Even though Sadie had only been physically close to one man in her entire life, her instincts recognized the emotion of that kiss. And it wasn't just Sadie feeling it. Sadie knew Howard had felt it, and responded to his emotions also. Sadie felt like a traitor to all of womankind. Sadie wanted to make her home here in Galesburg. And this was just not the way to do it.

Sadie's internal musings took her back to memories of Frank. She hadn't really thought about Frank in many days. He had almost left her mind. But now he was back showing himself to her off and on during the quiet times. Sadie shuddered to think what Frank would do to her, and to Howard, if he ever found out about their short-lived illicit liaison.

Sadie avoided Howard during his visit to the Boarding house on Thursday as long as she could. It wasn't very difficult, as Doris was in an extremely good mood. She showered Howard with more attention than usual. All Howard was able to get from Sadie was a quick confirmation that Sadie would be at the restaurant at eight that evening.

When Howard took Sadie's elbow to lead her into the restaurant, she pulled her arm away.

"No, Howard. Don't! I don't want anyone getting the wrong impression." Sadie knew she should be furious with him for playing this game with her. But she was already beginning to mourn the loss of the one bright thing in her life right now.

"Howard, we can't see each other outside of work anymore." Sadie began her exit.

"It isn't good for me to be seen with you. Or you to be seen with me."

"What do you mean, Sadie? I care about you! I can't imagine not having these evenings to look forward to. I really care for you and cherish my time with you."

"Howard, stop! It's no good. I'm not going to let this relationship, or whatever it is, to continue. You are not exactly good for my reputation, you know. I'm trying to establish myself in this town, and I have to be completely above reproach for that to happen." Sadie was angry at Howard. And she was angry at herself for letting the disappointment on his facts tug at her heart.

"I'm not good for your reputation? Your reputation? You breeze into town, obviously with no money and no family. You are working as a housekeeper. You won't even let me come to your house, so you must be hiding something, too. I'm not good for you? Honey, considering the prominence of my family in this town, you should be licking my boots in gratitude that I even noticed you!"

Sadie reeled back in shock at how hurtful his comment was. She was now past being angry. She was absolutely livid.

"Well, for a married man, you put on quite a show. Too bad that's exactly what it is. And you had better rethink your opinion of your family's prominence and great credentials. How do you think I figured out who you were? Especially since I'm new to this town and so obviously low in the social standings? Someone still had to tell me about you. Wonder how that happened."

"Oh, Sadie. I'm so sorry. I didn't mean that. Please forgive me!" Howard reached across the table to take Sadie's hand, only to have her pull her hand away and stand up to leave.

Sadie leaned down and hissed her final words into Howard's ear as she walked away from the table.

"Looks to me like there are a lot of people in this town who really have no right to walk around with their heads held higher than the rest of the world around them."

Sadie huffed and puffed and spit out her anger at the sidewalk as she walked hurriedly home. The audacity of that man! How dare he think she would be so stupid as to continue to buy those lies! And to intimate that she be lowly and should grovel. How dare he!

Then again, maybe she had been groveling a bit. She had been so grateful for Howard's attention in the beginning. She had even begun to equate those Thursday evenings as a sign of acceptance. If Howard accepted her, then soon the rest of the town would follow. Maybe Howard had picked up on her aloneness and used that to get to her. Howard wasn't entirely to blame. She had let him play his game and danced with him as soon as he had snapped his fingers.

But no more. Sadie felt strong, stronger than she had ever felt. She had never stood up to Frank like she had just stood up to Howard. Based on what Frank would do to her for just looking at him wrong, Sadie was pretty certain Frank would have pretty much killed her.

Yes, Sadie had come a long way. She would miss her times with Howard. But she would also remember this night as a turning point in her life. A grand turning point. She was one step closer to her dream of absolute freedom, and a whole lot stronger.

Laura was waiting on the front porch when Sadie walked up the sidewalk.

"I thought you would be home early. I was a little worried about you. How did it go?" Laura motioned for Sadie to sit beside her on the porch swing.

"It went well, Laura. It went well. As far as I was concerned anyway." Sadie patted Laura's hand as she gazed on the dew starting to form on the rose trellis at the bottom of the porch.

"I'm good, Laura. I'm really good."

Laura placed her hand over Sadie's and gave it a loving squeeze. The two friends sat rocking in silence for quite some time, each deep in their own reflective thoughts.

CHAPTER EIGHT

INNOCENT RESPONSES

Sadie was more focused on her work than normal on Monday. She was courteous to Mrs. Goshen and Doris but kept her head down and focused on finding every single little dust bunny that peeked its head out. Sadie finished her work a few minutes early, and Doris found it surprisingly easy to offer to let her go a few minutes early.

"Sadie, you did a really, really good job today. I'm pleased that you are finally beginning to take pride in your work." Doris walked Sadie to the door and slipped a small linen envelope in Sadie's hand as she stepped onto the back porch.

Sadie opened her envelope and hastily read the invitation as soon as she was out of sight of the boarding house. She was so excited that she jogged the rest of the way home.

"Laura! Laura! Guess what? I'm invited to a banquet at the college! Can you believe it?" Sadie burst through the kitchen door, her face flushed and eyes shining with excitement.

Sadie held her hands clasped to her chest while she waited for Laura to read the invitation.

"Well, a banquet in honor of the author Carl Sandburg. And at Knox college no less! Well, well, I see the Galesburg

Ladies Aid Society is hosting the event. Do you really know who these people are?"

"If you don't know them Sadie, let me tell you a little bit about them. When I went to the first function I came to realize that I, a nobody, had nabbed one of the most sought-after bachelors in town. The ladies literally backed me into a corner of the room and bombarded me with questions. I was just about to faint from claustrophobia when Saul came and rescued me."

"Did they keep picking on you the rest of the evening? Did you have to hide behind Saul?"

"Well, I was very young and had no experience dealing with women like these. So I hid in a stall in the rest room for the next two hours."

"Oh, my! Did Saul actually have to come into the ladies' room to get you?" Sadie's eyes were wide with curiosity. But yet she had to giggle at the visual. The stories Laura told her about what these women did to her were so unbelievably cruel.

"No, I thought if they couldn't find me, they couldn't hurt me. But they would come into the restroom in groups and just eviscerate me while they freshened their makeup and painted the smiles on. I finally snuck out, found Saul, and told him I had a headache. That was our cue for him to know that it was time to take me home."

"You actually resorted to feigning a headache? I've heard that women do that to get out of an uncomfortable situation. But I've never known anyone who actually did that."

"Oh, I didn't feign a headache. I truly had a migraine. I was in bed for two days after that event."

"I'm sorry, Laura. I didn't mean to insult you. So did you ever see them again? And are they all so mean and cruel?"

"I never went to another Society event. But I live here and know a lot of other people. I still hear stories regularly about who, or what, they are currently focusing on. And no, they are not all evil women. There are nice, good women like the woman who helped you when you were tripped. But the majority are just unhappy, mean-spirited women."

"Sadie, these are not nice people. Is Mrs. Lear still in charge?"

"As far as I know she is the president of the Society. And they don't seem to be all bad, Grace seemed to be a nice woman."

"Yes, Grace is very nice. But did you know that Mrs. Lear is her mother?"

"She is? That's a little scary. But I don't understand why you think I shouldn't go. They gave me an invitation with my name on it. And Doris talks to me every day now. And never criticizes my work. How can this be bad?"

"Sadie, I could be wrong. But I doubt it. It hasn't been that long since you had your first encounter with Mrs. Lear. Do you really want to go through that again?"

"But, Laura, It's a public gathering. There will be lots of other people there that are not part of the society. And I would really like to meet some other women in this town. I want to settle here and be comfortable in this town." Sadie was convinced that she had gotten the invitation because they liked her and wanted her there. And she really wanted to see Carl Sandburg.

"Sadie, you don't have to ask my permission. I'm sorry if I sound so negative. But I never had a good encounter with these women. They are deceitful, judgmental and self-righteous. And if you don't have just the right pedigree, they swarm around you like buzzards waiting for the chance to pluck your eyes out." Laura and Sadie both laughed out loud at the visions of Mrs. Lear with wings and feathers.

"Well, Laura. They know I don't have the pedigree. I'm the housekeeper for goodness sake. I think they just extended me an invitation out of courtesy. And out of courtesy, I should attend. Even if just for a little while." Sadie quelled the twinge in her stomach by thinking about how much fun it would be to go and watch. She had never been to a social function. The closest she had ever got was attending Frank's brother's wedding. And Frank got so drunk that they had to leave before the reception. She didn't even get to see the cake. Her own wedding was fifteen minutes in front of an evil judge. And then Frank whisked her off to the bedroom. None of that counted as a true civilized social gathering.

"Well, okay then. I will be more than happy to watch Gus for you. But what are you going to wear?" Laura laughed out loud as Sadie suddenly became serious and concerned.

"Well, I'll wear my best dress. It's all I have, and it will have to do."

"Sadie, I've seen you wear a total of two dresses since you have been here. And, based on your small satchel in the closet, I'm pretty sure those two dresses are all you have.

They absolutely will not do. I've attended these types of functions. Half of the women who come only show up to see who is wearing the latest styles. And whose dress cost the most. There will not be a woman there who is wearing a dress that cost less than one hundred dollars. If you want to stick out like a sore thumb, show up in one of your dresses. The banquet help will be dressed better than you will be. They probably wouldn't even let you in the front door."

"Oh, I hadn't thought of that. Then I guess I can't go. I have saved a little money, but I couldn't spend it on one dress for me. And the money I have isn't even close to one hundred dollars." Sadie looked so forlorn. She had thought, just for a moment, that she was going to be able to see the world that had always been out of her reach. The world that was still out of her reach.

"Well, I have a surprise for you, Sadie." Laura patted Sadie's hand and smiled knowingly.

"I used to do mending for a family that has since moved out of town. The man was a tenured professor with Saul, and they attended every social function that the college hosted. They had a daughter, Elizabeth, who died during childbirth. Elizabeth was only nineteen years old. I still have a few of Elizabeth's gowns. The family just couldn't bear reminders of her and left the gowns when they moved, asking me to find someone who would appreciate them. Elizabeth was a little larger than you, but I think we can do some altering. And it's only been a couple of years, so I think we can make them over and bring them up to date with the styles. What do you think? Want to give it a try!"

"Laura, you are wonderful! Yes, I want to give it a try! You are so good to me. I'm so thankful that I ended up on your doorstep!" Sadie had genuine tears of happiness in her eyes as she ran across the room to hug Laura.

"You are like a second mother to me, Laura!! And I do love you for that!"

"Well, just don't take Gus away from me. I really like the grandmother role. He is a real sweetheart. You two have brought me a lot of joy since you have been here. And, Sadie, you are just as deserving as any of those women that will be at the banquet. Maybe more so. And don't forget that!" Laura accepted Sadie's hug and hugged her back.

"We'll get the sewing machine out this weekend and see what we can whip up."

Sadie was thrilled and excited. Her new life was turning out better than she expected. Yes, there had been a few bumps in the road, but her future was looking brighter and better than what she could have dreamed.

Sadie bounced down the sidewalk to the boarding house the next day. She breezed through her tasks and chatted with Mrs. Goshen every time she passed through the kitchen.

"Slow it down, Sadie girl! What on Earth has got you going? I don't think I've ever seen you this bouncy. So out with it. What's going on in your life that's got you walking on air?" Mrs. Goshen shook her head with a smile as Sadie dipped her fingers in the apricot jam as she walked by.

Sadie laughed mischievously.

"There are no deep, dark secrets, Mrs. Goshen. Life is just good. That's all." Sadie smiled again as she helped Mrs. Goshen set up the serving tray.

"You are usually very quiet and spend most of the day hiding when the society is here. Did you forget that the ladies are probably on their way now?"

"Well, it's your turn to serve today so I don't have to interact with them. I get to hide in the kitchen. And I'm thinking they can't be all bad. Maybe they just have a lot of bad days."

"Sadie, girl, what have you been drinking? You had better take those rose-colored glasses off and watch your behind before they sneak up on you again. Trust me, if they haven't focused on some innocent lately, it's only because they haven't collectively agreed on which innocent to target in on." Mrs. Goshen shook her head and clucked at Sadie.

"Trust me. Watch your back. I've known these ladies a long, long time. And they haven't changed a bit."

Sadie patted Mrs. Goshen on the shoulder and smiled as she gathered up the dirty dishes. Mrs. Goshen could be right in general. But the ladies could change. They did give her an invitation. Maybe the Society was past the pettiness with Sadie and had decided she wasn't a threat. But deep down, Sadie was a little bit relieved that she was able to stay in the kitchen while the Society was there.

The afternoon passed without incident, and Sadie took that as a sign of better things to come.

Saturday morning, Sadie and Laura hurried through breakfast. As soon as the dishes were put away, Laura led Sadie to the closet in her spare bedroom. They rummaged through the gowns like schoolgirls, giggling and laughing, as Sadie held each gown next to her body for Laura to critique.

Laura had three gowns hanging in the closet. Sadie caressed each gown and couldn't decide which one she liked the best.

"I have one more, Sadie. This might just be the gown for you." Laura reached into the back of the closet shelf and pulled out a cloth bag. In the cloth bag was a moss-green dress that was twisted up like a skein of yarn. Laura unrolled the dress and shook it out to its full length.

"It's a Fortuny, Sadie. Made in Italy. I think you are one of the few women who have the figure to wear this." Laura beamed as Sadie held it up to her body and gazed into the full-length mirror. Sadie had never touched a dress so soft. The thin silk satin pleats felt like cool water on Sadie's arms and face.

"Oh, Laura! I don't know if I have the figure to wear this or not. But I really want to wear this dress! It just feels so wonderful. Almost magical!" Sadie couldn't help but notice that the green of the gown drew out the emerald in her eyes and enhanced the sparkles that were dancing there.

"This is the one, Laura. I really want to wear this one. Even if only for a few minutes. I already feel beautiful, and I haven't even tried it on yet!" Sadie's smile was radiant.

"Sadie, I think you are right. This is the perfect choice for you."

Sade modeled the alterations as Laura made them. It took almost all weekend to complete. The dress was made of fine silk pleats. The pleats were so fine that they were difficult to detect and impossible to work with on the sewing machine. Laura made all the alterations by hand and then restrung the striated Venetian glass beads to the shoulders and sides when she was finished. By early Sunday evening, they were finished. Sadie tried the dress on one more time. It was perfect. Sadie felt like a Greek goddess and did a little dance in front of the mirror.

"Laura, if I never get the opportunity to wear a gown like this ever again in my life, it will be okay. I shall remember this dress, and this banquet forever. Thank you so much!" Sadie was crying as she hugged Laura tight.

"Momma, you are so pretty!" Gus was standing a few feet away from Sadie and gingerly reached out to lightly touch the gown. The liquid silk satin gown flowed down Sadie's body, molding to her curves like the draped dresses of the ancient Greeks. The gold stenciled silk belt picked up the color of the Venetian beads. Gus had never seen or touched anything so beautiful.

"Thank you, Gus. You are my little man! I wish I could take you as my escort. I would be proud to walk on your arm. And I bet you would be so handsome in a little suit and vest." Sadie bent over to hug Gus and turned her face away from him so he couldn't see the tears. No one at the banquet could know about her wonderful little man. She felt really guilty for not stepping up and being publicly proud to be his mother. She told herself it was only temporary and necessary for both of them. Soon they would have a normal family. She didn't know when or how just yet, but someday they would walk the streets of Galesburg and hold their heads high.

"You'll need some shoes, Sadie. Will these do?" Sadie turned around to see Laura holding up a pair of white satin slippers.

"As my gift to you, I will take them to the shoe shop this week and have them died to match your dress. With these shoes and your ruby earrings, your outfit will be complete."

The next week, Sadie worked furiously, trying to make the days go by faster. Even with the extra chores from Doris, Sadie couldn't make the days go by fast enough. Doris found Sadie to be an eager participant in helping her get ready for the banquet. She carried messages back and forth from the caterers, helped Mrs. Goshen put the final touches on Doris's gown, and went to the laundry three times for Doris. All this was done with an eagerness and zest.

Howard came by on Thursday as usual, and he huddled in a corner of the kitchen with Mrs. Goshen and Doris. When Sadie walked by the talking ceased.

It was finally Friday afternoon, and Sadie reached home after work. She burst into the kitchen, face flushed from the July heat and the excitement of the evening to come. Her perfectly died satin slippers were sitting on the kitchen table, tied together with a big red ribbon.

"Laura and I got your shoes for you today, Momma. Do you like them?" Sadie gave Gus a big hug and smiled as she ran her fingers over the satin shoes and ribbon.

The banquet didn't start until eight, so Sadie helped with dinner and chatted with Gus and Laura while they ate. She didn't want to ruin her dinner at the banquet, but she also couldn't eat if she wanted to. She was too excited and nervous to eat.

After dinner, Sadie took a leisurely bath and then sat on the porch in her bathrobe with a cup of tea, letting the gentle evening breeze dry her long red curls. When her hair was dry, she got ready for the banquet slowly, savoring every moment. Sadie brushed her hair, added a little rouge to her cheeks and lips, and put on her ruby earrings before she slid into her gown. Once the outfit was complete, she twirled for Laura and Gus. Laura draped a soft, white crocheted shawl over Sadie's shoulders.

"Now you are complete. And I have called you a cab so you don't have to walk and soil your dress. You just have a good time and please be careful. You can tell Gus and me all about it over a late breakfast tomorrow." Laura hugged Sadie lightly. She and Gus stood on the porch as Sadie got into the cab and waved until the cab turned the corner and drove out of sight.

The ride to the Knox College campus took only a few minutes. Sadie stood in front of the alumni hall for a minute trying to gather her bearings. She had spent very little time on the campus, and the buildings and all they represented were overwhelming to her. She couldn't even imagine what it must be like to go to college.

Sadie studied the alumni hall looking for welcome signs. The brick building was a towering sight. Green vines climbed up the brick walls, and the cement steps were overshadowed by large untrimmed bushes. In the shadows of the sunset, the building was more menacing than inviting.

Sadie took one more deep breath and walked up the steps. Once inside, she followed the conversational noise to the banquet room. Before entering the room, Sadie stood to the side of the doorway and peeked in. She was looking for familiar faces.

It didn't take long to spot Doris, as Sadie already knew what her gown looked like. Doris had chosen a deco-beaded, tulle evening gown. The cut of the gown was meant to be sexy, with torso-clinging hips and a slight loose top, hinting at exposure on the deep open sides. The gown did not flatter Doris with her middle-aged, plump figure. The waistband was meant to emphasize the curve of the hips by dipping down from the natural waistline in front and forming a V shape around the navel. The black sequins on the waistband sparkled as they crawled over lumpy, oversized hips. And the V on the waistband was nearly hidden in front by excess belly fat. Sadie looked at the deep open sides of the top, then turned her head away when she recognized the overexposed pink flesh the silver beads were clinging to. Sadie had to chuckle. She did have one thing that was better than Doris, if anyone was counting.

Mrs. Lear was standing between Doris and a man Sadie did not recognize. Sadie assumed the man was Mr. Lear. Mrs. Lear was wearing a Worth evening gown. The gown was made of black tulle and completely covered with sequins. Mrs. Lear was a show-stopper with the plunging neckline, the floral spray design of the colored sequins, body-clinging style, and the back train.

'This must be wheat Laura was talking about.' Sadie thought to herself. "Every woman in this room is sparkling more than the Fourth of July fireworks. And based on their frozen smiles and the sideways looks, they are trying to figure out who sparkles the most. Thank God I am not sparkling, and thank God I don't have to play that game.'

Sadie walked quietly across the corner of the room toward the beverage table. Her throat was parched, and she really needed to sooth her nerves before making her way around the room.

While Sadie was waiting for the bartender to prepare her glass of wine, a slight figure excused himself from a group of gawking men and made his way over to Sadie's side. He gently touched her elbow as he softly introduced himself.

"Hello, Miss. My name is Carl Sandburg. And I would be honored to know the name of the most beautiful woman in the room." Carl Sandburg smiled as Sadie turned her blushing face toward him.

"Oh, my! Mr. Sandburg! I am so pleased to meet you. And thank you for the wonderful compliment. But the honor is all mine." Sadie held out her hand, and Carl took it between both of his.

"That wasn't just a compliment. That was the truth. I don't think I have ever seen a woman as lovely as you. If I would have known you were here in Galesburg, I would have moved back home years ago."

"Mr. Sandburg, my name is Mrs. Lear, and I am the president of the Galesburg Ladies Aid Society. I'm sure you remember the Society from your youth. We, the Society, are sponsoring this event in your honor. Please, let me introduce you to the prominent people of our town." Mrs. Lear interrupted the conversation and took Carl Sandburg's arm and steered him away from Sadie and back to the center of the room.

As she walked past Sadie, she hissed in her ear.

"You, girl, are nothing! You don't belong here, and you are not good enough to be here. I will make sure that before this night is over, you will regret ever stepping foot in this place! Mark my words!"

Sadie watched Mrs. Lear walk away from her, tears stinging her eyelashes. She had evidently done something wrong again. But she didn't know what it was. Well, she could still have a nice evening if she just avoided Mrs. Lear. The evening was already great. She had gotten to meet the famous Carl Sandburg.

Sadie thanked the bartender for her glass of wine and quietly walked to the back of the room. She noticed that the banquet tables had place cards at each dinner plate. Thinking that she could just sit and observe, Sadie started walking around the tables looking for her name.

Sadie wandered through the first two rows of tables, reading the place cards at each plate. Some of the names she recognized, most of them she didn't. She spotted Doris and Mrs. Lear talking to each other in a far corner of the room. Mrs. Lear seemed to be berating Doris. Doris was standing a few feet away from Mrs. Lear. She was nodding in agreement to something but not saying anything. Her head was down, and her arms were clasped in front of her in a defensive manner. Mrs. Lear finally walked away, and Doris headed back toward the tables.

Sadie walked up to Doris and quietly opened up the conversation.

"Doris, I was looking for my place card at the tables and can't seem to find it. Can you help me, please?"

"Sadie, why are you here? You don't belong here. I am just appalled that you thought you could just waltz in and make yourself at home. How dare you! Go home!" Doris turned to walk away.

"But Doris, you handed me the invitation. My name was on it. I don't understand. How could that be a mistake?" Sadie was shocked. She didn't understand why Doris would hand her a personal invitation, be extra nice to her for weeks, and then order her to leave the very party that she had personally invited her to.

"You stupid girl. Sadie, please, just leave now. You don't belong here, and the invitation was only to help you to see your place. You were born to the hired help, and you will stay with the hired help. Places like this are things that you know about, but you will never be able to attend. Or even think you should attend. No matter how good you look and how many airs you put on, you still have no right to mingle with the privileged. You never have, and you never will." Doris had trouble just getting these words out.

"But, Doris, I just don't understand." Tears were beginning to well up, and Sadie didn't know what she had done wrong. And she really, really needed to know. But her conversation with Doris was interrupted by Mrs. Lear and the other women from the Society.

"You little hussy! You think you can just come in here and flaunt yourself to the world? Well, you are wrong. You are white trash and belong on the dung heap with the rest of your kind. You do not deserve to be with good, upstanding people. You don't deserve to even be on this college campus, let alone at this banquet. Go back to the barn where you belong!" Mrs. Lear was smiling menacingly as she spit the words out of her mouth at Sadie.

"Yes, you little tramp. Go give that dress back to whoever you stole it from, and put your rags back on. They suit you." One of the ladies of the Society stepped up and continued the conversation with Sadie, her voice a little louder than Mrs. Lear's.

Sadie looked around at the faces and saw nothing but hatred and contempt. The banquet hall had become quiet, and all eyes were on Sadie and the little group. In total humiliation, Sadie started backing up. As soon as there was enough space between her and the ladies of the society, she turned and started walking quickly toward the door.

"Careful how you walk, dearie. You could trip on those heels. I'm sure your feet had never been in anything but working shoes. And that's where they belong. Big, ugly shoes. Big, ugly dresses. Perfect for an ugly piece of so-called humanity!" The women were yelling insults at Sadie as she walked toward the door. Sadie had tried to maintain her composure and walk swiftly with some semblance of decorum. As the insults came hurling at her, Sadie lost her last bit of composure. In total humiliation, Sadie let go of a huge sob and ran out the door of the banquet hall.

"Hey! You aren't good enough to use the front door. Remember, the hired help uses the back door!"

Sadie ran down the steps of the alumni hall building. She ran blindly, heading for any place where there were no people and no lights. She stopped at the edge of the college commons and leaned on a big oak tree in the shadows. The oak tree was beyond the sidewalks and the bushes lining the sidewalk. With no street lights reaching her hiding place, and the comfort of the trees reaching out to her, Sadie began to sob uncontrollably.

The sobs were slow at first, forcing their way out between deep, wretched gasps for air. As Sadie gave in to her hurt, the sobbing spiraled upward until it reached a hysteric crescendo. As the first wave of sobbing drained Sadie, she became quiet. With her eyes closed and thoughts empty, Sadie stared inwardly at the empty hole in her heart.

Sadie's eyes were still closed, and her thoughts were drifting when she felt a warm hand gently touch her shoulder. Startled, Sadie whirled around to face her accusers once again.

"Easy, Sadie. It's just me. I came to make sure you were okay." Howard had a look of genuine concern on his face, and his own eyes were misty. Sadie didn't know what he had seen or heard.

"Howard! How long have you been standing here? And why are you here? How did you know I was here?" Sadie was shocked to see Howard, but found some comfort in the softness of his face.

"I followed you when you left the banquet hall. I guess I've been here since you stopped here."

"I didn't see you at the banquet. How did you know I was there?"

"Well, I saw you. You could hardly have been missed. I was standing in the back of the room when you walked in. I normally don't stay at these functions. And I was getting ready to excuse myself when you walked in. You looked so beautiful, and it was such a surprise to see you that I decided to stay and watch." Howard was smiling at Sadie now. He reached out to touch her hair as a comforting gesture. But Sadie pulled away.

"So then you saw the whole thing. Guess you, too, are one of the privileged souls that have the right to treat me like dirt. Sorry, but I really don't think there is much to say now. I guess now I understand why you thought I would jump in bed with you at the snap of your fingers."

"Sadie, please. Yes, I saw the whole ugly thing at the banquet hall. I didn't hear it, but I could tell by the look on your face that the ladies had ganged up on you and were doing their best to destroy you. I've seen it and heard it all before. It's one of the Society's oldest and most self-appreciating games. I should know. My wife and mother-in-law are lifetime members of the Society and relish the thought of cutting someone to shreds. They don't need a reason. And they don't need the truth. They even practice their skills on me. Keeps the knives sharp that way." Howard chuckled softly.

"I am so sorry, Sadie. When I saw you come in the door, I knew you were their target. And I am sure they baited you with a gilded invitation to join them. I tried to come to you and warn you. But Doris and Mrs. Lear didn't give me any time. It all happened so fast. I know they hurt you deeply. And I am so sorry. I really want to be here for you. Can I help?"

Sadie smiled weakly and shrugged her shoulders. Having Howard here did help. She didn't feel so alone.

"Howard, I just don't understand. I did nothing wrong. And it hurts. It really, really hurts." The waves of sobbing started again. Howard reached out and engulfed Sadie in his arms.

"Then just cry it away. I'm here as long as you want me here." As Sadie's strength waned from the sobbing, Howard gently pulled her to the ground with him. Together they laid under the oak tree in the silent darkness, Sadie sobbing into Howard's chest.

Sadie's soul began to quiet itself. She could feel the warmth of Howard's body around her and the moist evening dew on the grass. Sadie sat up and wiped her face.

"The grass is wet. I'm going to ruin Laura's dress." Sadie picked at the moist spots on her dress. She didn't know how much of the moisture was tears and how much was dew.

"I can fix that. How's this?" Howard took off his suit jacket and spread it out on the ground beside him. Sadie's body was so small that they both had room to lie together on the jacket. Howard gathered Sadie up in his arms again and gently kissed her forehead.

"There, my little China doll. I'll keep you warm. Just snuggle in and forget the world for a while."

Sadie snuggled into Howard's chest and absorbed his warmth. The shaking of her body was beginning to subside as she allowed Howard's arms to lull her into peacefulness.

No words were spoken between them. Sadie had her eyes closed and her head nestled under Howard's chin. Howard was caressing her back with his hand and making small guttural sounds as if he were soothing a baby.

Sadie shifted her body slightly so she could see Howard's face. She saw only warmth and caring in his soft eyes and was comforted. Howard looked down at Sadie and smiled. Her eyelashes were still wet with tears.

Howard began to kiss the tears away. First her eyelashes, then her cheeks. Sadie closed her eyes and savored his touch. When Howard lightly kissed her on the mouth, Sadie responded by opening her mouth slightly and breathing in his warmth.

Sadie's heartbeat picked up. She could feel Howard's breathing quicken. The feeling was instinctive and mutual as she moved slightly to allow the full palm of Howard's hand to rest on her stomach.

Sadie and Howard both gave in to the loving needs welling up within them. There were no words spoken, only loving caresses and soft moans of fulfillment.

After the passion of the moment had subsided, Sadie and Howard lay in the dark on the soft bed of grass for what seemed like hours. Sadie had never felt so loved in her entire life. She wondered if this was what making love felt like. It was so different than being forced to have sex with Frank. So sweet, so fulfilling, so delightfully giving and draining at the same time.

As Sadie came back to her senses, she knew that this was only a moment in time. And the only moment. Howard would go back to his wife and family. Sadie would go back to Laura, Gus and the boarding house.

"I have to go now, Howard. It's a long walk home, and we've pretty much finished things off here." Sadie stood up, shook out Howard's suit jacket, and brushed off the grass that was clinging to the cloth.

"Sadie, I'm sorry. I never meant for this to happen. I had no intention of taking advantage of you while you were so vulnerable. My only thoughts when I followed you here was only because I knew you were hurting, and I just wanted to help." Howard looked so forlorn and so serious in his confession that Sadie had to smile. She patted his cheek.

"I believe you, Howard. And I do thank you for being here for me. I think I might have completely lost my mind if you hadn't come here for me. And I thank you for that. What happened just happened. I guess we both needed it. Or wanted it. And I thank you for that too. But now the moment has passed. You need to go home to your wife, and I have a long walk ahead of me." Sadie was putting on her satin slippers and frowning at the tiny, protruding heels. It was going to be a long walk in those shoes. But she planned on taking them off as soon as she was in the quiet, dark neighborhoods. It was late enough that most people would be in bed. They wouldn't notice the lonely, barefoot woman on the sidewalk.

"At least let me get you a cab, Sadie. There will be plenty at the alumni hall waiting to drive the drunk's home. I'll go get a cab and bring it here so you won't have to face the Society again tonight."

"That would be wonderful, Howard. I'm so tired. I would be so grateful if you would do that for me." Sadie stood in the shadows, holding her shoes, for what seemed like an eternity before Howard returned with the cab.

Howard gave the cab driver a ten-dollar bill and instructed the drive to take the lady anywhere she wanted to go. As Howard helped Sadie into the cab, he squeezed her arm and kissed her on the cheek.

"Go with the angels, my sweet baby doll. Sleep the sleep of the innocent, as that is who you are. And just for the record, you were stunningly beautiful tonight. You still are stunningly beautiful. Inside and out. The most beautiful woman I have ever had the privilege to meet."

"Thank you, Howard. And you sleep well also. Your kindness meant everything to me tonight. Good night. And good-bye."

CHAPTER NINE

HIDING HER SHAME

Sadie opened her eyes to the smells of breakfast and laughter between Laura and Gus. Sadie stretched and yawned and then rolled over for a few more minutes. She knew Laura would want to know all about the evening before. But she wasn't ready to share just yet. And she wasn't sure what she was going to share. Sadie was still sifting through the events herself. She still didn't know what was good or bad.

There was also going to be a need for censoring for Laura. Sadie had grown to love Laura, and she couldn't hurt her by revealing her transgressions with Howard. Sadie didn't really regret it, but she was afraid Laura would lose some respect for her.

Sadie emerged from her bedroom about thirty minutes later and padded into the kitchen.

"Oh, Sadie." What happened? You look awful! Last night must have been horrible for you. Can you talk about it? It might help some." Laura hugged Sadie tight, pulled out a chair for her, and prepared her coffee as Sadie pulled Gus onto her lap.

"Yeah, it was pretty awful. You were right, Laura. Those women of the society are mean, vicious, and cruel. And they totally sucked me into their trap. I guess I just couldn't imagine a group of women so mean that they would spend days and weeks planning and scheming against someone. I should have listened to you." Sadie shook her head in disbelief. She was still having trouble processing the events of the previous evening in her mind.

"Laura, I still don't know what I did to deserve such meanness. I have never hurt those women. They don't even know who I am. They've only seen me at the boarding house. And I just work there! All I did was try to make an honest living."

"Well, Sadie. Maybe you frighten them. You are young, pretty, and they know nothing about you. Some of those women are just existing in a world their families created for them. And they don't even know why they are here or what they want in life. They live in loveless marriages because that's what they are supposed to do. And just follow the leader because everyone else does. Or because they are afraid of Mrs. Lear. Everyone has secrets, and maybe they want to keep their secrets to themselves for fear of Mrs. Lear doing the same thing to them that she did to you. Who knows? Maybe they are jealous of the freedom they see in you. Kind of like misery loves company."

"I don't know, Laura. All I wanted when I came here was peace and safety. And I have found neither, outside of this house anyway. I think it would be easier if they would just beat on me and be done with it. At least maybe then I could see it coming. Bruises will heal over time. But I'm not sure these emotional wounds will ever heal." Sadie shook her head in disbelief and despair.

"I just don't know what I'm supposed to do. I don't know how to make this work. And I have to go back to the boarding house in two days and face the evil witch again." Sadie was totally devastated by the attack of the women at the banquet. And especially Doris. Doris had been so gracious to Sadie in the last few weeks. Sadie had thought that maybe they were becoming friends. Or at the very least, Doris was learning to allow Sadie to interact with her in peaceful coexistence.

Sadie wanted nothing more to do with Doris and would give anything to just walk away. But Sadie had no place to go. She felt trapped. The same way she had felt trapped with Frank. All she had done was replace one prison with another.

"Laura, I don't know how I can go to work on Monday. I simply can't face Doris. And she's probably going to fire me anyway. Maybe I should just give it up and not even go to work on Monday."

"Sadie, that's what they want you to do. They want you to just skulk away. If you do that, you just give them more power. And they will keep attacking more women because you will be proving their tactics work. I know. I gave in to them years ago. I went to two Society functions when I first married Saul. And yes, I was their target. I let them make me so miserable that I not only stopped going to the functions, I stopped going anywhere I thought the ladies might be. In a way, I let them control my life for many years. It was so unfair to Saul. And unfair to me. All I did was feed their egos and make them stronger. I've always regretted that."

"I say you go to work on Monday and just do your job. And do it well. Make Doris fire you if that's what she wants to do. And make her look you in the eye when she is doing it. You know you and Gus have a home here as long as you want it. And if you do get fired, something else will turn up. You have options, Sadie. You just can't see them yet."

"Your words make sense, Laura. But It's easier said than done. You didn't see the evil in Doris's eyes."

"Maybe not. But I've known Mrs. Lear for a long time. And I have watched her destruction."

"I guess I have lots of thinking to do and some decisions to make. Now that I know I won't lose my home and Gus won't starve, things look a little better." Sadie was pensive. Her fear wasn't quite so overpowering. She decided to put Doris and the Society in the back of her mind for the rest of the weekend. Hopefully an answer would come and a plan would form before Monday morning.

"One good thing did come out of last night. I got to meet Carl Sandburg. He told me I was the most beautiful woman in the room." Sadie laughed as she told Laura how Carl Sandburg was so wonderful. They had started to have a delightful conversation, and then Mrs. Lear whisked him away.

"Yup. Just as I thought. Those women are so jealous of you that they absolutely can't stand it. You should be proud."

"Well, enough of this for a while. It's such a beautiful day. I think we should make a picnic lunch and go to the park. What do you say, Gus?" Sadie got an immediate hug from Gus.

"Yes! Yes! Let's go!" Gus squealed with delight, pulled Sadie out of her chair, and led her down the hall to the bedroom.

"Get dressed, Momma! I'll get my baseball and glove so we can play catch." Sadie whirled around and grabbed Gus by the shoulders. She kneeled down so she could talk to him face to face.

"Gus. Where did you get a baseball and glove? We didn't bring any of your toys with us."

"Laura gave it to me, Momma. We play catch in the backyard almost every day. Was it bad for me to take it? Do I need to give it back?"

"Sadie. I did give him the ball and glove. They belonged to Saul and have been sitting in the closet for years. I just thought someone should get some use out of them." Laura was standing in the hallway behind Sadie. The frown on Laura's face startled Sadie and brought her back to her senses.

"Oh, I should have known that. Gus hasn't been anywhere but here. And, Gus, I do know you wouldn't steal. I'm sorry to you, Gus and to you, Laura. I guess I've been so focused on myself and my own worries that I forgot there was another world right beside me." Sadie hugged Gus and smiled at Laura. She was a little jealous of Laura. Laura was spending more time with Gus than she was and probably even knew him better. Sadie didn't like that. She vowed to herself to make more time with Gus and just love and appreciate him. He was the one who made all of this worthwhile.

The weekend was delightful. The trio spent all Saturday afternoon at the park. Sadie and Laura took turns playing catch with Gus. Gus fell asleep on the blanket for a while, and the two women took advantage of the quiet time to catch up on each other's lives.

Sunday found Sadie and Laura lingering over the morning paper and their coffee. Later in the morning, Laura and Sadie sifted through the rest of the clothing that had been left by Elisabeth's parents. They mixed and matched skirts and blouses. After the alterations were made, Sadie had two more outfits to add to her closet. Gus helped by running back and forth for sewing supplies and keeping the glasses of tea filled. Gus was a great cheering section when it came time for trying on the outfits.

After Gus was tucked into bed Sunday night, Laura and Sadie took their tea to the front porch. The front porch had become the safe haven for the two of them. The place where tears were shed, joy was shared, and difficult decisions talked through.

"Well, Sadie. Have you decided what you are going to do about the boarding house and Doris?"

"Yes, I have. I'm going to go to work because of Gus. And because you believe in me. If Doris fires me, I'll make her look me in the eye when she does it. If I can work for Doris, I can work for anyone. And maybe with the next job, I can be the real Sadie with a wonderful son and a great friend. If she doesn't fire me, then I can just do my job and life goes on. However, I will make sure to watch my back with Doris and the Society. They won't catch me again." Sadie felt strong about her decision. She knew she could, and would, do whatever was necessary to support and protect Gus.

"That's my girl! I knew you would make the right decision. Just stick to your guns, and be true to yourself. It will all work out. Besides, Monday is only twenty-four hours in a lifetime. It can't last longer than twenty-four hours. "Laura and Sadie laughed together at the simplistic approach to healing that they had defined.

"I hadn't thought about it that way before. But you are right, Laura. It's only twenty-four hours. I can live through that." Sadie stopped talking and seemed lost in her own thoughts for a few minutes.

"Laura, I kind of hope Doris fires me. If she does, It's over. If she doesn't, I have to go back to the boarding house on Tuesday and start all over." Sadie didn't know what was around the corner for her life. But she did know that she was getting tired of the turmoil. She wanted some peace.

"Just remember that Tuesday is also only twenty-four hours. One day at a time. As Saul used to tell me, 'Stop borrowing tomorrow's troubles.' Laura patted Sadie's knee. For the remainder of the evening, the two rocked silently and kept their thoughts between themselves and the stars.

Sadie trudged to work on Monday, head down as she counted each block in the sidewalk that she stepped over. By the time she walked in the back door of the kitchen, she had steeled her body and mind to whatever might come next. She reasoned that nothing could be worse than if she was still living with Frank.

"Morning, Sadie girl! Hope you weekend was good. Let me warn you, Doris is in a foul mood today. This is going to be a long day for both of us. So be prepared." Mrs. Goshen kept working as she talked to Sadie. She was almost finished preparing the breakfast tray for Doris.

"How come you are fixing the breakfast tray? That's my job." Sadie knew this was not a good sign.

"I have no idea. Doris was in here way earlier than usual, and just told me that this was my job from now on. She said you had too much to do." Mrs. Goshen winked at Sadie.

"I think she is beginning to like you."

"Or beginning to do away with my job." Sadie had conflicting feelings. She wanted the pain to end, but she also, at this moment, wanted to keep her job.

"That won't happen, Sadie girl. No one else in this town will work for Doris. Why do you think she pays so well? Doris should thank her lucky stars that she has you." Mrs. Goshen took the tray and left Sadie alone in the kitchen.

Sadie took a deep breath and started her chores. No matter what was going to happen, time would go faster if she were busy. And she only had to suffer through about ten hours of the twenty-four-hour day. She could do that.

Doris was very sullen the few times that Sadie passed her in the hall. She did not speak to Sadie and did not look at her. Most of her day was spent in her office with the door closed.

Toward the end of the day, Doris summoned Sadie to her office. Sadie knew this was the end. She came in to the office and closed the door quietly behind her. She then sat motionless on the hard oak chair opposite Doris's desk until Doris finished her paperwork.

"Sadie, it's time to discuss your job performance. You've been here several months now, and if you will remember, we made a deal." Doris was not looking at Sadie. She had not raised her eyes from the papers on her desk. Her fingers fidgeted with the edges of her hair with one hand. The other hand was hidden in her lap.

"Yes, I remember." Sadie knew that Doris was going to fire her. She had set herself up by making the deal, and now Doris was using it as an excuse to fire her. But Sadie was relieved that Doris was doing it quietly. The viciousness that

Doris had displayed on Friday evening didn't seem to be here today.

"If I remember, you took a pay cut on a trial basis. You have since proven your work. This is to notify you that you will now be getting the full ten dollars a week, starting with this week's pay." Doris stood up from her desk and turned her back to Sadie. She stared out the window while waiting for Sadie to answer.

"But, Ms. Steinway, I really don't understand. After last week I thought…" Sadie was stunned. Doris cut her off before she could finish her protest.

"Don't look a gift horse in the mouth, Sadie. Take it and be grateful. That is all. You may get back to work now."

"Thank-you, Ms. Steinway." Sadie muttered as she quickly left the room. The full impact of what had happened didn't hit her until Laura asked about Sadie's day once she was home.

"Laura, you'll never believe it in a million years. Doris gave me a raise! She said I had proved my work and was giving me the full salary starting today! Can you believe it?" Sadie shook her head. She was still stunned and wasn't sure if this was another setup by the Society or if it was real.

"Well, good for her! And good for you! Maybe she does have a conscience and is trying to apologize for the banquet. You just never know."

"Do you think it's really real?" Sadie just couldn't believe Doris could be generous on her own. Or make a decision without Mrs. Lear being involved.

"You'll know on Friday when you get paid. In the meantime, enjoy the day. Gus is waiting to show you the cookies we baked today." Laura opened the front door for Sadie. Sadie smiled and left her workday on the porch.

Doris and Sadie fell into a silent routine over the next few days. Mrs. Goshen continued to serve Doris her breakfast, and Sadie and Doris only spoke to discuss work-related items. The conversations were brief with Doris never looking directly at Sadie. Even when they passed each other in the hallways, Doris was always looking at something in the distance. True to her work, Doris included the full ten dollars in Sadie's pay envelope on Friday.

Sadie was quite pleased with the way her life was unfolding. She and Doris had made a truce, and the rest of the Society had seemed to forget that Sadie existed. Sadie knew that this was due, in part, to Doris's keeping Sadie in the kitchen or out on errands when any of the Society members were at the boarding house. Sadie was grateful for that.

Encounters with Howard were also brief and painless. Howard always acknowledged Sadie when he came to the boarding house and then spent the rest of his time with Mrs. Goshen and Doris. He would always find Sadie to say good-bye for the day, and their brief conversations were a delightful interlude. Howard was very respectful of Sadie and never hinted at their earlier tryst or made any attempt to further their relationship. He always hovered uncomfortably just out of Sadie's physical space and seemed to have trouble standing still. There was softness in his eyes, along with a bit of sadness about him. Sadie didn't know why, and her heart always twitched a bit when she recognized the sadness. But Howard had his own life, and Sadie had hers. And those lives were separate. Their time together was brief and wonderful. But it was in the past.

Sadie was enjoying the life that she had carved out for herself and Gus. She had a good job, great pay, and a true friend in Laura. Soon she would have enough money saved up to look for a house of her own. And Sadie knew her next home would be close to Laura. They all needed each other. And they all cared deeply for each other.

Frank was a distant memory. It had been three months since Sadie's escape, and there had been no sign of him. Sadie had convinced herself that Frank had given up on her and moved on to his next victim. Or maybe he had died at Grand Central Station. With either one Sadie lost no sleep with guilt. She had moved on with her life, and Frank was not in her future.

Sadie's work had become routine and satisfying. The evenings and weekends were spent with Laura and Gus. Sadie and Laura would take turns cooking, and Gus was always assigned to the kitchen help.

"My goodness, Sadie. I don't know how you eat so much and stay so thin. I hate you for that!" Laura had commented on Sadie's third helping of ham Sunday evening.

"Must be the physical exercise I get at the boarding house. And the fact that I am so very happy. Does being happy make you hungry?" Sadie grinned at Laura and offered herself another brownie.

"In your case, I guess it does! Eat away. I love to watch! It makes me feel really good that my little adopted family is happy and healthy."

By late August, Sadie was beginning to feel the heat of the late summer. She would sweat profusely on her walks to and from work. Breakfast smells were nauseating to her, and she would sometimes get dizzy when she moved or stood up too quickly. She would have to stay perfectly still until it passed.

Sadie was feeling particularly ill one morning and was not the least bit amused when Mrs. Lear showed up at the front door unexpectedly. Sadie stood aside and motioned Mrs. Lear into the boarding house. Sadie refused to meet her gaze and looked down at the floor until Mrs. Lear had passed.

Sadie waited until Mrs. Lear was out of sight before she left the boarding house for the day. It had been an especially arduous day at work with the unrelenting August heat. Sadie found the thought of adding a confrontation with Mrs. Lear to her day to be intolerable.

Sadie walked slowly home. There was very little shade on the sidewalk. She was so hot she could barely move. Every step was harder than the step before it. Sadie stepped out of view and removed her wool stockings and shoes, even with the freedom and additional air movement that she had gained from removing some of her clothing, Sadie still found the heat unbearable.

Sadie's face was flushed, and tears of exhaustion were forming when she finally arrived home. Laura had a fan going in the dining room and Sadie headed straight to the moving air.

The fan was a floor fan and was doing a good job of cooling her feet and legs. Sadie bent down to turn the fan up to her face, and dizziness overwhelmed her. She fainted onto the floor with a thud.

When Sadie came back to consciousness a few minutes later, Laura was kneeling beside her. Gus was on his hands and knees staring fearfully into Sadie's face.

"Sadie! You had us scared to death! Are you okay?" Laura was alarmed. She insisted that Sadie stay on the floor. She felt Sadie's arms and face. She was burning up.

"You stay right there on the floor. We need to bring your body temperature down. Gus, stay with your mother while I go get some cold water. Don't let her get up!" Laura came back with a bowl of cold water and a kitchen towel. She wiped down Sadie's face, neck and arms with the cool water. Sadie's body temperature began to come down, and her skin color faded back to a healthy pink.

"I'm better now. Just let me sit up for a few minutes." Sadie sat up and allowed Gus and Laura to help her lean herself against the leg of the dining room table.

Sadie closed her eyes, and the room started to spin again. She opened them immediately, and threw out her arms to grab the table leg. The quick movement caused her stomach to lurch. Her face went ashen.

"I'm going to be sick. I need to go throw up." Laura ran for a bucket and held Sadie's hair while Sadie emptied her stomach. Once she was finished, she leaned back against the table leg. Laura got Sadie a glass of ice, and Sadie gratefully let the ice chips melt slowly in her dry mouth.

"I think I'm okay now. I must have just gotten overheated walking home." Sadie closed her eyes again and leaned her head back against the table. This time nothing was spinning, and Sadie's stomach was calm.

"Sadie, this is not good. You were overheated. I'm worried about you. I think I should go get the doctor to take a look at you."

"I don't need a doctor. And I can't afford a doctor. I'm fine. I just need a little rest under a cool shade tree. Thank you, Laura, for the thought. But I'll be fine in a few minutes." Sadie stood up slowly and Gus walked with her to the porch. Together they sat in the porch swing while Laura cooked the evening meal.

"Gus, why don't you go help Laura? We don't want her to have to do everything by herself."

"No. I want to stay here with you. You might need me to get something for you." Sadie could see that Gus was still frightened. His hands were wrapped around her arm, and his little body was pushed up against Sadie. The closeness of Gus made Sadie uncomfortably warm, but she knew he needed to be there. She pulled her arm up and pulled him a little closer.

"Okay. We'll just stay here for a while then. I'm sure Laura won't mind at all."

"Dinner is almost ready. Are you two up to it?"

"Oh, yes. I don't know about Gus, but I am famished!" Remembering the earlier episode, Sadie stood up slowly. She made sure she was perfectly balanced before taking Gus's hand and walking into the kitchen.

Laura had fixed cold corn beef sandwiches and potato salad. Sadie brought the sandwich up to her mouth for her first bite. The smell of the meat ran up her nose and instantly turned her stomach.

"I can't eat this. The smell is making me sick to my stomach. I'm sorry." Sadie put the sandwich down and pushed her plate away.

"You need to probably just rest a bit."

"I think I will just go on to bed. I'm still feeling pretty weak. And if I don't show up for work, I will lose my job. I just need a little more rest." Sadie kissed Gus good night and apologized to Laura for leaving her with the dishes.

"I'll handle dinner tomorrow night. Laura, you and Gus can have the night off as thanks from me for being so considerate today." With that, Sadie padded down the hall and crawled into bed. It was barely seven, and she was bone tired. She had been going to bed earlier than usual for over a week now. She just couldn't seem to get caught up on her sleep.

The next morning Sadie drug herself out of bed. She felt horrible and dreaded another day at the boarding house.

"Sadie, you look awful! You look worse than you did yesterday. Did you not get any sleep?" Laura felt Sadie's forehead for a temperature, but didn't find one.

"I'm not sick, Laura. I'm just really, really tired. I must have caught a flu bug or something. I should feel better in a couple of days. I certainly hope so. I'm not sure I could feel much worse and still be standing." Sadie smelled the cup of coffee Laura handed her, grimaced, and put it back on the counter.

"I think I'll just have water this morning. My stomach is still a little queasy."

"At least try to eat some dry toast. Maybe that will help settle your stomach. The bags under your eyes are so dark you look like you've been in a fight. And you definitely lost! You could scare people with that face." Laura sat with Sadie at the table, ready to insist if Sadie refused to eat her toast.

Sadie chewed slowly, swallowed hard, and slowly began to feel a little better. By the time she was ready for work, Sade was almost convinced she could handle the day.

Not wanting to have a repeat episode of the night before, Sadie paced her work. She was exhausted by the time the day was over. But she had been able to keep the dizzy spells to a minimum and had only thrown up twice.

Sadie contemplated her physical symptoms on the slow walk home. She was absolutely miserable, but there was something familiar about it. She had been here before.

Laura and Gus were waiting for Sadie on the porch. Sadie assured them that she was feeling much better.

"And I'm keeping my promise. I'm cooking tonight. Just let me throw some water on my face to cool it off a bit." Sadie splashed cold water on her face and then looked up at her reflection in the mirror. A stranger stared back at her. She saw a face surrounded with dull, lifeless hair, blotchy skin, and huge dark circles under her eyes that hung almost to the chin.

"I've seen this face before." Sadie said to the reflection. 'I've seen this face staring back at me.' Sadie paused in mid-thought.

"Oh, my god! No!" Clarity came to Sadie in a flash. She hadn't had a menstrual period for several years due to Frank's physical abuse. Her body had finally healed, and Sadie had been surprised by having a menstrual period in June. She had one in July, and she should have had one in August. She was over two weeks late.

Sadie had slept with Howard in a moment of passion. Sadie hadn't even considered the possibility of getting pregnant. Sadie knew what she had needed at that moment, and she was certain she would have done it no matter what the possible consequences. If she had taken the time to think about the consequences.

The possibilities flooded into her mind. How could she support another child? She was just getting by now. And could she really do all that physical labor while she was pregnant? Could she even keep a job or get another one if Doris fired her? What would the ladies of the town think of her then? What would Laura think of her? What would Gus think? How could she even explain it to Gus?

'No more, God! Please, no more!' Sadie said to herself as she shut off her mind. She fluffed her hair, put a smile on her face and started dinner.

The evening was excruciatingly long for Sadie. She tried to concentrate on the matters at hand, but her mind kept slipping back into the dark space. Sometimes she couldn't see Laura and Gus clearly. Their faces seemed to be floating in a fog. Sometimes she couldn't hear their voices.

Sadie, Laura, and Gus all worked together to clean up the kitchen after dinner. It was easier for Sadie to move around and keep her mind busy with trivial things that didn't cause pain.

"I've had my bath, and the bathroom is all yours now. I checked on Gus on my way by your bedroom. He is fast asleep. So, you can lounge and indulge as long as you like." Laura peeked her head out of the porch door. Sadie was sitting quietly with a cup of tea.

"Thanks, Laura. But I think I'll just sit out here for a while. It's peaceful. And the evening breeze feels really good." Sadie smiled in Laura's direction for just a moment. Then she returned her gaze to the dark shadows in the front yard.

"Want me to sit with you for a while?"

"No. No. You go on to bed. I'm enjoying my own company. I'll be in in a little while." Sadie only took her eyes away from the dark front yard long enough to take a sip of tea.

"Okay. Don't stay up too late, Sadie. You still need a lot of rest." With that, Laura closed the porch door. Sadie waited until she heard Laura's bedroom door close before she allowed her thoughts to focus on the tiny life growing inside her.

Sadie quickly dove into deep despair. A pregnancy was something that Sadie had never considered for herself at this time in her life. She had no answers. She didn't know how she could be able to continue on now or how she would ever give Gus the home that she wanted to give him.

Sadie cried no tears. Tears came during emotional crisis. This was no crisis. This was the end. Laura would throw her out, and then there would be no place for her and Gus. As soon as the other women in town found out about her pregnancy, she would be marked for life.

Sadie's thoughts drifted back to Frank and her life with him. He had always told her that she was too stupid to live on her own. Her stupidity was one of the reasons he beat her all the time.

'A beating might be a blessing at this point,' Sadie thought to herself. The beatings always ended. And there were always periods of quiet before the next beating. Sadie saw no end to this dilemma. It was constant, churning self-deprecation.

Life was hard. Harder than Sadie could have ever imagined. She thought leaving Frank would give her the peace and safety that she had longed for, for so many years. A peace and safety that, at the time, she thought she deserved.

But her life had been in constant turmoil since she had left Frank. The beatings had stopped, but the emotional pain just kept coming and coming. Sadie hadn't allowed herself to feel for many years. And now she regretted opening that door to her heart. It was easier when she was stone cold.

The face of her son, Gus, popped into her mind. He was smiling at her. That innocent, wonderful I-love-you-no-matter-what smile that Sadie loved so dearly.

Sadie's heart skipped. She fell to the bottom of despair when she realized that she was pregnant with Gus. She didn't think she could bring an innocent life into her home with Frank. She had felt extreme guilt for allowing the pregnancy.

But she now had no regrets. The pregnancy was difficult and fraught with physical trauma from the beatings. Frank did everything he could to cause Sadie to abort. He did not want another child. He wanted Sadie all to himself. And he wanted her youthful, taut body to stay a trophy for him.

The bigger Sadie's belly got, the more Frank loathed touching Sadie. For a few months, Sadie felt no beatings and learned to tune out the yelling. Frank's mother was looking forward to another grandchild, so Sadie knew Frank would only go so far.

Once Gus was born, Sadie forgot all her misgivings about bringing a child into her world. Gus had become her personal blessing from God. She lived and breathed for him. Gus was the reason Sadie got out of bed every day.

Sadie's mind started taking little steps forward. A small flicker of light was forming in the corner of her heart. Sadie still had Gus. And he was still her reason for getting out of bed. She still considered him a blessing.

Now she could maybe have two blessings and two reasons to get out of bed in the morning. If she still had a bed once the world knew about her pregnancy.

Sadie didn't think even Laura could forgive her this time. Laura was the dearest friend Sadie had ever had. The only friend. Laura knew Sadie better than anyone else. But she didn't know about Sadie's past. Adding an illegitimate child as an ending to that story would push even Laura over the edge.

Sadie could never go back to Frank. Even if she wanted to. Frank held her virginity in high esteem when they had married and had made it clear that one man was Sadie's destiny. Frank often lectured to Sadie about the vows she had taken. And the repercussions if she ever broke them. As soon as Frank found out she was pregnant with another man's child, the punishment would be swift and final.

Sadie also couldn't stay in Galesburg. The work at the boarding house would soon become too much to handle physically. Sadie could do the work, but not at the pace Doris demanded. And Sadie was certain that Doris would give no consideration to an unwed mother. Doris already thought that Sadie was a childless widow. All Doris would have to do was simple math to know that the father of Sadie's child was not her dead husband. Doris would not tarnish her reputation by even being in the presence of such a tainted woman.

And the Society! They would crucify her. Sadie could even envision them marching her out of town. Or worse.

Out of town. That might be an option. Sadie had arrived in Galesburg with no money, no job, and no place to live. That part of her life she had handled well. And she had even learned a lot about how to live on her own as a single mother.

Sadie could do it again. She had more money saved now than when she had left New York City. She and Gus could just move to another small town. Sadie could continue to present herself as a widow and get another housekeeping job. If she could please Doris, she could please anybody. And she knew that most housekeepers had much lighter demands on them than the demands that Doris placed on her. Or she could work in a laundry like Laura had done. There was work out there. And Sadie now knew that what she did for a living was no reflection on who she was. It was honest work. And that was what really counted.

No one in the next town would need to know her history. Sadie understood how that worked and had learned to be convincing in her deceptions. And Gus was still young enough that he would never question where the baby had come from. He would simply delight in a little brother or sister to play with.

Sadie settled on the option of leaving town. There were still a lot of questions to be answered and lots of planning to do. But this time, Sadie had the time to plan. She just needed to go before she started to show. She had a couple more months to plan if she needed it.

Sadie knew she was betraying Laura's friendship. Laura had saved her from the street. And Sadie knew she would not have made it this far without her friendship. Laura and Gus had become very close. It would be hard on both of them when Sadie announced they were leaving.

Sadie made the decision to tell Laura the real reason she was leaving. She owed her that much. And hopefully Laura would let them stay until Sadie had her plan in place. Sadie was fairly certain Laura would let them stay because of Gus. And as long as she left before the pregnancy started to show, there would be no shame on Laura. Besides, she didn't know Laura before they came to Galesburg, and she wouldn't know Laura after they left. Telling Laura the truth couldn't hurt Sadie any more than she already hurt. But it just might make her feel a little better for doing the right thing.

Sadie also decided to tell Howard that she was carrying his child. Due to Howard's marital status, she knew he would tell no one. Sadie didn't want anything from Howard. But as the father, Howard needed to know that his child may someday come looking for him.

Sadie slept fitfully that night but with resolve. She had a good plan. Starting over with the promise of a new life gave Sadie hope. Gus was everything to her and her reason for living. She didn't think she could take care of Gus before he came either. She was so afraid. But when he came, she loved him instantly and never looked back. So if there was another new life growing inside her, she would accept her future and embrace it. Another child would give her more reasons to live and could just possibly double the joy in her life. Life would be different, but life would be just fine.

CHAPTER TEN

Planning to run Again

Sadie awoke the next morning feeling better than she had felt in many weeks. She knew why she was so tired now. And she could work with that. She also knew she had another chance to make her life better. And she would give this baby a safe and happy home from day one.

The thought of leaving Galesburg invigorated her. The only bright spot here had been Laura. The Society and Doris had made Sadie's life away from Laura's rooming house a living hell. But she had gained experience from that. Sadie was confident she would be able to see the warning signs and stay away from any vicious societies in the next town.

Breakfast with Laura was delightful. Sadie used her memories from her last pregnancy as a guide as to what to eat. Dry toast eaten slowly and hot tea was just the ticket.

"Sadie, you seem so much better. You still have those dark circles under your eyes, but you seem so much more rested. Whatever you are doing, keep doing it. You'll be back to your old self soon."

"Yes, Laura. I'm so much better. I know I'm going to be fine." Sadie meant every word. Just saying the words out loud helped cement her decision to move on.

"And your dill pickles are great, Laura! You really need to teach me how to make these!" Sadie was cleaning off the kitchen counter, and on impulse had plucked a pickle out of the jar.

"Well, I've never seen anyone eat them for breakfast. But I guess you can appreciate the flavor any time of the day."

The vinegar in the pickles had cut through a lot of the goop in Sadie's throat and calmed her stomach. She wrapped a couple of the pickles in foil and stuck them in her dress pocket. They would be good to have around if her stomach became uncontrollable during the day.

"Got to go to work. I need a little more time so I can walk slowly. Laura, see you tonight. Give Gus a kiss for me when he wakes up. Love you both!" Sadie was more encouraged every minute. Daylight had shed capability to her plan, and chased away the evils of the what-ifs.

Sadie's pickles were gone by noon. Between the smells of breakfast and the pungent cleaning detergents, Sadie was light-headed and had a headache. But she had been able to avoid the embarrassing questions that would have ensued if she spent the morning running to the bathroom.

Doris had noticed the slow-down in Sadie's work. She had not started the white glove inspections, but she walked through each of the rooms at least once when Sadie was cleaning and once when she was finished. No words were spoken between them, but Sadie knew she was being watched.

Sadie was mildly irritated by Doris's interruptions. She knew the scowl on Doris face was meant for her to see. Sadie chuckled when she thought how surprised Doris would be when she turned in her resignation.

'Wonder how much fun Doris will have doing her own cleaning. I think Doris should have Mrs. Lear do the white glove inspections. They would make a perfect team. Knowing that her time was almost over made the day much more enjoyable.

The weekend soon came, and Sadie and Laura lingered over their morning coffee. Gus was soaking in the bathtub making bubble castles with Laura's bubble bath.

"Sadie, I do so enjoy Saturday mornings with you and Gus. It reminds me of Saturday mornings with Saul. Time would just stop, and we would enjoy each other's company as long as we wanted. The rest of the world was not allowed in, and we didn't greet the world until we were ready. It made the weekends almost like little vacations."

"I enjoy this very much too. I'm totally going to miss this." Sadie sat her coffee cup down and took a deep breath.

"Laura, let's go sit on the porch. I have something I need to tell you, and I would be more comfortable out there." Sadie took Laura by the hand and led her outside. They each had a full cup of coffee. Sadie tucked an afghan around Laura's lap to protect from the early morning chills.

"Okay, Sadie. We're both here now. What'd you want to tell me?"

"Laura, I have a story to tell you. You need to understand how I came to be in Galesburg so you can better understand when I tell you why I have to leave." Sadie started her story with the trip she and her parents took to New York City when she was a teenager.

"When I met my husband, Frank, he was a dashing figure. He was in his late twenties, tall, dark and handsome. My family took the train to New York City for a vacation, and Frank was our porter. By the time we got to the City, Frank had become our official tour guide"

"Frank took us to all the popular sites, paid for theatre tickets, got us the best tables in the best restaurants. It was a fantasy vacation. Frank doted on us. Frank doted on me. He lavished me with flowers and gifts and was the perfect gentleman. I fell head over heels in love with him."

"Did your parents approve, Sadie? He was a lot older than you."

"Oh, yes. They approved. Especially when the cars and letters kept coming after we got home. He even came to Ohio to visit. On the second visit, he proposed and I accepted."

"Did you have a big wedding with all of your family there?"

"Well, no. My wedding day should have been the first sign that something was wrong. Frank proposed on Friday, and my parents came with us to the courthouse on Monday. I didn't even get a new dress. We got married in the morning, and Frank took me back to the City with him that afternoon."

"Did you have a honeymoon? Go anywhere special?

"No. As soon as we got to the City, Frank quit his job as a porter and started working at a local salvage yard with his brothers. And then my training began."

"Training? What do you mean?"

"I was instructed on how to act, when to act, what to say, when to keep my mouth shut, how to dress. Basically, it was total control by Frank. I was totally controlled, and if I did not act properly, I was beaten. Anything would set him off. My dress might be too short, my hair might be an inch too long, he might find a crumb or two on the kitchen table after I had finished cleaning the kitchen. I could never get any peace because the rules kept changing. It got to the point that I wore long sleeves and high collars all year round just to hide the bruises. And for the last two years, he reminded me every day that if I ever tried to leave him, he would kill me." Sadie spared Laura some of the details of the abuse.

"Okay, Sadie. I fully understand why you did what you did. Believe me, I've been there. Before I met Saul. You should be proud of yourself and your strength. Not many women would have been able to do what you have done. You've come so far! But I don't understand why you say you are leaving Galesburg. Frank hasn't found you, has he?" Laura had tears in her eyes.

"No. Frank hasn't found me. Galesburg wasn't part of my escape plan. I didn't plan to run away to Galesburg. I picked a destination after I got to Grand Central Station that was far away from Frank and hopefully a place he would never look, I never heard of Galesburg, Illinois before I saw it on the ticket board. I had absolutely no ties here. I had very little money, no home, and no income when I stepped off the train. You saved my life. And have been a dear friend ever since. That is why I'm telling you my story. Gus and I owe you so much."

"Then why are you saying you are leaving? You like it here. Gus likes it here. I like having you here. I don't see the problem."

"Well, there's more to the story. Remember the dinners that I used to go to with Howard? I broke off the relationship as soon as you told me that he was married. But by then we had gotten close and enjoyed each other's company when he would come to the boarding house."

"Go on."

"Well, remember the night of the banquet for Carl Sandburg? I told you part of the story. But I didn't tell you all of it."

"Sadie, you don't have to tell me everything. I know how the Society works. There is no need for you to relive that pain for me."

"It's not the Society, Laura. Well, the Society is part of it, I guess. What I didn't tell you is that I left the banquet hall in tears very early in the evening. I found a quiet spot on the college campus and just let all my hurt out. Howard had also left the banquet hall and followed me. He stayed with me most of the night and comforted me." Sadie got up from her chair and paced back and forth across the porch. She didn't quite know how to explain the rest without offending Laura.

"Define comfort. Did he comfort you or did he take advantage of your vulnerability?"

"I'm carrying his child, Laura."

Laura was quiet for a moment.

"Oh. I don't know quite what to say."

"But he didn't really take advantage of me. It was mutual. If it hadn't been for Howard, I would have let the

Society totally destroy me. It's hard to explain. At that point in time, I really needed what Howard was offering me. And I know he didn't plan on taking advantage of me when he followed me out of the building. It just happened." Sadie finally stopped pacing and looked straight at Laura. It was all out in the open now, and Sadie braced herself for Laura's response. No self-respecting, God-fearing woman would want anything to do with Sadie now.

Laura stared into her coffee cup for a few moments. With tears streaming down her face, she walked over to Sadie and put her arms around her shoulders.

"My dear child. You have been through so much. I am standing by you no matter what. You've done nothing wrong, and you are a good person. A good mother and a good friend. We can get through this together. I'll help you any way I can."

"Laura, I'm so glad you don't hate me! I was so worried." Sadie hugged Laura back. Until this moment, Sadie had not known how deep and true Laura's friendship was.

"But I do need to leave Galesburg. I don't want to leave you, but I do need a fresh start. And the more I think about leaving, the more excited I get about being in a place where there is no Galesburg Ladies Aid Society. I hate those women and what they did to me!"

"Where will you go? Do you know yet?"

"I don't know yet. But I still have some time. I won't start showing for a couple more months, so there is time to plan."

"And time to say good-bye. I'll help all I can with your planning. And I even have a little money saved up if you need it. I still think you can stay in Galesburg and have a wonderful life. But I understand and respect the reasons why you think you have to leave. In the meantime, you are safe here. And you will always be welcome here any time you want to visit. And I will have a place to visit and two grandchildren to spoil!" Laura and Sadie walked arm and arm back in the house. Gus was done with his bath and was excited to get on with the day. The three of them had started a practice with Gus on Saturday mornings. It was a practice of planning for the weekend

Saturday evening Sadie and Laura found themselves out on the porch again with their tea.

"Laura, I have made a promise to myself that wherever I end up, I will have a house with a front porch just like this one. I have so enjoyed this comforting porch." Sadie's mood had lightened considerably. Now that her secret was out and Laura was still her friend, Sadie felt great freedom in planning and dreaming. She didn't have to hide this time. And she really wasn't running away from her life. She was walking deliberately forward to an improved life. She was definitely making progress.

"I'm rather attached to this porch, myself. It's going to be lonely out here after you leave. And I'm going to miss Gus so much. You two are my family. I don't know what I'm going to do without you."

"You can always come to visit. Gus needs you in his life. You are the first grandmother he has ever known. And I need you. I don't ever want to lose touch with you." Sadie smiled warmly at Laura.

"Speaking of visiting, are you going to tell Howard why you are leaving? And where you are going? Do you expect him to have any part in his child's life?"

"Yes, I'm going to tell him. I'm going to tell him that I am carrying his child mainly because he deserves to know. And the child may want to have a relationship with him someday. Howard needs to be prepared for that. But I'm not going to tell him where I am going. I don't want anything from Howard. And believe me, I certainly don't want to start any rumors in my new town. I'm going to show up as a widow whose husband died recently. And I'm going to keep it that way. I'm done with letting men in my life. My life will be absolutely fulfilling without them." Sadie was practicing her new story on Laura. She watched Laura's face to see how believable it was.

"Well, that's a good story. And you can almost tell it with a straight face. But your eyes are giving you away. You couldn't live the life of a young widow for too many years. You are too beautiful and vibrant to grow old alone. Some nice man will come along someday and sweep you off your feet. That's when you will want more in your life. Or when your children are grown and gone. The quiet gets to you. Days and days and days of quiet make you see what you missed out of in life."

"That's a lifetime away. I'll worry about it when I get there."

"I think you should make Howard pay you to leave town. He needs to suffer a bit. It's not fair that he gets off scot-free and you bear the whole burden. Besides, he can afford it. And you need it. It's only right." Laura brought the subject back to Howard with startling force.

"I don't need or want his money. And I want to cut the ties. I don't want to have to keep looking over my shoulder in the next town. If I just leave, Howard will be so grateful that he still has his perfect little life. He will never come looking "for me" Sadie wanted finality. She wanted to do the right thing and tell Howard. But then she wanted to be done with all the drama and heartache. She wanted Galesburg and all it represented to be part of her past.

"It's your decision. And I will support you. But I still think he should feel some pain in this."

Laura and Sadie smiled knowingly at each other. They had formed a deep friendship. A friendship that allowed each of them to be the individuals they were without judgment.

Sadie was well rested on Monday morning. As she was getting ready for work, she was able to smile at her reflection. Her hair was bouncing back, and her eyes were sparkling above the dark circles under them. Sadie knew the dark circles were temporary. As long as she took care of herself and continued to honor the needs of her changing body, the dark circles would fade. And once the child was born, the dark circles would disappear.

The physical work at the boarding house was hard, and Sadie was having a difficult time pacing herself. She needed to respond to her body and arrange her schedule to accommodate.

Doris was extremely displeased when she noticed that Sadie had changed the order of her tasks. The light duties were done in the early morning and later afternoon, while the heavy tasks such as waxing floors was now being done midday. Doris tried to intimidate Sadie into going back to the prescribed routine by following her around. Doris would cluck and frown behind Sadie and then stomp out of the room.

Doris repeated this routine on Tuesday and Wednesday, but Sadie just kept working at her new pace.

Howard came to the boarding house as usual on Thursday. He nodded hello to Sadie and then got down to business with Doris and Mrs. Goshen. Sadie knew Howard would come find her to say good-bye before he left. She wanted to talk to him privately.

Sadie eavesdropped on the conversations as she continued her work. She had saved the dining hall dusting chore for Howard's visit. That way she would be just behind the kitchen wall and could listen in.

As soon as Sadie heard Howard begin to gather his papers and thank Doris for her order, Sadie moved quickly to the front porch. She knew Doris would walk Howard as far as her office and then leave him to find his own way out.

When Howard stepped into the enclosed front porch, Sadie was meticulously dusting the table and lamp on the far corner of the porch.

"I'm leaving now, Sadie. It was good to see you again." Howard tipped his hat to Sadie and was about to step out the door when Sadie's response stopped him in mid-stride.

"Hello, Howard. It is good to see you too. I need to talk to you. I have something to tell you. But I don't want to talk about it here. Can we meet some evening and talk for a few minutes?" Sadie was smiling, but not looking at Howard, as she continued to dust.

When Sadie looked up at Howard for his response, she had to laugh. He was actually blushing. He was shuffling his feet from side to side and would not meet Sadie's gaze.

"I could be free this evening. But I'm a little surprised. Has something changed that I didn't know about?"

"A lot has changed, Howard. Good things, I might add. I just really want to talk to you but not here. Shall we meet at the restaurant at eight?" Sadie knew that Howard would have different expectations for the evening than she did. She knew she was leading him on, but she didn't care. She found great satisfaction in it. This time, she was in charge.

"I'll be there with bells on!" Howard tipped his hat again and bounced out the door.

'Poor man.' Sadie thought to herself. 'He's in for the shock of his life.'

That evening Sadie chatted with Gus and Laura while they ate dinner. She was more excited about seeing Howard than she wanted to admit to herself. But she was also very nervous. This was a situation that she would not have expected herself to be in. Never in a million years.

"Sadie, at least make him pay for dinner. And have dessert!" Laura admonished as Sadie walked down the porch steps.

"Yes, mother Laura!" Sadie said over her shoulder as she kept walking down the sidewalk.

Sadie turned the corner toward the restaurant a few minutes before eight. Howard was waiting for her on the other side of the street with a bouquet of red roses in his hand.

Sadie was impressed. Howard was risking being noticed by someone who knew him. Howard usually had the flowers delivered to their table after they sat down.

"Well, here we are again. Just like before. Like the last few months didn't happen." Howard held out his arm to Sadie and led her to their table. The little round, discreet table in the back, partially hidden by the huge rubber tree plant flourishing next to the doorway.

"Shall we order spaghetti and pretend like this is our first time here? And that nothing ever happened?" Howard was dashing in his dark green wool jacket. His hair was jet-black and slicked back shiny. Sadie could really understand why women would fall for him. He had charm, he had looks, he had money, and he had heart. Sadie felt envious of Howard's wife just then. "Let's have the spaghetti. I love it! But let's not pretend. And let's not forget the last few months. I certainly don't want to live through them again." Sadie tipped her glass of wine to Howard and took a tiny sip. She wasn't sure how it would go down. As expected, it didn't.

Sadie excused herself and hurried to the restroom. She spit the wine out in the sink and washed her mouth out with cold water. Then she leaned against the cool brick wall of the restroom until the dizzy spell subsided. When she got back to the table, the spaghetti was being served.

"So, Sadie. What did you want to talk to me about? Or am I being a cad in hoping that I'm going to get to see you again on a regular basis?"

Sadie put down her fork and folded her hands in her lap. She didn't want Howard to see them trembling.

"I'm sure you remember the night of the banquet for Carl Sandburg. Before anything else, I want to thank you for being there for me. I'm not sure I would have made it through without your help."

"Sadie, I told you. My intentions were honorable. I never meant ……………" Sadie held up her hand to stop him.

"Shut up, Howard. Let me finish. I need to get this said." Sadie put her hand back in her lap, closed her eyes, and took a deep breath.

"Anyway, I've been sick a lot lately. And finally realized that I am pregnant. I'm carrying your child."

Howard slowly put his fork down and reached for a piece of garlic bread. He looked across the table at Sadie. She wasn't joking. Quietly he drew his arm back, resting his chin in the palm of his hand.

"You sure It's mine?"

"Howard! That was so cruel!" Sadie was shocked. She never expected that to come out of Howard's mouth.

"I'm sorry, Sadie. I didn't mean it. And I know better. I'm a little shocked. I don't know what to say, honestly. I have no defense. Or plan."

"I take full responsibility for this, Howard. I don't blame you. And I'm going to deal with it. I just thought you had the right to know."

"Deal with it? How do you intend to deal with it?" Howard spoke softly.

"I'm leaving town as soon as I can get organized. I'll start a new life somewhere else, and no one will ever know what really happened. But when the child is old enough, I do intend to tell him, or her, who their father is. The child just might come looking for you someday."

"Where do I fit in between now and then?"

"You don't. I want nothing from you. I know you have a wife and children. And I won't interfere. I take full blame, and I'll deal with the consequences." Sadie had said the magic words.

"Really? You want nothing from me? You're just going to disappear?"

"I've done it before. Seems to work."

"So that's it? Just like that?"

"Just like that." Sadie cocked her head to one side and smiled back at Howard.

"Now let's eat. I'm famished." Sadie felt free. She chattered through the meal about her plans and the timelines she was putting together. And about how glad she would be to leave the boarding house, Doris, and the Society behind.

Howard was cordial and added his thoughts to her plans as she described them.

Sadie kissed Howard lightly on the cheek as they were leaving the restaurant.

"I don't know if we will get to talk again before I leave. If not, let me tell you that I will always remember you. And always be grateful for your kind heart."

"Sadie, at least let me drive you home. In your condition you shouldn't be doing all this walking in this heat. And I do worry about you walking alone at night. You're leaving anyway. What's it going to hurt for me to know where you live?"

"I guess you're right. It doesn't really matter now. And, if someone sees you with me, you'll just have to deal with it. It's not my problem anymore." Sadie gave her bouquet of roses back to Howard while she climbed in his car. Once she was settled, Howard gave them back to her and closed the door.

Saturday morning found Laura and Sadie in their favorite chairs on the front porch. Gus was having his bath, and Sadie was recapping her dinner with Howard for Laura.

"Laura, I like Howard and don't blame him for the pregnancy. But I must admit that I did get a bit of guilty pleasure putting him on the spot. He was so shocked that he almost stopped breathing! It was quite delightful!" Sadie sighed the sigh of the victor.

"I can't believe you thanked him for getting you pregnant. That is the strangest thing I have ever heard." Laura shook her head.

"Laura, I feel like it is a blessing in disguise. This child was conceived from love, if only in the moment. And it gave me a reason to look beyond what was happening now. And helped me to get the courage to do what I needed to do to be happy. I am thankful for that. I have hope now. I'm not stuck."

"Well, did you at least ask him for money or some kind of compensation?"

"No. But the look on his face was priceless when I told him that his child might come looking for him someday. That was definite compensation." Sadie and Laura giggled together. The future was still unknown. But it was getting brighter.

A black Ford Coupe pulled up to the curb in front of Laura's hose and stopped. A man got out of the car and started up the sidewalk.

"Who on earth is that?" Laura asked. The three gentlemen who rented rooms from her never had callers. And they never used the front steps. They came and went through the side door facing the driveway.

"That's Howard. I let him drive me home last night. Guess he knows where I live now." Sadie was very surprised to see Howard on her sidewalk. And very pleased. She had already started to miss him.

"Want me to stay out here or go inside?"

"You can stay. I have nothing to hide from you. And I might need some womanly support." Sadie stepped off the porch and met Howard on the sidewalk.

"What on earth are you doing here, Howard?"

"I couldn't sleep last night, Sadie. I wanted to talk to you."

"There's nothing left to say, Howard. You're off the hook. Be grateful, and get on with your life."

"But I don't want to be off the hook. I really need to talk to you, Sadie. Can we go somewhere? Take a walk or something?" Howard put his hands in his pants pockets and smiled weakly at Sadie.

"I suppose it wouldn't hurt. Just let me make sure it's okay with Laura." Sadie was intrigued. She really wanted to find out what he meant by not wanting to be off the hook.

"Laura, would you mind watching Gus while I talk to Howard? He seems to really need to talk to me. We won't be gone long. We'll just go to the park around the corner."

"Are you sure it's safe? He isn't going to hurt you, is he?" Laura had only trusted one man in her life. She didn't know Howard personally, and was concerned for Sadie's safety.

"No, Laura. I know he won't hurt me. I don't know Howard all that well, but I do know he is not violent. Besides, he already knows he has nothing to worry about."

Sadie and Howard walked the two blocks to the park in silence. They found a picnic table away from any other park visitors and sat down across from each other.

"All right, Howard. What did you need to say to me?"

"Sadie, I can't live without you. I don't want to live without you. I really want you in my life." Sadie could tell Howard was nervous and scared.

"Just listen to me before you say anything. I need to get this all out on the table." Howard took one of Sadie's hands and placed it between both of his.

"When you told me you were carrying my child, I was scared to death. All I could think about was that I was going to lose everything here in Galesburg. And then when you told me you were leaving town, I was so relieved. I was actually patting myself on the back for sliding through one more time."

"We had such a wonderful time after you told me your story. I thought it was because I was elated that you were taking care of things and not expecting me to help. I have since realized that is not the case."

"I've done a lot of thinking the last day or so. And a lot of observing. I've been looking at what I have and where I'm going. Sadie, I now know that I didn't pursue you initially because you were the new girl in town and could be my next conquest. I know several places that I can visit any time I want and get my needs met."

"I pursued you because I was drawn to you, Sadie. The more I got to know you, the more I wanted you. But not as the next conquest. I think I knew that night after the banquet that I was in love with you. I just didn't know what to do with those thoughts."

"I love you, Sadie. I need you and want you in my life. If you will have me."

Sadie was stunned. Here was this wonderful man, right in front of her, professing his love to her. It was incredible.

"Just exactly what does that mean, Howard? Are you begging me to stay so you can continue this illicit affair? Do you want me to love you back? What do you expect me to do with this information?" Sadie was not about to continue her miserable life in Galesburg just because Howard said he loved her. And she certainly was done living in secret. At least in secret with the people she cared about.

"I want you to let me leave town with you, Sadie. I want to start a new life somewhere else with you. There's nothing for me here, and no one will miss me." Howard's eyes met Sadie's and never wavered. He waited for her answer.

"Nothing for you here? You have a wife and family. You have an established business. Are you just going to walk away from all of that?"

"Yes, I am. I am prepared to walk away with you and never look back. My wife won't miss me. There's no love lost there. Besides, she thinks more of her mother than she does me. And my children already have no respect for me because of my wife and mother-in-law. So they won't be missing a thing without their father there. It's not a home, Sadie. It's a prison. I'm not the father. I'm just the guy who comes and goes and the guy my children's mother yells at."

"I don't know what to say, Howard. I thought your life was perfect." Sadie felt empathy for Howard. But so much was coming at her so fast. She didn't know what she was supposed to do.

"Well, now you know. There's more, but it's not important right now. Right now I want you to absolutely know that I want to go with you. And I will go with you wherever you say. Whenever you say. I love you, Sadie. And I know you have feelings for me. I want a chance to be a real partner and a real father. You and this baby give me that chance."

"But you lied to me Howard. When you first met me, you told me you lived alone. I had to find out from other people that you were married. I won't tolerate being lied to. "Sadie wanted to believe him, but there was that one great big lie that she couldn't get past.

"Sadie, I did not lie to you. At least not totally. I do live alone. But no one knows that. My wife and I stopped sleeping together months ago. And it just got so painful to be around her that I rented a sleeping room. As far as the town goes, my wife insists that we play the part of the married couple. Outside of social events, my wife would rather I just stay away. As far as her friends and socialites, I travel a lot, which is why I am not home at night. I should have told you the rest of the story, Sadie. But at the time I wasn't looking for anything more than friendship because I was so lonely. And then there never seemed to be a good time to tell you after that. I am sorry that I didn't tell you everything from the beginning."

"I don't know what to say."

"Just say yes!"

Sadie's heart was beating wildly. Could this be the answer to her prayers? Could she really have it all? A normal life, a normal family, a normal home? Sadie was studying Howard's face and feeling her heart move. And then Frank's face popped into her head.

"Howard, you've really put yourself out on a limb here. But you don't know the whole story. My sordid story." Sadie then gave Howard a shortened version of the story she had told Laura just a few days ago. A story that she had not intended to ever have to repeat. Howard wept with Sadie as her emotions overcame her.

"So you see, Howard, I have a husband and a son. And a past that may catch up with me someday. I'm not free to marry. A life with me will have lots of strings attached to it."

"Well, look at it this way. I'm also married with children. And a past that would most definitely haunt me the rest of my life. And I couldn't divorce my wife and then marry you. First of all, the divorce would take forever, if my wife allowed it. And she would fight it tooth and nail, just to save face in the town. Secondly, the Jewish faith, my father's faith, would never allow me to pollute the gene pool and marry a Christian. Besides, you are already pregnant with my child. It's a little late to worry about what other people think. What you and I want is the only thing that counts right now." Howard smiled engagingly at Sadie.

"Howard, you should have been a lawyer! You have made a very convincing case for yourself." Sadie was laughing. A carefree laugh. She stood up and hugged Howard.

Howard gave Sadie a big bear hug in return. In the morning sun, in front of all the park visitors, Howard tipped up Sadie's chin and kissed her full on the mouth.

"Just say yes, Sadie. Let me run away with you. Say yes to happiness for us both." Howard whispered in her ear.

"Maybe. Maybe yes. I have to think about this for a while. And you have to meet my son, Gus. If he doesn't like you, you are history!" Sadie kissed Howard back. And then kissed him again.

CHAPTER ELEVEN

Found by Frank and left for Dead

Howard joined Sadie and Laura for lunch on Sunday. Laura was courteous but guarded.

The initial introductions to Gus seemed confusing to the boy at first. But he eventually relaxed and began to respond to Howard.

The afternoon flew by. Howard played catch with Gus, and the three of them spent some time in the park. By the time Howard was ready to leave, everyone was relaxed. And there was an air of familiarity about the house.

Sadie walked Howard to his car, and he hugged her tight.

"So, do I pass inspection? Is the answer, yes?"

"I'll let you know on Thursday. I need to think about it for a little while." Sadie touched Howard's nose with her finger, grinned at him, and skipped back up the sidewalk.

"Sadie, are you sure you know what you are doing? Howard seems genuine, but it's just such a new thing for him. I can't help but worry that it won't last." Sadie could sense Laura's concern.

"I know Howard loves me. And I know he is sincere. I'm not really convinced he is actually going to leave with me, though. That's why I won't tell him yes or no yet. I want to see if he still feels the same way in a few days. Does it bother you that Howard is married with children? Do you think I'm the evil witch luring him away from his responsibilities?"

"Heavens no, Sadie! He came to you, remember? Besides, just because you made a bad decision once doesn't mean God expects you to be miserable the rest of your life. I believe God wants us to be happy. And I believe God expects us to pursue that happiness. But I also believe God expects us to be decent human beings while we are doing it."

"Amen to that! Happiness seemed impossible not too long ago. But now I have such hope." Sadie was happier than she could remember in her adult life. She had a new life growing inside her that seemed to be a sign of happy days to come. This new life could have a loving father and a loving home and a wonderful older brother who now had a chance to become a healthy, happy young man.

Sadie didn't know if she loved Howard. She wasn't really sure what love was supposed to feel like. But at this point in her life, she didn't think it really mattered. What she had with Howard was better than anything else she had ever had. Sadie was very attracted to Howard, and so far, he had displayed no violent tendencies. That was the key to Sadie's choice right now.

Monday morning dawned hot and humid. Sadie was dreading the walk to the boarding house. She knew that she would be sick by the time she got there in this heat.

Howard was waiting alongside the curb when Sadie turned the first corner.

"Your chariot awaits, my dear." Howard was standing beside his car, holding the passenger door open.

"Don't you think you are being just a little foolish? If Doris sees us together, that will be the end of both of us. We'll be run out of town before we get a chance to leave of our own free will."

"Doris won't see us together. I will drop you off a couple of blocks from the boarding house. And if my wife is any indicator, no one from the Society stirs before seven thirty or eight. So we're pretty safe right now."

"Well, then. I accept your kind offer." Sadie said as she got in the car.

Riding with Howard put Sadie at the boarding house way too early. Rather than go straight to work, Sadie sat under the oak trees in the front yard for a spell. Before today she had not even noticed the beautiful front yard at the boarding house. She hadn't seen any beauty, only fear and intimidation. Sadie thought she could really learn to appreciate the clean beauty of the Midwest. Time was on her side now. She could afford to relax and enjoy her new surroundings.

Howard was waiting for Sadie a couple of blocks away from the boarding house that evening. The ride home was refreshing and fulfilling.

Thursday, Howard came to the boarding house for his usual rounds. He nodded to Sadie as he walked in and then proceeded to the kitchen. Once his business was done, Howard found Sadie out on the front porch. He didn't touch her. He only came close enough to keep their conversation private.

"So is it a yes? Are you going to allow my biggest dream to be fulfilled?" Howard took his hat off and covered his chest with it as a symbolic token of surrender.

"I'll let you know tonight when you pick me up. I have lots of work to do right now. I'll talk to you later." With that, Sadie sashayed back into the boarding house and out of sight.

When Howard picked Sadie up that evening, there was a single red rose lying on her seat. Beside it were two road maps, a bottle of wine, and a tiny pillow.

"The rose is a symbol of my everlasting love for you." Howard explained.

"The wine is to celebrate our new life if you say yes. The road maps are a symbol of the beginning of our adventure through life. And the pillow is to tell you that you can sleep peacefully from now on. I will always be there for you, and I will never let any harm come to you."

"That is so sweet, Howard! And the answer is yes! We both deserve to be happy." Sadie smiled and Howard beamed. He simply reached down and squeezed her hand then drove her home. Sadie took the maps and the wine to keep until Saturday morning. Howard would come early, and they would start putting details to the plan. Sadie hung the rose on her bedroom mirror and tucked the tiny pillow under her large bed pillow. She wanted to dream about what that pillow represented.

Saturday morning Howard arrived promptly at ten. Laura and Gus took off for the grocery store while Sadie and Howard spread the maps out on the table.

"Let's see. We have a map of Illinois and a map of Iowa. Are these the two states where you think we need to be, Howard?" Sadie had unconsciously slipped into an old habit of deferring any decisions to the man.

"Nope. We can go anywhere you want to go. I picked Illinois because you were already here. I know you don't want to go any farther east because of Frank. Farther south would be hotter and not good for your pregnancy. I chose Iowa because it was next to Illinois and would probably have close to the same environment and weather as Illinois. And I know you like Illinois. There are by all means not your only choices. I'm going with you. Not taking you. If you want to look at another state, I'll go down to the store and get another map."

"Thank you, Howard. You are really going to be good for me. Just don't change." Sadie liked what she saw and heard. She prayed to God that he didn't change.

"Let's check these out first. I really don't know where I want to go. You are right in that I won't go east. In fact, I wouldn't mind going a little farther west. Just in case. I want a small town, maybe a little smaller than Galesburg. A place that's not quite so busy. A farming community. Maybe we can live in the country! Can you see yourself digging in the dirt, Howard?"

Howard looked down at his light wool suit, silk shirt, and matching tie. He studied his black leather wing tipped shoes and pretended to flick a spot of dust off of them.

"Well, it would be a new experience. My father says that the Jews own the land, so maybe I should try working with it."

"Howard, I'm not a city girl. I grew up in the country in Ohio. And I really miss the stars, the fireflies, the sounds of the coyotes at night. And room to just be yourself. I don't need fancy dresses or parties or the theater or any of that stuff. I want peace and quiet and security."

"You can be whoever you want to be, Sadie. And don't think the traveling salesman with the silk shirts is necessarily me. I have no idea who I am. This is just what was expected of me to be. I never got the choice to decide. But we'll figure it out together."

"Okay, then. Let's go to Iowa. Let's just drive until we find a town we like. We can stay a few days, check it out, and then make a decision." Sadie was getting more excited by the minute. The idea of just driving and picking a place that felt good was like embarking on a pleasant adventure.

"Then that's settled. We'll go to Iowa. When are we going? It needs to be soon. We need to be settled so that you can relax and enjoy this pregnancy. We could be on the road for a couple of weeks."

"That soon? I still need to give Doris two weeks' notice. And I need to prepare Gus. I still don't know what I'm going to tell him. He is so attached to Laura." Sadie wrung her hands. Thinking about leaving was a whole lot easier than actually doing it.

"Sadie, you owe Doris nothing. She has treated you like dirt and spit on you since day one. Besides, if you tell Doris too soon, she will hound you for details. And then the Society will get involved and start snooping. And they just might find us, which would bring Laura pain. Also if you start to work on Monday, you will have to wait until Friday to get paid. I say we just leave. Let Doris wonder where you are."

"Your reasons are valid. I hadn't thought about it that way. So when do you think we should leave?"

"I think we should leave Monday morning. Let's just be moving on. We can write Laura as soon as we know where we are going to stay, and she can come and visit us before winter. We can also get Gus enrolled in school. He's old enough, you know." Howard was pacing the floor now.

"But, Howard, I don't know if I have enough money saved up to last us until I can find another job. I wasn't really prepared to up and leave just yet. I'm still enjoying just the thought of leaving." Sadie was worried. And still thinking that she was totally responsible for the welfare of herself and her children.

"Sadie, dear. I don't want to tell you what to do. But I don't think you need to worry about taking care of yourself and your children. That's my job now. You can work if you want to, but you won't need to. I'll take care of you and Gus and the baby. You just need to settle in and continue to be the good mom that you are."

"I really want what you have to offer Howard. I want us to be a family. But when does this family thing start?" Sadie was giddy. She hadn't thought about just being able to be a mother and enjoying her family. She had been in survival mode way too long.

"It started when you said yes. My intentions when I told you I wanted to go with you were to provide for my family. We'll stay in the town you choose, and I'll provide for my family. As far as I'm concerned, you don't ever have to go back to that boarding house. You can be done starting today. No matter when we decide to leave town."

Sadie jumped up and down with glee.

"Oh my! Oh my! I like the sound of that. But I need to let Doris know I won't be coming back on Monday. I just can't disappear. And now, I have no fear of that conversation."

"So, then we are leaving on Monday? You ready to go?" Howard sounded hopeful.

"Well, maybe. Let's talk to Laura when she gets back just to make sure she is okay with that. I owe her time to say good-bye to Gus. But in the meantime, I'm going to go to the boarding house and tell Doris I'm done. I've definitely made that decision. I can't wait to see her face!" Sadie was giggling like a schoolgirl.

"Okay. I'll drive you and drop you off a couple blocks away. Then I'll come back and tell Laura where you are. And then come back and pick you up. We can take Gus and Laura out for ice cream when you are done."

Howard dropped Sadie off a couple of blocks from the boarding house. As Sadie walked up the sidewalk, she debated as to whether she should use the back door as required for the hired help, or if she should be bold and walk in the front door.

Sadie was bracing herself for a confrontation with Doris as she walked up the sidewalk.

'I no longer work here. Doris just doesn't know it yet. So I'm not the hired help. And what is she going to do to me? She couldn't fire me now if she wanted to. I'm using the front door.'

Sadie opened the screen door and went into the enclosed front porch. She tried to open the door into the main house and found that it was locked.

'That's strange.' Thought Sadie. It was summertime, but some of the college boys had already moved back in. 'I wonder how they get in and out. This door is never locked during the day.'

Sadie rang the doorbell and waited. After a few minutes, the door swung open to an empty hallway. Sadie walked in and looked behind the door for Doris.

Sadie gasped as she recognized Frank. He grabbed her roughly by the arm and threw her down the hallway. Sadie was so surprised that she didn't have time to catch herself before she hit the floor. Her head banged hard on the oak floor.

"Well, well. If it isn't my little loving wife. Welcome home, honey!"

As Sadie got to her feet, Frank pushed her down the hallway toward Doris's office. He had a butcher knife in his right hand, and the knuckles on his left hand were bloody.

Sadie stumbled into the office. Doris was crouched in a corner, with one hand tied to the overstuffed chair by the fireplace. Blood was dripping from her nose, and her upper lip was split open exposing bloody, broken teeth. Her bodice had been ripped open, and the camisole underneath ripped away from her breasts.

"I'm sorry, Sadie. I'm so sorry, Sadie. I didn't know." Doris's whimper could barely be heard. Frank took a step toward her, and she cowered, covering her face with her free arm.

"You should thank your friend here, Sadie. If it hadn't been for her, I wouldn't have any idea where you were." Frank grabbed Sadie's shoulder and pushed her down into Doris's office chair. He pulled a rope out of a satchel that was on the desk and tied Sadie tightly to the chair. Once Sadie was secure, he rolled her out into the middle of the room.

"Now that I have your undivided attention, where is Gus?" Frank leaned into Sadie's face and softly stroked her cheek with the pointed end of the butcher knife.

"He isn't here. And I won't tell you where he is." Sadie knew Frank would kill her. But he wasn't going to get Gus. No one knew where she lived, and Gus would be safe with Laura.

Frank responded by putting pressure to the tip of the butcher knife and running it from Sadie's ear to her chin, breaking the skin. The blood oozed out behind the blade as it cut.

Sadie turned her head away from Frank and his knife, wincing in pain.

"Do not turn away from me! I told you what would happen if you ever tried to leave me!" Frank pulled his fist back and struck Sadie hard across the face. Her head jerked back on her shoulders. Sadie's head slumped to her chest as she lost consciousness.

Sadie opened her eyes a few seconds later, only to find Frank waving the knife menacingly at her face. She was startled when she saw Howard quietly standing in the doorway of the room, several feet behind Frank. Frank did not seem to notice that there was someone else coming into the room.

Acting on instinct, Howard let out a war whoop and ran into the office. He jumped on Frank's back and knocked the knife out of Frank's hand before Frank could turn around.

"Yeeow!" yelled Frank. He reached behind him, grabbed Howard by the back of his shirt, and threw him on the floor in front of him.

"Who are you?"

Howard didn't answer. Instead, he got up, ran at Frank, and tackled him. Howard was on top of Frank, ready to pound him with his fists. Frank regained his senses in time to stop the first blow with his left hand and counter with a right-hand cross to Howard's chin. Frank rolled out from under Howard and pulled him up to his face by the front of his shirt. Frank punched Howard full in the face. Howard slumped to the floor.

"Who is that? He your new man? If so, he ain't worth much. But now he's going to have to die with you. You have one more chance. You tell me where Gus is, or I will kill him right here and now. You are going to die regardless. But if you want this man and that ugly wench over there to live, tell me where Gus is right now!" Frank walked over to Doris, jerked her head up with her hair, and laid the blade of the knife across her throat.

"Frank, no. Please." Sadie was weak and her voice barely audible. She couldn't let Frank kill Doris and Howard. But she couldn't let him have Gus either. She knew that

Frank would have to kill them all in order to escape cleanly. As soon as he knew where Gus was, they would all be dead.

"Please, Frank. Let her go. I'll tell you what you want to know. But if you kill her, you will never see your son again." She prayed desperately that an escape route would form in her mind.

Frank pulled the knife away from Doris's throat. Before he let go of her hair, he pulled her head back hard and then let go. Doris's head hit the back of the chair and popped like a watermelon. Her eyes floated back in her head, and she crumpled to the floor.

"It's about time, Sadie. What did you think you were doing when you ran away? Did you really think you could find a place where I wouldn't find you? You are stupid, stupid, stupid! And soon dead. Now tell me where Gus is!" Frank walked over to Sadie, placed both hands on the arm of the chair, and leaned into her face.

Sadie saw a flicker of movement out of the corner of her left eye. She turned toward the movement and saw Laura holding a heavy, lead crystal flower base over her head.

Frank turned to follow Sadie's glance. He stood and started to turn to face Laura. Laura was only a few steps away and closed the gap without hesitation.

Frank instinctively turned slightly as the vase was swung at his head. Laura was a good foot shorter than Frank, and he bent slightly to see what was coming at him. Laura swung the vase with strength and accuracy.

The vase smashed against the side of Frank's chin and neck. Frank stumbled backward but did not lose his balance.

A broken shard of glass stuck in Frank's neck. Surprised, Frank looked down at Laura and pulled the piece of glass out of his neck. Blood gushed from the side of his neck once the glass plug on his arterial wound had been removed. In just a few moments, Frank bled out and fell to the floor dead.

Laura slowly sunk to her knees where she had been standing. Her gaze was fixated on Frank's body. As the blood pool oozed across the floor, the horrific events of the last few seconds began to become real.

"Sadie, I think I killed him." Laura was still kneeling where she had stood, her hands clasped over her mouth, and her voice barely audible. She was still staring at the growing blood pool.

"Sadie, there's a lot of blood. Did I kill him? I didn't mean to. I just wanted to stop him from hurting you."

"Laura, look at me!" Sadie was still tied to her chair, feeling very helpless. She couldn't help anyone as long as she was held captive by the rope.

"Laura, look at me!" Sadie stomped her foot on the hardwood floor as she spoke hoping to jolt Laura back into reality.

Laura turned her head slowly and looked directly at Sadie. A flicker of recognition flashed across her fac.

"Oh, my! Sadie! Let me get you loose from those ropes!" Laura managed to get across the room to Sadie, still in a partial daze. She fumbled with the knots in the ropes and was finally able to free Sadie's legs and arms.

Sadie flung the ropes off her body as she stood up. She took Laura by the shoulders and looked into her eyes for a few moments. Assured that Laura was okay, Sadie rushed to Howard and knelt beside him.

"He's out cold. But he's still breathing regularly. I don't think anything is broken." Sadie shook Howard gently, but he didn't respond.

"I'll get some water and a cloth." Laura rushed down the hall to the kitchen. A couple of minutes later, she reappeared with a basin of water and a hand towel from the kitchen. Sadie was bending over Doris. She was laying very still, her body crumpled in the corner.

"Sadie, we need to help Howard. He comes first. Doris can wait."

Sadie took the basin of water from Laura, and the two of them knelt beside Howard. The cool water on Howard's forehead quickly brought him to consciousness. He opened his eyes and, with a painful groan, sat up slowly.

"Laura. Where is Gus? I left you both in the car."

"I left him in the car, Howard. We heard you yell, and then I came in. He was pretty scared. I don't think he'll leave the car." Laura was matter-of-fact in her reply. She was still in shock.

"Laura, call the police and then go to the car. Sit with Gus and make sure he knows that his mother is okay. But don't tell him anything. Sadie and I will take care of Doris and wait for the police." Howard pushed Laura gently to her feet and took charge.

Howard and Sadie knelt over Doris. She began to stir as Howard felt for broken bones.

"I suppose that man laying on the floor is Frank?" Howard directed his question to Sadie but did not turn to look at her.

"Yes." Sadie answered. It was all she was able to say. Doris was coming back to consciousness and beginning to moan loudly in pain.

CHAPTER TWELVE

THE INQUEST

Sunday evening Laura, Sadie and Howard lounged on Laura's front porch discussing the events of the weekend. Gus had been put to bed for the night, and the locusts were beginning to wake up the night air.

Sadie was especially quiet that evening. Laura and Howard had told Sadie the events leading up to Howard coming after her and then Laura coming into the boarding house herself. Howard had been concerned that Doris might be giving Sadie a hard time about quitting her job, and he didn't want Sadie to have to endure another minute of being disrespected by any of the women in town. He had intended to just sneak in and check on things and then go back to the car if things were okay. Howard was totally surprised to find Frank there and had lost all common sense when he saw Sadie hurt and bleeding. He had not even given a thought to whether he could subdue Frank. He just rushed in.

Laura knew Howard's plan and decided to come in to support Sadie and Howard when too much time had passed. She too felt the need to quietly come in after she heard Howard yell. Laura told Sadie that when she saw the scene, her mind instantly flashed back to her days of childhood abuse and the stories Sadie had told her of what Frank had done to her. Laura said she picked up the vase and swung at Frank instinctively, and was completely surprised when he slumped to the ground. She did not feel good about killing him, but she felt good about stopping a man who would continually hurt everyone around him.

The police had arrived at the boarding house on Saturday afternoon within fifteen minutes from the time Laura called them. After the police interviewed everyone, it was decided that an inquest needed to be held regarding Frank's death. It was scheduled for the following Wednesday morning. Sadie, Laura, Howard and Doris were all required to testify.

Doris had been taken to the hospital with multiple bruises and lacerations, a broken arm, and several cracked ribs. The medical team at the scene reset Howard's nose and informed him that he would have at least two black eyes. The cut on Sadie's face was superficial, and she was expected to heal with no scarring. Sadie had had worse beatings from Frank and knew her body would heal quickly. Both Howard and Sadie refused to be taken to the hospital.

The entire town was buzzing about Frank's death, and rumors were flying as to the events that may have precipitated it. The street in front of the boarding house had been lined with curious people by the time Sadie and Howard had walked out of the boarding house. Howard had had to take Sadie's arm to steady her when they walked back to Howard's car. The Galesburg newspaper reporters and cameras were everywhere, flashing snapshots within inches of their faces.

"I wonder how Frank found me. I had no clue whatsoever that he knew where I was. And he knew to go to the boarding house. I just don't know how he pulled that off." Sadie was truly puzzled. Both Laura and Howard rolled their eyes at Sadie.

"You can bet the Society had something to do with it. And Doris. How else would he have known to go directly to the boarding house? The police said he had just arrived in town Saturday morning, judging by the time stamp on his train ticket." Howard had stopped at the police station on his way to Laura's. He wanted to know what they knew. Partly to protect Sadie, partly to protect Laura, and partly to protect himself. As much as he was committed to Sadie, he still needed to be able to be out of town before the rumors started flying. He dreaded the day his family found out that he was gone for good.

"And I'm sure Mrs. Lear was involved. I've seen her do this many times. And just because Mrs. Lear wasn't attacking you directly Sadie, doesn't mean that she had forgotten about you. Once she had someone in her sights, she doesn't stop until someone is destroyed." Laura shuddered.

"Have you told Gus about his father yet?"

"No, not yet. I just told Gus that a bad man was there, and there was a fight. And that you saved us. He doesn't need to know anything more. He's only six. Someday I'll tell him that his father passed away. But not now. He doesn't ever have to know anything more than that." Sadie knew that Gus would eventually ask about his father. She could stall for a while and make up reasons why Frank wasn't with them. And when the time was right, she would tell him his father was dead. Now that Frank was dead, Gus would never have to know about the ugly side of Frank. And Sadie would make certain that Gus would never know that Laura had been the one who had killed his father.

"Sadie, I am so sorry! I didn't mean to kill him. I just wanted to stop him from hurting you. I just couldn't stand by and let it happen again."

"Laura you saved our lives! All of us! If you hadn't came in when you did, we would all be dead. You have nothing to feel guilty about. Besides, under normal circumstances, a glass vase upside the head would not have killed Frank. It was an accident." Sadie held Laura as she broke down and sobbed.

After several minutes, Laura blew her nose and wiped the tears from her eyes with the handkerchief that Howard had placed in her lap.

"That's the first time I've cried. I've been trying to bury my memories for all of these years. I thought if I pretended that it never happened to me it would go away." Tears started streaming down Laura's face again.

"Laura, do you have something that you need to tell us? You know we love and respect you. And there is no judgement here." Howard spoke softly.

"Yes, I have something about my past that I want to tell you. I need to tell you things that I never even told Saul." Laura took a deep breath.

"You both know that when I married Saul at sixteen, I was working and living at the Galesburg laundry. There was a storage room in the back of the laundry that the owners let me sleep in. I had been working there and living there for two years before I met Saul."

"So how did you get there? Did you lose your family, or did you run away like me?" Sadie was pretty sure that Laura had run away.

"My family lived in Macomb, Illinois. I had an older brother and a younger sister. My father started to sexually abuse me when I was about eight. At that time, I didn't know that this behavior was not normal. He was always gentle and always told me it was his way of showing me how much he loved me. So I just accepted it."

"One day when I was ten, my father and my uncle were drinking heavily. My father sent me to the kitchen for another whiskey bottle, as I was the only other family member home at the time. My father was so drunk he ordered me to sit on his lap. And then he began touching me and bragging to my uncle about it, who was watching the whole sordid scene. Before the afternoon was over, my father and my uncle took turns with me. There was no gentleness and definitely no words of kindness."

"They hurt me so bad that I was in bed for two days and bled for a week. I tried to tell my mother about it, and she just slapped my face and told me I was an ungrateful little tramp. Then she told my uncle what I had tried to say. And I then received a severe beating from him so that I would understand what would happen if I tried to tell anyone else."

"This went on until I was fourteen. I was raped and then beaten at least once a week. My mother not only turned a blind eye to it all, she would reinforce the beatings if I so much as shed a tear."

"I had no intentions of running away when I did. It just sort of happened. One afternoon, my uncle had raped and beaten me in the neighbor's cornfield. Then he just left me there and walked away. The beating was so severe that I was disoriented and didn't know how to get home."

"So I just started walking. I walked until I was exhausted and then just lay down and slept where I was. And then got up and walked again. I was sleeping on the back steps of the laundry a few days later when the owners found me. They fed me, gave me a place to sleep and a job. Two years later I married Saul. My life started when I married Saul."

"But why didn't you call the police or tell someone when you got to Galesburg? You were safe here." Howard asked.

"Was I really safe, Howard? I was only fourteen years old. Who was going to believe me? My father was the county magistrate at the time. Plus, I would have had to go back to my home county and face him again. And also face my mother and my uncle. I considered myself absolutely fortunate to have found Galesburg and Saul. I certainly wasn't going to temp fate." Laura was walking back and forth across the porch, allowing her words and admissions to finally begin the healing process.

"Now I understand why you couldn't deal with the Galesburg Ladies Aid Society. It was kind of like going back home, wasn't it?" Sadie had a renewed, tremendous respect for Laura. She now understood why she had always felt such a strong bond with Laura. They were kindred spirits.

"Yes, Sadie. Mrs. Lear and the ladies were too much like my mother. Although she wasn't Mrs. Lear at the time, she was single and trolling for her man of influence when I married Saul."

"So why did you have to tell your story now, Laura? It's all in the past and no longer affects your world."

"That's not entirely true, Howard. I never told my story. And I never healed. I just buried it in the back of my mind and closed off my heart to everyone and everything but Saul. I realize now that made for a very lonely life. I let my uncle and my father continue to abuse me by hiding myself from the world. I could have had so much more in my life. And been a much better wife to Saul."

"I always had one regret. and that was I didn't take my sister with me when I left. She was twelve at the time. And I always wondered if they just moved on to her. I've always felt guilty about that."

"So you see, when I saw Frank and what he had done to Doris and Howard, and what he was about to do to Sadie, I lost control. I didn't mean to kill him. But I saw my sister tied to that chair. I couldn't let it happen again. I don't remember anything between seeing my sister in the chair and Frank pulling the piece of glass out of his neck." Laura smiled ruefully at the two of them.

"Laura, you are like a sister to me! I had always felt like you were a great replacement of my mother until now. But after hearing your story, we are definitely sisters. We have a bond deeper than blood." Sadie and Laura hugged for a long time.

Howard arrived early Wednesday morning to drive Laura, Sadie and Gus to the courthouse. He dropped them off a couple of blocks away and then drove home to pick up his wife.

The Knox County Courthouse faced east onto Cherry Street. The formidable exterior was limestone and spread over two square blocks of land covered with huge shade trees and walkways. Laura and Sadie lounged among the century-old oaks on the courthouse lawn while they waited for the hearing to start.

"See, over there, Sadie. That building is City Hall. That's where Saul and I were married. The building was brand new at the time. Saul and I were one of the first couples to be married there. I haven't been in that building since."

"Laura, you really need to get out more. You are much too young to retire to the porch. Have you ever thought of marrying again?" Sadie wanted Laura to have a full life. She was still young and deserved absolute happiness.

"Oh, I don't know. No, I've never considered marrying again. Saul was fifteen years older than me. He died suddenly of a heart attack. And he was young. He wasn't even sixty years old. Up until you and Gus came into my life, I thought I had my shot at happiness. And I was content to live with my memories. Now I'm not so sure. You two have given me some spark back." Laura smiled at Sadie and squeezed Gus's hand.

"I don't think I could go back to my old life. I might just have to do some traveling." Laura winked at Sadie.

People were beginning to congregate on the courthouse lawn. Howard and his wife had arrived along with Doris. Mrs. Lear was also entering the courthouse along with her daughter, Grace Henderson.

"Well, I see the old goat just couldn't stay away. I'm sure she had something to do with Frank being in Galesburg. Probably came today to evaluate her handiwork." Laura spoke with much bitterness.

"Mrs. Lear? You really think she had something to do with this? I'd find that hard to believe. She hasn't said two words to me since the banquet for Carl Sandburg. You really don't like her, do you Laura?" Sadie was surprised at Laura's bitterness. She also knew there had to be a logical reason behind Frank finding her at the boarding house. But she didn't want to guess and blame a possible innocent. What was done was done. Sadie just wanted to move past it.

"There's a history between us. And Mrs. Lear doesn't have to speak to you to put a mark on you. But I guess it really doesn't matter. It's pretty much over now, isn't it, Sadie? Let's go inside and get this over with. Let's finish and get on with the good stuff." Sadie agreed with Laura as she set Gus down under a big oak tree with his colors. Admonishing him to stay put until she was back, Sadie then took Laura's arm and they walked silently into the courthouse together.

The sheriff's office and the courtrooms were on the second floor. Laura and Sadie checked in at the sheriff's office to let the court officers know they were there. The court clerk led them to the third courtroom and instructed them to wait outside the courtroom until their name was called.

Sadie and Laura sat on one of the wooden benches outside the courtroom door. Howard and Doris were already sitting on the bench across the hall. Howard smiled at them when they sat down. Doris was studying the tile floor and did not look up.

Sadie was called into the courtroom first. The courtroom was small and crowded with furniture. The judge's bench was in the corner of the small room with the witness stand right next to it. There was a long oak table in the middle of the room for the lawyers and court officials and a jury box with barely enough room for six jurors. There were only three short rows of benches in the back that might seat twenty-five people at the most.

The room was full to capacity. Seated at the lawyer's table were the sheriff and two deputies, the county coroner, the court bailiff, and the court recorder. Although there was no jury appointed for the inquest hearing, the jury box and the benches in the back of the room were overflowing with spectators. Sadie recognized Mrs. Lear, Grace Henderson, and a couple of other ladies from the Society. Sadie surmised that the woman sitting to the left of Mrs. Lear was Howard's wife. She had dark green eyes, jet-black hair, and a prominent, crooked nose. She was a tall, big-boned woman, as Mrs. Lear's head barely came to the woman's shoulders. The woman was not immediately handsome, but she did have a stately air about the way she held her head.

"State your full name for the record, please." The court bailiff was standing in front of Sadie with a large, black Bible in his left hand.

"Sadie Alza Adams." Sadie spent the better part of an hour answering questions about her relationship with Frank and the details of exactly what happened at the boarding house. Sadie was truthful in her responses but didn't offer information that wasn't asked for. Her relationship with Howard was not relevant to the matter at hand, especially with Howard's wife sitting in the audience. If Howard wanted to offer the information, he could do so when it was his turn to testify. Doris was called in next and was in the courtroom for over an hour. Howard took his turn, and Laura was last.

It was Mid-afternoon before the hearing was over. The judge determined that Laura acted in self-defense and ruled Frank's death as accidental. As the courtroom emptied, Mrs. Lear marched past Sadie and Laura with her head held high, even as her daughter stopped to talk.

"Sadie, I'd like to offer my condolences. Not just for the events of last weekend and your husband's death. I want to apologize for the City of Galesburg. I'm sure your time here with us has not been all that pleasant." Grace Henderson was sincere in her apology and extended her hand in friendship. Grace studied Laura's face and felt some recognition.

"I think I know you. Weren't you Saul Blumenthal's wife? I used to see you on the college campus with him. I would see Saul at Society functions, and my mother always talked about him a lot. But I've never seen you around a lot."

"Yes, Grace. I was Saul's wife. I'm still Saul's wife. Saul passed away a few years ago. And I did attend Society functions when I first married Saul, but you were not even born then. Your mother and some of the other members made it so uncomfortable that I stopped attending."

"Well, Laura, I would really like you to consider joining us again. I am heading up a campaign to remove my mother from power. This last episode was the final straw. Even though the judge never asked Doris if she knew how it came to be that Sadie's husband was in town, I know without a doubt that my mother was involved somehow. I've seen it too many times before. And I've stood aside and let it happen too many times. Well, no more. I've been talking to the ladies in the Society, and there are only a handful that rally with my mother. And we are going to remove them from office. And if they don't become decent, respectful human beings, we will be barring them from the Society and Society functions."

"Grace, you have my blessings and my support! This should have been done many years ago. As soon as you have your Society cleaned up, let me know. I would love to join in and help out the community."

Laura and Sadie gathered up Gus on the courthouse lawn. They saw Howard leave with his wife but knew he would come and find them soon. Gus was whining with hunger, so Laura and Sadie decided that it would be a good day to grab some homemade sandwiches at the National Biscuit Company. It was only a few blocks away.

As they headed down the sidewalk, Sadie heard someone calling her name. She turned to see Doris slowly limping towards her.

"I guess I have to talk to this woman one more time. Laura, you and Gus go ahead, and I'll catch up with you. There's no need for Gus to have to wait any longer to eat." Sadie waved good-bye to Gus and then waited for Doris to catch up with her.

"Sadie, is that your son walking with Laura? He is certainly a nice-looking young man."

"Yes, that's my son. He is six years old. Doris, I'm sorry I lied to you on my job application. But at the time, I was desperate and needed that job." Sadie still felt a little intimidated by Doris and still had a need to do the right thing.

"You have no need to apologize. I fully understand why you did what you did. I would have done the same had I been in your shoes. I'm the one that needs to apologize."

"What do you need to apologize for?" Sadie was more curious than anything else. She didn't need to know what was behind Frank being in Galesburg. But she never expected to hear Doris trying to apologize about anything. If Doris wanted to talk, Sadie would listen.

"When you first came to the boarding house to apply for the housekeeping job, I was so jealous of you. You were so young and so pretty. I was almost married once. But before my man could pop the question a young socialite, who you reminded me of, blew through town and took him away from me."

"That's it? That's what you wanted to apologize for?"

"No, there is more. Mrs. Lear and the Society never let me forget that I was a spinster and they weren't. My life was so lonely, and I wanted the happy married life that I thought they had. And I always looked up to them because they were married and had children. I would have done anything to gain their approval. In fact, I did anything that Mrs. Lear asked me to do. Even though I always knew someone would get hurt. As long as it wasn't me, I didn't care. Sadie, when Mrs. Lear and I were searching for the dark secrets that we knew you must have, I never once dreamed that your husband would come back here and that he would be so violent." Doris was broken and humbled. All the while she talked, she kept her head own, never meeting Sadie's gaze.

"Mrs. Lear kept insisting that you had a husband somewhere. She was so jealous of your beauty that she couldn't imagine someone like you being alone. And she was so worried that her husband would find you attractive and leave her for you. And I also had some jealousy. You reminded me of the young woman that took my fiancé away from me years ago."

"Mrs. Lear convinced me to place an ad in the New York City paper asking for responses from you relatives. We had tried the papers here in the Midwest, and had received nothing. So, we branched out. Frank responded. But he said he was your brother and he had to get in touch with you due to a family emergency. Sadie, I never dreamed it would come out like this. I am so sorry!"

"You were behind Frank coming here? Doris! How could you be so cruel! And all the time you were pretending to be my friend." Sadie was angry. This was too much. She couldn't be nice to Doris for another minute.

"And I suppose you were behind the awful things that were done and said at the banquet too?"

"Well, I knew Mrs. Lear was going to do something. But I didn't know what it was. I was just hoping that, as the hired help, you would consider the invitation as a courtesy only and not show up. But when you did show up, I felt I had no choice but to do Mrs. Lear's bidding. I did try to tell you to go home. Remember?"

"So, I should thank you for that? Doris, you still don't get it. Why didn't you stand up for me? You knew nothing about me, and yet you judged me because I was younger and prettier than you. You did the same thing to me that the Society had been doing to you all your life. You, of all people, should know how that feels! That is so wrong!" Sadie was no longer intimidated by Doris. She was very angry and wanted her to feel some of the hurt that she had felt.

"Yes, Sadie. That was wrong. I know that now. What I did to you and what I allowed the Society to do to you was absolutely unconscionable. And it almost cost me my life." Doris shifted on her cane, taking her weight off her bruised hip.

"As a woman, how could you do this to another woman? You've felt the pain that Mrs. Lear and the Society can inflict. How could you, in good conscience, let it continue?

And be part of it?" Sadie just could not understand how another woman could be so hurtful.

"I guess I just got used to it and considered it normal. It's been so long since I felt good about myself. I was jealous of you, Sadie. I wanted you to hurt the way I did. Until Frank showed up, I just thought you must have the perfect life. The life I wanted but didn't think I could have."

"And you only felt a few hours of Frank's beatings and terrorizing. Try nine years of him! Talk about the perfect life!"

"Sadie, you are a strong, wonderful woman. You are much stronger and much more capable that I will ever be. And I do want you to know that I'm done with Mrs. Lear and the Society. I'm not going to be a part of it anymore. I'm going to be a good woman. From now on I will respect everyone, no matter where they live, how they live or where they came from. You taught me that life is precious and beautiful for everyone." Doris was looking directly into Sadie's eyes now.

"What do you want from me, Doris? Those are just words, and I've seen your handiwork. A man died because of your handiwork. I'm done with you." Sadie was finally free of the chains she had let the Society bind her with the day she arrived in Galesburg.

"I want your forgiveness. Someday. I know you can't see your way to it right now. But maybe someday you can find it in your heart to forgive me. And I want you to come back and work for me. I promise you that you will receive the utmost respect from me and anyone who comes into the boarding house. And as of today, the Galesburg Ladies Aid

Society will no longer hold any meetings at the boarding house."

"Doris, I'm done. The reason I came to the boarding house last Saturday was to tell you that I quit. I'm leaving Galesburg and not looking back."

"Well, then. I understand. And I wish you all the luck in the world and a wonderful, happy life."

Sadie was up early on Thursday morning. Today was the day that she, Howard, and Gus were leaving for Iowa. Gus was still sleeping as Sadie and Laura padded around in the kitchen. Laura had fixed a big breakfast of ham, eggs, and toast.

"Should we get Gus up or let him sleep for a while?" asked Laura as she cracked the eggs into the skillet.

"Let's let him sleep until he wakes up. He's got an exciting day ahead of him, and I'm sure he's not going to sleep through any of it." Sadie knew that Gus would be watching the world go by from the back seat of the car. Taking a road trip was new to him, and he would be so excited that he wouldn't be able to sit still.

"Have you told him yet that you two are leaving Galesburg?"

"No. I wanted him to get some rest. If I had told him we were leaving before today, he would have been anxiously waiting. I want this to be fun for him, and I don't want him to even think about not being with you until he has something else to think about. I don't know if that's being cruel to Gus or not, but I think it's the best thing for him. He thinks in the moment, so I want to give him something new in the moment so he doesn't have time to dwell on anything." Sadie popped the last bite of toast in her mouth and then got up to put some ham in the oven to keep warm for Gus.

"Well, I agree it's probably the right approach for Gus. But not for me. It won't give me much time to say good-bye. Before you yank him out of my arms." The tears were welling up in Laura's eyes.

"Are you sure you have to go, Sadie? Frank is gone now, so he can't hurt you. And everyone knows you have a son. And Doris is willing to give you your job back. I don't think anyone in town holds anything against you now. After yesterday I think they really respect you."

"Yes, Laura. I have to go. Frank is not an issue anymore, which is wonderful no matter where I am. And yes, I could go back to work for Doris, and I'm sure things would be much more pleasant. But what about the baby? I'm going to start showing in a few months, and then the tongues will start wagging again. All that will do is give Mrs. Lear and her cronies a reason to say 'I told you so'." Sadie did not want to knowingly place herself in the position to start the cruelty again.

"But that's a couple of months away. You still have choices, Sadie. We could think of some story to cover that. I don't know what just yet. Worst case, you could just quit and stay here with me. I have enough money to support us both. We could just continue as we are. If we stay in this small area of town, you could still be a recent widow. We could change your name, and no one would ever connect you to the news stories. I could even tell people that you are my sister or cousin or some close relative that's come to live with me."

"Laura, I'm really going to miss you too!" Sadie gave Laura a big hug and wiped away the stray tears on Laura's cheeks.

"But what about Howard? He can't stay in this town and be a father to this baby. And he can't keep coming over here every day. It won't be long until someone figures it out." Sadie paused, thinking about how hurt her children would be if they had the time to develop a relationship with Howard and then have him taken away from them.

"And I'm tired of living a lie, Laura. I want to hold my head up in the next town. I want to be able to live a normal life as a wife and mother. I've never had that, and I really, really want it."

"But Howard is married. You are, in effect, running away with a married man and having his baby. How are you going to explain that to your new neighbors? Isn't that still living a lie?" Laura had her arms crossed in front of her chest in a self-defense stance.

"What's so wrong with just admitting you had an affair if someone asks? After all, it is 1930. Most people now realize that everyone makes mistakes. Two years from now, no one will even remember who you were. Let alone question the fatherless state of your children. Then you are no longer living a lie. You are just not sharing the details of your life with the nosy creatures that inhabit every town and every neighborhood."

"But what about Howard? Staying in town will not work for him." Sadie had to admit that Laura's argument made sense. Up to a point.

"What about Howard? So far, no one, including him, has been affected by his actions but you. You owe him nothing. You owe yourself happiness. And the ability to sleep peacefully at night. Sadie, you are free of Frank. You are free to do whatever you want to do. I just need to know that you understand how free you are to choose right now. And I need to know that the decisions you are making are decisions that will be the best for you. Don't make decisions that will be the best for everyone else while you are left out in the cold again. Including me, Sadie. I desperately want you to stay. But more importantly, I want to see my Sadie standing on her own two feet, making her own decisions."

"I hear what you are saying, Laura. And I completely agree with you. And I am pretty sure that my decision to leave is based on what I want for myself and my children." Sadie was pensive and slow to respond back to Laura. She had never really stopped to evaluate her reasons for leaving, especially now that her circumstances had changed.

"I know I want to be with Howard. Which means leaving. I know I want a normal life as a wife and mother. Which means leaving. I know I can't work at the boarding house past my fifth or sixth month. Which means leaving if I want Howard to support us. I know I want a home of my own, even though living with you has been so wonderful. Which means leaving. I know I want my children to have a positive male influence in their lives. Which means leaving. And I know I will miss you terribly, Laura!" Sadie took a deep breath. She was relieved. For a minute she was afraid her reasons for leaving wouldn't stand up under any type of scrutiny.

"Okay, then. This conversation is over. I won't bring it up again. But I will tell you that you will always have a home here. No matter what. Never feel like you are trapped in a life you don't want. You can always come home. And I expect to get a letter from you as soon as you are settled. I will be visiting my adopted grandson and my new grandbaby as often as possible!" Laura had just finished her sentence when Gus came bursting into the kitchen. He had his shirt half-buttoned over his pajama bottoms, and his hair was still tousled from sleep.

Howard pulled up to the curb before Gus had finished his breakfast. As Sadie helped Howard pack the car, she had to know what he had told his wife.

"How did you leave things with your wife? What did you tell her?"

"I didn't specifically tell her anything. I packed my car and then drove over to the house to say good-bye. I kissed each sleeping child good-bye. I don't know if I will ever see them again. And as soon as my father figures out what I have done, he will excommunicate me from the family. I will never see a dime of my father's fortune. It will all go to my younger brother."

"You didn't tell you wife anything about us?"

"Once she figures out that I left with you, her wrath will be unstoppable. Between her and her mother, my children will be taught that I am evil and languishing in prison somewhere. Which isn't much different than it is now. So not much will change there."

"How will she support herself and her children? Howard, you do have a responsibility to your children." Sadie was getting concerned at how easily Howard could just pick up and leave without saying a word.

"My wife and I have a sizeable amount of money put away. We aren't rich by any means, but we live quite comfortably. And she should still get another month of commissions from my job. These savings, combined with assistance from my father, will provide very well for them for a long time."

"So, It didn't bother you to just walk away from all of that? Howard, we don't even know where we are going. All we have is what is in this car and in your wallet."

"Sadie, we will be fine. I am free to love the woman I choose and free to start a great life with my little family. No, it doesn't bother me. It gives me great joy to begin this new life with you." Howard walked over to Sadie, hugged her tight, and kissed the top of her head. They walked back into the house hand in hand.

"Well, are we ready to go?" Howard directed his questions to Sadie and Gus, who were sitting at the kitchen table.

"Go where? Are we doing something special today?" Sadie could see that Gus was excited.

"Yes, Gus. We are doing something very special today. We are going to find our new home. You and me and Howard. We are going on a road trip. Another great adventure." Sadie answered for Howard. She wanted to make sure that Gus heard exactly what she wanted him to hear. And nothing more.

"Is Laura coming?"

"No, dear. I'm staying here. But I will come and visit you as soon as you get settled in your new town. Then you can tell me how much fun you had on your road trip and show me your new bedroom." Laura hugged Gus tight and hid her tears.

"Is Daddy going to be able to find us?" Sadie took a deep breath before she answered him.

"Honey, Daddy is really busy off doing other things. He is okay with us leaving with Howard. But you won't see him for a long, long time."

"So, little buddy, can I be your dad in the meantime? I would love to have a son just like you." Howard butted into the conversation before Sadie could stop him.

"Okay, Howard. You can do that. But do I have to call you Dad?"

"No, son. You can call me anything you want. Whatever feels good to you. Now go get your stuff so I can put it in the car. Don't forget your ball and glove. And when we have the car packed, I have a surprise for you. It will make this adventure even more memorable." Howard gently pushed Gus in the direction of his bedroom. Sadie smiled appreciatively at Howard. It was going to be nice to have a whole family.

Before long the car was packed and ready to go. Laura had made ham sandwiches for them to take on the trip, and Gus made sure they were in the backseat next to him. Howard started up the car, waved quickly at Laura standing on the porch, and patted Sadie on the knee.

"Well, sweetheart, we're off. Off to a new, wonderful life. You won't be disappointed. I promise." With those words, Howard winked at Sadie, put the car in gear and let it roll down the street.

    Sadie and Gus waved to Laura until her house faded out of sight. Sadie had the Iowa map on her lap, and Gus was in the back seat with his face glued to the window. Howard was beside her, gently and respectfully moving their lives forward. A new life was growing in her belly, pushing against the waistband of her skirt. Her life was moving forward. The momentum had begun, and Sadie looked forward to the ride.

CHAPTER THIRTEEN

SNEAKING OUT OF TOWN

Sadie and Howard drove through the back streets of Galesburg in silence. Sadie had not seen this part of town and was mesmerized by the difference in economics. The houses were smaller, closer together, and unpainted. Scattered among the blocks of small, narrow houses were large vacant lots of sand, dirt and rocks. Lots of middle-school children were in the lots playing kick ball and just hanging out

"What part of town is this, Howard? I don't think I have been here before. Everything looks so pressed down, and so, well, poor. Are we still in Galesburg?" Sadie wasn't concerned for her safety, but she was hoping that they had no car trouble and this could just be a drive through.

"Well, I don't know if most people will call this the slum area or not. And yes, we are still in Galesburg. We are on the North side of town." Howard patted Sadie's hand in a caressing way, then deftly turned the car to the left. Down a badly maintained gravel road.

"You seem to know where you are going, Howard. Do you have clients here?"

"No, Sadie. No clients here. Friends, yes. I went to school with a lot of the people who live down here. And I visit quite often. Brings back good memories. These are just normal, hard-working people with no pretense. And I like that."

"So are we visiting someone here? Do you have a need to say good-bye to old friends?

"Not good-bye, Sadie. I would say It's more like 'I am ready now.' Remember the surprise that I promised Gus? This would be it. And hopefully you'll find the surprise a pleasant one also." With that, Howard turned into the next vacant lot and pulled alongside a pickup truck.

"Wait here. I'll be right back." Howard jumped out of the car and walked into the storage building that was in front of the old pickup. A few minutes later Howard emerged through the doorway with another man. The man was taller than Howard, and had plain features. His skin was suntanned and dark, with black hair and deep brown eyes. His white teeth glistened through his smile as he held out his hand and extended it to Sadie through the car window.

"You must be Sadie, Jack's girl. Good to meet you. I'm Fernando." Sadie shook his hand, and allowed Fernando to help her out of the car.

"Gus, just stay in the car for a minute. Please?" Sadie did not want to try to explain to Gus what was going on until she knew herself. And she needed to know who these people were. She totally did not understand what was going on here.

Jack shook Fernando's hand heartily. As the men hugged each other, Sadie watched in amazement as a small group of men and teenage boys gathered around them. After Jack shook hands and chatted with each man, he turned to Sadie with an impish grin on his face.

"Well, Sadie, we are here. First stop on the way to our new home."

"Who are these people Howard? And why do they call you Jack?"

"I grew up with these men, Sadie. Or rather we all became friends over the years. They lived on the other side of town from me and I used to frequent the area when I was bored and out walking the town. They looked like they were having so much fun playing kickball and football in the vacant lots that I joined in. And the rest is history. We all became friends and I still come down here and visit often. These are true, life-long friends, Sadie. My true friends."

"And why do they call you Jack? That is not your name."

"Oh, that. Well, Fernando had a serious lisp when we met, and he couldn't say Howard. So he just started calling me Jack instead. And it stuck. I don't think anyone here knows my real name."

Gus was looking out the car window as Jack explained the scene before them. Sadie then relaxed and pulled Gus out of the car and around to the front of her.

"It is okay, Gus. These people are good friends of Howard's. But they call him Jack instead of Howard. I think we all came here to say goodbye to them."

"Well, not exactly Sadie. I cannot take the only family car with me. My wife and kids will need it. I don't need to stay here, but the car does. So I have a plan. And hopefully Sadie, you and Gus are okay with my plan. Gus, remember the surprise I promised you? This is it."

"I don't understand, Howard."

"Well, I thought we should leave my car here and hop this potato truck to Iowa. Fernando's friends will get the car back to my family. And we will have an adventure on our trip!"

"And why did you not explain this to me earlier, Howard? It's kind of important information to leave out of our plans, don't you think? And then just spring it on us at the last minute."

"I wasn't sure you would allow it, Sadie. And I didn't know how to make you understand this thing I needed to do."

"Howard, I know you are used to not talking, and just doing. But you need to get over that! It's not just you that this affects. It's all of us."

"I know, Sadie. And I'm sorry I didn't tell you earlier. I really will work on this communication thing – later. But for now, I guess I was hoping Gus would love it and talk you into it."

"Do not pit my son against me, Howard. And furthermore, as a couple we need to present a united front." Sadie was mortified. Howard, on the other hand, was smiling as he studied his perfectly polished, wing-tipped shoes.

"It will be an adventure, Sadie. I will help with the potato crop on our way to Iowa, and that will pay our way plus get us some additional cash. And, Gus can even help us in the fields if he wants. These are great people, Sadie. Loyal people. They will take good care of us and get us where we need to be." By this time Gus had left Sadie's side and was checking out the pickup. One of the older boys had hoisted Gus up and put him in the bed of the back of the pickup. Gus was smiling and laughing and having a great time. Sadie had never seen Gus so relaxed and confident among strangers.

"I don't know, Howard. This is a major change in our plans. We need to be settled somewhere before this baby comes. And while I can still move around like a normal person. How long will this trip take? Especially if we have to harvest and sell potatoes along the way. "

"Maybe six weeks. Maybe eight. We still have time. You still have time. And it will be a wonderful adventure for Gus. You can sit up front in the cab, and Gus and I will sit in the back with the crew. You can work, or not, with us. It's your choice. It will be fun! And these people will take very good care of us. Very good care of you. Fernando knows you are carrying my child." The look on Howard's face was so impish and childlike that Sadie had to laugh.

"Howard, that's the first time I have heard you openly talk to anyone other than Laura and me about being a new father! How can I yell at you for that?"

"So it's okay? My plan? We can take the truck ride and work our way to Iowa?" Howard seemed so excited that Sadie just couldn't argue anymore.

"Howard, this is not what I had envisioned. It was the farthest thing from my mind. In fact, I don't think I could have thought about this if I wanted to. It's not normal. But, on the other hand, what is normal What a way to leave town. No one their wildest dreams would ever think to look in this direction. So, yes! Let's do it! Oh my god, the stories I am going to have to tell my grandchildren!"

"I love you, woman! I have looked for you all my life, and here you are in front of me! With me! Thank you! I will love you forever after this! My conscience is now clear, and I can walk this new adventure with you and Gus forever! Life begins now. Come on, Gus. Let me show you the new ride we are taking for a few weeks. And tell you about the surprising adventure we are going to love!" With that, Gus and Howard looked over the pickup truck, the truck bed, and kicked the tires just because they could. Sadie laughed gleefully as Howard introduced Gus to Fernando and all the farm workers that were coming along on the trip.

Most of the farm workers were young men, and took Gus under their wing immediately. Sadie rode in the front of the truck, but Gus rarely sat with her. Most often he was in the back with the others, sitting on the potato sacks. Howard usually rode in the back with Gus, which comforted Sadie. Howard and Gus were bonding quickly and Sadie was thankful for that.

It was now late September and the leaves on the trees were starting to change. Sadie was content with where she was in her life, and was enjoying the people around her. Fernando got Sadie involved in the planning sessions as she had a very organized head. Fernando appreciated her planning knowledge, and felt like he had a partner. Sadie knew they had three more farms to dig potatoes at, and they would be in Eldora by the end of the month.

Eldora was the city that Sadie and Howard had chosen to put their roots down in. It was the last stop for the potato truck, and from all indications seemed to be the perfect small town to raise a family in. Sadie was just hoping it was more open and less judgmental than Galesburg was.

Howard and Gus were in the back of the truck with the other workers. As they pulled out onto the farm road towards the next potato field, Sadie's body bounced when they hit the first rut in the dirt road.

"Slow down, Fernando! These ruts are going to be the death of me." Sadie grabbed the door handle and braced her feet on the floor boards. The next rut was small, but made Sadie extremely queasy.

"I don't know about this, Fernando. I'm getting sick to my stomach hitting all these bumps. Maybe you could pull over and I'll walk the rest of the way?" Fernando looked at Sadie with concern as he pulled over to the side of the road.

"Sure, Sadie. You can walk if you like. But are you okay? You never seemed to even notice the ruts before. And it's quite a walk to the other field."

"I'm going to go slow, Fernando. And don't wait on me. I know you have a schedule to keep. I'll be okay. I'll just walk slow. I need even ground underneath my feet."

"You okay, Sadie? Why are you getting out?" Howard looked worried, and jumped out of the back of the truck to help Sadie.

"I'm okay, Jack. It's just that these ruts are making me sick to my stomach. I asked Fernando to pull over so I could walk the rest of the way." Sadie squeezed Howard's hand and smiled weakly as he helped her to the side of the road.

"It still feels odd calling you Jack. That is so far from your real name. But no one here seems to know you other than by Jack." Sadie gigged a little, and then instinctively put her hand to her stomach.

"Oh, Sadie. I don't think they know my real name. And Jack sounds more like who I am anyway. I'm just a common man in love with a beautiful woman. So call me Jack. Or call me Howard. Whatever you like. The name does not change who I am, or who I am in love with. You, okay now, Sadie?"

"I'm okay. I'm okay, Jack. Just let me walk a little. I might sit under those trees up there and wait for you all to finish. But don't worry. I'll be fine." Sadie waved at Jack and headed for the trees. She knew that she just needed to sit for a while.

This pregnancy was a little different then when Sadie was pregnant with Gus. She would be winded easily with Gus. But not until later in the pregnancy. This tiring easily, and nausea, worried her a bit. But she was healthy and strong. She was eating and sleeping well so her head told her there was nothing to worry about. As Sadie lowered herself to the grass under the trees, she breathed a sigh of relief. The grass was cool, and the shade felt good. Sadie closed her eyes in contentment.

Within minutes, Sadie felt a gentle touch on her shoulder. She looked over to see Gus standing next to her.

"We are done now, Mama. Are you ready to go? Are you okay? I can help you up if you want me to." Sadie smiled and patted Gus on the shoulder.

"Wow. That was quick. I must have taken a little nap. Yes, please. Help me up, if you don't mind." Sadie took Gus's hand and put her other hand on the tree beside her. As she stood up, she felt a sharp pain in her side. Instinctively she moved her hand to her lower abdomen in pain. As she stood very still, with her eyes closed, the pain lessened.

"Wow, Gus. I think I stood up too quickly. I'm sorry about that."

"Stay here, Mama. I'll be right back." And with that, Gus dropped Sadie's hand and ran toward the truck. Sadie watched from under the tree as Gus stopped Jack and Fernando. And then all three of them started running towards her. Jack got there first.

"Sadie, you okay? Gus is really worried about you."

"I'm okay, Jack. I'm just really, really tired. I'm so tired that I'm dizzy." Sadie was still clinging to the tree. She was afraid if she let go she would fall.

"Maybe riding in the truck is too hard on your body, Sadie. Especially in your condition. And we've been pounding the roads pretty heavy the last couple of weeks. I know we only have a couple more weeks in the season, but do we need to slow down? If we need to, we need to. No questions asked. We still have time to finish the season well. Just a yes or no. I'll do whatever you think we need to do Sadie." Sadie could tell that Fernando was nervous about her being ill, and that he also had her best interest in mind.

"That's a great suggestion, Jack. And thank you Fernando for assuring me that we are not running behind. I think I'll take you both up on the offer. And for now, I'll just rest here by the creek and enjoy the scenery while you finish the other field. By the time you all get back later this afternoon, I'll feel much better. I just need to stop for a while and rest."

"We can dig the rest of the potatoes we have on schedule for today. And then get these potatoes to the store in Union. It's only a few miles from here and we would be back before sunset. You can stay here Sadie, and rest. We have water we can leave for you, and extra blankets we can leave with you. We will finish up and then we will be back." Sadie smiled as she watched the boys pulling out blankets and water for her. It looked like the decision had already been made for her as everyone knew what to do, and they couldn't even hear the conversation. But that was awesome to her. This will be a good group of people she was with; they took care of each other, and her, very well.

Sadie leaned against the tree and let Jack and Fernando get her settled with the blankets and the water. She watched the truck bump on down the dirt road. Gus had decided to go with Jack and the boys in order to speed the process along. Sadie was going to miss him while he was gone. But Gus was growing up, and Sadie was pleased that the bond between Gus and Jack was growing. And, she was also glad to be alone for a while. She was going to enjoy the rest.

Sadie spread out the blankets a little more under the shady tree next to the creek, and settled in for the afternoon. She was letting the chirping of the birds lull her into sleep when the cramping started

At first the cramping was light, and kept Sadie from falling asleep. So she rolled over on her side to take the weight off her back and stomach. The cramping came with sharp, piercing pains that ravaged through her body and sat her straight up from her fetal position. Sadie closed her eyes and took deep, slow breaths to calm her fears. And to alleviate the pain.

But it wasn't working. Each breath in caused the pain to go deeper. The pain and cramping was so sharp that it brought tears to Sadie's eyes. She needed to find a better position to find a little more comfort. But it wasn't possible to escape from the pain. As Sadie lay on one of the blankets, all she could do was concentrate on dulling the pain. Sadie wiggled and writhed as she wiped the tears from her eyes. Her body was spasming with each sharp and long cramp. Then she felt it.

A warm liquid had begun to flow between her legs. Sadie didn't move her body, but reached down between her legs to feel the fluid. When she looked at her finger, Sadie gasped in dismay. Her fingers were covered with blood.

"No, God. Please, No! I can't lose this baby! Not now. Not ever!" Sadie sobbed quietly as the cramping and the bleeding continued.

Sadie lay still as the cramping pain continued. She sobbed openly as she knew that she was losing her baby. But maybe if she lay perfectly still the cramping would cease. And she and the baby would be okay. But deep down she knew that there was nothing she could do to stop nature.

After a few minutes of quiet, Sadie's body was swayed by one huge, painful pushing cramp. As Sadie's body slowed it's shaking from the final unwanted, forcing push, she instinctively knew it was over. She lay quietly sobbing, grieving for the new life that was never going to be.

Sadie eventually fell asleep where she lay, awakened only by the sound of a vehicle coming down the bumpy path by the river. She laid where she was, her body too weak to move her hips. Eventually she breathed a sigh of relief when she heard Jack calling for her. As soon as Jack looked over the small bulge and saw Sadie's body lying in a bloody pool, he ordered Gus back to the car.

"You stay there Gus, until I come to get you. I need to check out your mother first." Jack watched until Gus had shut the door of the back seat, and then hurried down the river bank to Sadie.

"Oh my God, Sadie! What happened to you?" Fearing that Sadie was dead, he bent over her checking for a pulse.

"It wasn't me, Jack. I think I'm okay. But I couldn't stop the pain or the pushing. I'm so sorry!" Jack took Sadie's hand, brushed her hair from her face, and kissed her lightly on the forehead.

"It's okay, Sadie. I'm here now. We'll get through this!" As Jack took his eyes away from Sadie's face, and viewed the scene before him, his heart sank. He soothed Sadie as if to comfort her and then moved to the small lump in the leaves between Sadie's legs. He felt for a heartbeat, a pulse, anything. But there was nothing. Jack stopped as tears streamed down his face. He closed the baby's eyes with his hands and then went back to Sadie. He pushed her back to the ground as she tried to sit up.

"No, Sadie. Stay where you are. I think you have lost our baby. But I need to make sure you are okay. Stay where you are and rest until I get back with a doctor." Sadie started sobbing when she saw the tears in Jack's eyes.

"I'm so sorry, Jack! I tried so hard. I didn't want to push, but I couldn't help it."

"Sadie, no one is blaming you. Please stay here. Rest and don't move! We can talk later. Please, Sadie." As soon as Jack was convinced that Sadie was going to stay, he patted her on the shoulder and ran up the hill to the car. Sadie dozed off to sleep again as she listened to the vehicle bumping back down the road.

Jack returned quickly with the doctor. The doctor checked out Sadie, noted the death of the baby in his papers, and turned to leave.

"Sadie, you are fine. I see no reason for you to have miscarried this baby, other then sometimes these things happen. And we don't know why. I cannot see any reason you can't bear a healthy child in the future. I'm sorry, but I could not have stopped this even if I was here. It would have been less painful. That's all. If you rest for the next few weeks you'll be as good as new. I am sorry for your loss. But just rest here for a few hours. I don't want to move you until the bleeding stops. Which it will do soon. So come see me in a few days, or Jack can come get me if he needs to."

"Thank you, doctor." Sadie voice was soft and weary as she forced the reality into her heart.

"I would like to stay here with my child if it's okay with you. And maybe bury her by the river. It is pretty here. Is that okay?"

"No one owns this river bank, Sadie. You do as you need to. Jack will help you, I am sure. And again, I am so sorry." With that, the doctor walked back up the bank to his car, and then left.

"I have some tools in the car. I'll see what I have, Sadie, and check on Gus. You just stay and rest." Jack worked his way back to the car and dug around in the trunk until he found a shovel.

"Gus is asleep, Sadie. We can explain all of this to him tomorrow. Right now I need to do something constructive. So where would you like the grave dug?" After Sadie pointed out the perfect place, Jack started digging while Sadie took the blanket Jack had brought from the car and wrapped the lifeless form as best as she could. Sadie hugged the body tightly to her chest until Jack finished the grave.

Sadie slept fitfully that night, even though Jack was right beside her. Gus was sound asleep in the back seat of the car. Sadie contemplated on what to do next. Her connection to Jack was now buried next to the river, never to grow up and know them. She was too far away to walk back to Galesburg with Gus. And she knew Jack could, and would, walk away soon.

Sadie's dreams took her to a place that was a fairy dream at best. She was in a home, Jack and Gus were tending to the fields, and Sadie's little Katherine was scampering around her legs and begging for a bite of the warm bread. Sadie knew a life like that was not to be, but it was a life she had wished for and dreamt about the last few months. Sadie was startled awake by Jack stirring beside her.

"Good morning, Sadie girl. I know you didn't sleep well, but things will get better. I promise." Jack finished tying his shoes, got up, and held his hand out to Sadie for assistance.

"I guess we had better tell Gus together. He should see a united front with us."

"Why, Jack? You are not tied to us anymore. You can come and go as you please. Probably mostly go." Sadie smoothed out her skirt while she was talking. She did not want to look Jack in the face. Whether he was ready to admit it even to himself, she knew it would come to Jack soon. He was free now, whether he knew it or not.

"Sadie, what are you talking about? You are scaring me!" Jack walked over to put his hand on Sadie's shoulder, but she shrugged his hand away.

"Jack, I know you will come to the realization soon. You probably already have. The only tie to us as a couple is gone now. Like dead. You can walk away any time you please, without guilt." Sadie had tears in her eyes. She really wanted Jack to confront her. But she also knew that she needed to get over that feeling.

Jack took Sadie by the shoulders and turned her to face him. He wiped a lone tear away that had snaked down Sadie's cheek.

"Sadie, dear. What on Earth are you talking about? I'm not going anywhere. I am totally committed to you and Gus, with or without that baby in the ground over there. I'm the happiest I have ever been, and am so looking forward to spending a life with you and Gus!" His face blanched white as another truth hit him in the chest.

"Sadie, do you want to leave? Was that baby the only thing holding us together?"

"No, Jack. It's not that. I would like to know that I can stay and that we are still building a life together. But you have a wife and children back in Illinois. Maybe this was just a lark for you. You could play house with someone else for a while and then go back home and just carry on again with the life you already had. Just keep doing what you were doing until you got the wandering eye again." Jack laughed out loud at the comical thought.

"Wow, Sadie. How long did it take for you to dream up that story?" Sadie had to smile at that comeback from Jack. She absolutely loved, and would miss, Jack's quick sense of humor.

"Pretty much all night, Jack. I couldn't sleep." Sadie smiled up at Jack and lightly shrugged her shoulders.

"Sadie, first of all, I did not want to lose that baby. I wanted to enjoy that child right along with you and Gus. And hopefully many more children. It broke my heart to lose that baby, Sadie. I am just so grateful that I didn't lose you too." Jack again steadied his hands on Sadie's shoulders and bent down to look her directly in the eyes.

"Now, hear me good, Sweetheart. And never forget this because once this conversation is over and we have an agreement we are done. We won't discuss this matter again."

"It took me quite a while in town today, Sadie. I found us a house at the edge of town. It's close enough for you to come out here to the gravesite any time you want. And I got a job at the grain elevator. I not only want to take care of you, I AM taking care of you."

"Yes, Sadie. We are putting down roots here. This is where our baby is buried so this is where we belong."

"I'll make a deal with you Sadie. I will not commit to you with a ring and vows. Partly because I am already married and can't afford to get a divorce. And partly because my heart is already committed to you and Gus. I won't ask you to commit either. We will stay 'uncommitted' so that you have a free will. You can go at any time and just walk away from here if you so choose. But my hope is that you and Gus will walk with me awhile. Check me out before you make a decision." Jack had that little impish grin on his face as he raised his eyebrow with expectation.

"I will walk with you for a while, Jack. I have nothing to go back to anyway. So Gus and I will go forward with you. We will see what's out there together." Sadie slipped her hand into Jack's hand, and walked towards the car and Gus with him.

"Well, Sadie girl, let's share our terrible news with Gus and show him the grave that you all can visit any time. Then let's go home."

THE END

www.ingramcontent.com/pod-product-compliance
Lightning Source LLC
LaVergne TN
LVHW021806060526
838201LV00058B/3249